All Things Hidden

Books by Tracie Peterson

www.traciepeterson.com

House of Secrets • A Slender Thread • Where My Heart Belongs
All Things Hidden*

LAND OF SHINING WATER
The Icecutter's Daughter
The Quarryman's Bride
The Miner's Lady

LAND OF THE LONE STAR
Chasing the Sun
Touching the Sky
Taming the Wind

SONG OF ALASKA
Dawn's Prelude
Morning's Refrain
Twilight's Serenade

STRIKING A MATCH
Embers of Love
Hearts Aglow
Hope Rekindled

ALASKAN QUEST
Summer of the Midnight Sun
Under the Northern Lights
Whispers of Winter
Alaskan Quest (3 in 1)

YUKON QUEST
Treasures of the North
Ashes and Ice
Rivers of Gold

BRIDES OF GALLATIN COUNTY
A Promise to Believe In
A Love to Last Forever
A Dream to Call My Own

DESERT ROSES
Shadows of the Canyon
Across the Years
Beneath a Harvest Sky

HEIRS OF MONTANA
Land of My Heart
The Coming Storm
To Dream Anew
The Hope Within

LADIES OF LIBERTY
A Lady of High Regard
A Lady of Hidden Intent
A Lady of Secret Devotion

LONE STAR BRIDES
A Sensible Arrangement
A Moment in Time

WESTWARD CHRONICLES
A Shelter of Hope
Hidden in a Whisper
A Veiled Reflection

*with Kimberley Woodhouse

All Things Hidden

TRACIE PETERSON
and
KIMBERLEY WOODHOUSE

BETHANYHOUSE
a division of Baker Publishing Group
Minneapolis, Minnesota

Published by Bethany House Publishers
11400 Hampshire Avenue South
Bloomington, Minnesota 55438
www.bethanyhouse.com

Bethany House Publishers is a division of
Baker Publishing Group, Grand Rapids, Michigan

Printed in the United States of America

Library of Congress Cataloging-in-Publication Data
Peterson, Tracie.
    All things hidden / Tracie Peterson and Kimberley Woodhouse.
        pages cm
    Includes bibliographical references.
    ISBN 978-0-7642-1119-5 (pbk.)
        1. Physicians—Fiction. 2. Alaska—History—20th century—Fiction.
    I. Woodhouse, Kimberley. II. Title.
    PS3566.E7717A794 2013
    813'.54—dc23   2013032758

Song lyrics quoted: "'Tis So Sweet to Trust in Jesus," Louisa M. R. Stead, 1882.

Scripture quotations are from the King James Version of the Bible.

This is a work of historical reconstruction; the appearances of certain historical figures are therefore inevitable. All other characters, however, are products of the author's imagination, and any resemblance to actual persons, living or dead, is coincidental.

Kimberley Woodhouse represented by The Steve Laube Agency

Cover photography, illustration, and design by Brandon Hill

14 15 16 17 18 19   7 6 5 4 3 2

This book is lovingly dedicated to

Lori Healy

Through all the TV craziness, home schooling, the writing of books, traveling with us on book tours and signings, and sorting millions of phone calls and emails— you've been a constant friend and trusted assistant.

Thank you, precious lady.

Authors' Note

The novel you are about to read is fiction, though it is bathed in historical detail, facts, and yes—a few factual characters. We loved researching and discovering these fascinating people who were pioneers of their time, but most of the personality traits and characteristics were fleshed out in our own imaginations and should be construed as such.

The Hillermans and Dr. Vaughan were not historical people of this time period, but many of the other characters were. Please see our note to the reader at the end of the book to see the list there. (Yes, there really *was* a man chosen with a wooden leg, there was a teenage girl who had a bear cub as a pet, and one of the colony houses was torn down three times and restarted.)

In addition to the characters, a major part of the story is the grand setting of Alaska. Were you to visit the Mat-Su Valley today, you would see a landscape much different from the time of our novel. In fact, the cities of Wasilla and Palmer didn't exist yet. But thanks in part to the colony and the other homesteaders who stuck it out during the Great Depression, the valley flourishes today.

Our great country's history is rich, and we invite you along on a journey to discover one of Franklin Delano Roosevelt's New Deal projects: The Matanuska Colonization.

Enjoy the journey.

Tracie and Kimberley

1

FEBRUARY 1, 1935
ANCHORAGE, ALASKA TERRITORY

Fear twisted Gwyn Hillerman's stomach just like her fingers twisted the delicate handkerchief into a knot. If she wasn't careful, the fabric would be ruined. Forcing her hands to still, she glanced out the picture window on the southeast side of the large lodge. Wind whipped at the jagged peaks surrounding the small town of Anchorage, the snow whirling around like a dance. But even the rugged beauty of her beloved mountains couldn't calm her spirit. Usually the daily sight of God's handiwork cheered her, no matter how hard the wind blew, how low the temperature dropped, or how deep the snow drifted. It was Alaska, after all—the most beautiful place on the planet.

But today was different. A heavy sigh left her lips. How long must they be kept waiting?

She closed her eyes for a moment and took a deep breath. The warm glow from the fireplace couldn't ease the chill of anxiety. What was this new board? And what would it mean for them? Would a group of total strangers make life-changing decisions without concern for what others in the area might want?

As much as Gwyn loved people and loved helping her father doctor the few families in their remote area, she held an equal amount of hate at the thought of change. Maybe because Mother always wanted change.

Which was why she'd left them.

Gwyn glanced at her father. Gray hair, shoulders straight and strong, twinkling gray eyes as he read the *Anchorage Daily News*. His face held an expression of expectance. Almost joyous. The exact opposite of what Gwyn felt inside.

This beautiful and grand territory was her home. Not here in the bustling little town of Anchorage, but in the quiet valley—the snow-covered mountains of the Chugach and Talkeetnas on the east and the north. The Knik Arm joining them to the Cook Inlet in the south. The moose, the bear, the spruce, the snow . . . The Matanuska valley was *her* valley. The people were *her* people; she'd known them almost all of her life. But more than that, she belonged here. It was etched on her soul.

Gwyn's thoughts went back to their comfortable place— worry. What would the government board members require of them? Would they ask her father to take another post? How could she leave her home?

She had a few memories of life back in Chicago, but they were disconnected. Unreal. This place—Alaska—held her in its mesmerizing grip. She didn't want or need change.

Change meant new. Different.

But most of all, change meant heartache.

Gwyn unwound the fabric from her fingers and attempted to press it flat. Each tick of the clock seemed to span longer with each beat. She folded the kerchief in rhythm, feeling as if time almost stood still. She allowed herself to dart a glance to the clock over the fireplace in the large meeting room. It couldn't be working properly.

Good grief, she'd allowed her nerves to get the best of her once again. With a huff, Gwyn blew a few curls off her forehead. She stood and walked around the room before she could mangle the monogrammed cloth in her hands. Again.

Time to get her mind off these worrisome thoughts. Worry never helped. Besides, it was a sin. She could almost hear Nasnana's voice—in her gentle singsong way—drilling those words into her as a child. A lesson she still needed to learn. The older native woman had taken Gwyn under her wing at an early age, when Gwyn formed an attachment to Nasnana's granddaughter, Sadzi. The two girls had been inseparable, and Gwyn would always be grateful for the woman's guiding hand in her life.

But even with Nasnana's advice and direction, Gwyn's habit of giving in to worry had gotten her into trouble on multiple occasions. A glance down at the frayed fabric between her fingers proved she hadn't conquered it yet. But she would.

With a nod to emphasize her point, she tucked the hankie into her pocket and focused her thoughts on the furnishings around her. Dark wood beams covered the ceiling, but the log building's interior walls were plastered and painted a creamy white. Three long tables surrounded the room, but they wouldn't do at all. Crossing her arms, Gwyn cocked her head to the right and narrowed her gaze. The chairs sat in a crooked line, if one could even call it a line. There seemed to be no rhyme or reason whatsoever. Well, she could fix that.

Gwyn scurried around the room, straightening chairs and

the several sets of wooden benches that took up residence in the middle.

Another glance at the clock. Bother. That spent all of two minutes. She blew a stray curl off her forehead. She needed something to occupy her mind. Something other than worry. As the fire roared in the grand fireplace, Gwyn looked out one of the windows. Snow dwelt two inches above the ledge and they still had a good bit of winter left. A memory surfaced.

"Father?"

The newspaper crinkled. "I'm sorry, Gwyn, did you say something?"

"Do you remember the winter we had blizzard after blizzard and the snow reached the roof?"

"I do." He chuckled and the paper rustled some more in his hands. "You dug tunnels all the way around the house. Oh, the energy of youth."

She laughed with him and crossed her arms. "If I recall, you helped." It had been a tough winter. Their first without her mother and sister.

"I did." He patted the chair next to him with the now-folded newsprint. "Come, sit."

Plopping down onto the seat in a manner her mother would deem unladylike, Gwyn fidgeted some more.

Her father reached out a strong hand and covered both of hers. "I'm sure it will be good news, my dear. What's causing all these nervous jitters?"

Gwyn met his gaze. Harold Hillerman was a handsome man. Add to that, he was caring, positive, helpful, a wonderful doctor, and he loved the Lord. How could her mother have ever thought to leave this man? It didn't make sense. Gwyn shook her head to rid her mind of the negative thoughts.

It'd be best if she didn't cause him more concern. When she worried, he hovered and tried to fix everything. Father hadn't quite recovered emotionally since Mother and Sophia abandoned them for the amenities of "civilized society." Oh, he was strong and steadfast, as always. But Gwyn never wanted to see the same pain in her father's eyes again. More than that, she had no intention of being the source.

She pasted on a smile. "Of course. It was just a bit of a shock—the request that we attend a meeting, when we have no idea what it's about." She squeezed his hand and released it with a long sigh. "I'm not very good at surprises. Or waiting."

Father chuckled. "With this, I'm all too familiar." He gave another pat to her hands. "Change is coming, my dear."

Of course it was. And that was the exact thing she *didn't* want.

The clock chimed, bringing her attention back to her impatience. What could be taking so long? They'd taken the time to travel to Anchorage and now were kept waiting. Although the board technically wasn't late . . . yet. She and Father were just early. But the waiting . . . oh, she abhorred waiting.

She placed her hands on her knees, straightened, and breathed deeply. Gwyn longed for the crisp, frozen air outside and the cabin she called home. Meeting with a bunch of government bigwigs in town was not her idea of an outing.

Outings were for friends, a hike in the woods, snowshoeing up the pass, catching salmon in the stream, picking berries, or helping her father deliver a baby. Meetings in town would never be on her wish list of outings.

A slammed door made her jump. Heavy footsteps followed, echoing on the wooden floor. Finally. The waiting would be over. Her spine straightened out of habit as her fingers fidgeted with the hankie again.

A stout man walked into the room, followed by an assortment of five well-dressed businessmen. The leader carried a mess of papers. When he reached the table at the front of the room, the others began to take chairs and sit. The stout man's papers slid in disarray as he dropped them in a heap. Gwyn longed to reach out and straighten the pile.

A heavy sigh preceded the leader's drop into his chair. "Good afternoon, Dr. Hillerman, Miss Hillerman." His smile seemed genuine. "I'm George Townsend. I've been asked to head up this new board of the Alaska Rural Rehabilitation Corporation—ARRC—until President Roosevelt gets everything in place. These gentlemen are here to assist as well."

Gwyn's father walked to the table to shake each man's hand. "We're eager to hear what news you have and how we may be of service."

Mr. Townsend nodded his head and leaned forward. "Thank you. Have a seat and let's get right to it. President Roosevelt has initiated some new experiments to help the country through these tough times. The ARRC will be a part of that. On January fifteenth, the decision was made to move forward with what the president calls the Matanuska Colony Project."

Gwyn drew her eyebrows together. The Matanuska Colony Project? Referring to *her* valley? The president of the United States?

Her father sat back and nodded. "January fifteenth? You're moving forward pretty fast."

"That's why we summoned you as soon as we heard and why we're a little unorganized." Mr. Townsend shuffled through the messy pile. "Forgive me as I work to be clear on this matter. It will progress even faster as we approach the end of winter." He pulled out a sheet of paper and continued. "The Matanuska Project is to bring relief to a portion of the American people and bring settlement to Alaska. The president wants them here by May to prepare for the next winter."

Gwyn's stomach dropped. Settlement? They meant to settle the valley? Mr. Townsend continued speaking to her father, but her ears clamped shut. She loved Alaska. Truly, she did. And she loved to share with others. Hadn't she always wanted the world to know what an incredible land she lived in? To give people glimpses of the wonderland that was her home? But she'd only done that twice. And those were wealthy tourists wanting to explore the Last Frontier. But they came and went and left the valley in peace.

"Approximately two hundred families will be chosen for the colonization of the Matanuska valley," she heard the board chairman say as she started listening again. The man slid his glasses to the end of his nose and held out two of the sheets of paper from his stack to read. "Families will be selected from those areas with a climate closest to Alaska's and those hardest hit by the droughts: Michigan, Wisconsin, and Minnesota."

She swallowed. Her throat was so dry. What she wouldn't give for a huge glass of water.

Her father chimed in. "Will there be any medical personnel coming as well?"

The man to Mr. Townsend's right responded. "Not at this time. The Red Cross will hopefully send some nurses, but right now this is all we know. That's why we asked to meet with you. We would like to avoid any epidemics or deaths that would cast a poor light on the area to the rest of the world."

Her ever-calm father crinkled his brow. "You should know by now my dedication to healing people, but this is a *large number* of people we're talking about. I can't guarantee the health of everyone just so we look good to the press—besides, we haven't had any press up in our area for some time, sir, so why are you concerned?"

"We appreciate your honesty, Dr. Hillerman, and we're asking you to do this for the benefit of future Alaskans. These people will need medical care. As to the press, the president's declaration has caused quite a stir in the newspapers. We'll probably have a lot of tenderfoot reporters up here as well." The man at the end of the table puffed on his cigar. "I wouldn't be surprised if we're all in the papers every day."

Discussion erupted around the table as the men voiced their excitement about the chance for Alaska to make its mark on the world. Other people would surely see the beauty and opportunities in this Last Frontier. *Hope* would be Alaska's new motto.

Gwyn bowed her head. *Two hundred families.* That could be well over a thousand people. With no clue how to survive in the often harsh land that was Alaska.

Her brain replayed those three words again and again like a stuck phonograph.

Two. Hundred. Families.

She attempted to swallow again and almost choked. Her throat felt like it was stuffed with cotton.

Two. Hundred. Families.

Heat rose up her neck and into her face. She attempted to breathe.

But the air in her lungs fought for space to move around the words. . . . *Two. Hundred. Families.*

And they would be here in less than four months.

Harold watched his daughter stare out the window of the train. For twenty-two years he'd been blessed by her quick mind and quiet spirit. This wouldn't be easy for her, all the chaos and upheaval. Gwyn liked things stable. Organized.

And steady. She enjoyed the quietness of their lives. But even though he understood her underlying fear, she'd done a great job in front of the board, showing her strength and ability to assist and tackle a project. It'd been obvious she was dumbstruck at the beginning of the meeting, but as the plan unfolded, his brave Gwyn had straightened her shoulders, cleared her throat, and answered their questions without any hesitation.

The Matanuska Project. His heart sped up a little at the thought. The president's task was unprecedented. But the biggest question dangled out there: Could they be ready in time?

Harold allowed his thoughts to go back to the meeting. What little facts they knew for certain were overwhelming. The colony families would be chosen by each state's local aid workers. The federal government would pay for their transportation and for shipment of two thousand pounds of household goods per family, and would build them a house and a barn on their forty-acre parcel, which would be purchased for five dollars an acre and given out by lottery once all the colonists arrived. Each family would be granted a loan to pay for their land, farm equipment, and household goods as needed. For all of that, the colonists must agree to live in

Alaska for thirty years. Eighty thousand acres were already set aside in the Matanuska valley.

As the train chugged the forty-plus miles toward their valley, Harold considered the needs of the colonists. Adding another thousand people—if not more—to care for in a very rural area would tax his time and energy. What would this mean for him? He was the only white doctor outside of Anchorage for hundreds of miles into the interior. His heart had always been for the Alaskan Indians. If that many people moved in, how would he have time to travel to the remote villages? He already cared for almost a thousand people.

And what of the hundreds of transient workers the board planned to bring up? They would help provide jobs and also help out the colonists, but they were going to be in need of medical care as well. Especially when clearing land and building on an insane timeline were involved. The rush plus the people not being acclimated to Alaska could prove to be disastrous. Harold prayed not.

His thoughts drifted to Edith. His wife's disdain for his work bothered him to this day. She had never liked the native Alaskan people and disliked his work with them even more. When she left, she'd blamed him. Could he have done something more to keep her here?

But her goals and wishes for him had always been her own visions of grandeur. Raised in wealth and in the city, she'd jumped at the chance to marry a promising doctor from a good family. Harold had fooled himself to think it was because of love. Their first few years had been wonderful, but very busy with his work at the hospital in Chicago and the addition of their two baby girls.

Edith's true heart appeared several months after the Hillerman family arrived in the Alaska Territory in 1916 to homestead. With the railroad's work to connect the interior to the ports, four hundred homesteads had been applied for the previous years. Harold knew he could build a medical practice and work to help build the hospital in Anchorage. The territory was exciting to all the wealthy people in society. Edith and her friends seemed so supportive of this new move. But once they left Chicago, she'd followed like a ghost as a dutiful wife with two young children. And her demeanor changed. After the difficult journey and the realization that the comforts of home wouldn't be in Alaska for years, possibly decades, her silence turned to rage.

In his heart, all these years, Harold knew he'd married a spoiled girl, but she'd always been sweet. And she was so beautiful. But after the fateful move to this beautiful land, in private she unleashed her anger on him. He worked hard to please her, and Edith's pride kept her by his side until her father suffered a massive heart attack after the stock market crash of '29.

It was all the excuse she needed. And she left.

Harold glanced at Gwyn again. Her hands folded tight in her lap, eyes closed. Probably praying about the changes to come. As he gazed at his older daughter, he pondered what he'd done to deserve her loyalty, and where he'd gone wrong with her sister, Sophia.

When Gwyn had followed him around like a young pup, wanting to learn anything and everything there was to know about helping people, Sophia wanted more ribbons for her hair and soaked up every word Edith told her about how the "real" world lived. All the talk of grand dances, lavish dinner parties, and society occasions filled the young beauty's head with the same ideals as her mother.

And he'd allowed it. Allowed one daughter to be spoiled while granting himself the adoration of the other.

Guilt squeezed his heart in time with the chugging of the train. If only he'd been a better husband, a better father, maybe they would have stayed . . . maybe . . .

No. This wasn't an easy place to live. Beautiful and fertile, yes, but darkness, harsh winters, and death caused more than one family to abandon their homes and farms. Only about a hundred of the original families were left.

Edith tried to convince Gwyn to leave "this Godforsaken country" with her and Sophia, stating that no young woman should be left in the wild, untamed land. But as much as Edith argued and yelled, Gwyn dug in her heels and stayed by Harold's side.

Edith left with not even a hug for her husband and daughter. Harold would never forget the sting of her expression as she looked over her shoulder at him, grabbed Sophia's hand, jutted her chin forward, and walked away.

And they hadn't returned.

His heart shattered that day.

A tear rolling down Gwyn's cheek caught his attention and brought him back to the present. A wife abandoning a husband was one thing, but a mother abandoning a child was quite another.

He reached into his pocket and pulled out a handkerchief. Gwyn wasn't one for coddling or sympathy, so he pressed the kerchief into her hand. Even though she never expressed it to him, he knew. The worry in her eyes every time he left without her. The tears every time she received a letter in Edith's handwriting.

Her heart had never healed either.

She dabbed at the tears and straightened her shoulders. "Well, I guess we have a lot of work to do." The weak smile she gave him couldn't erase the fear he saw in her eyes.

"Yes, it sounds like we will have our hands full."

She looked forward and sniffed. "I know you are excited about this, Father. I will do whatever I can to help."

"I know you will."

Gwyn turned back to the window.

Harold let his thoughts roam. Excited? Yes, he was excited. New people. New families. New homes. New farms. New businesses.

Their beautiful valley would thrive.

But Gwyn didn't share his excitement. At least not yet.

His mind couldn't quite take in all the thoughts as it jumped from one subject to another. He longed to be able to discuss them with his daughter but knew she needed time to digest all the information thrown at them in the meeting.

America needed encouragement through these tough times. Alaska was bountiful. This was sure to be a successful project. But the thought of more than two thousand people for one physician to care for overwhelmed him. Gwyn's gifts as a nurse were valuable. She had no formal training, no hospital work, no experience whatsoever except what she'd learned from him. Would the government consider sending him another doctor? Most of his patients lived off the beaten path in small villages. And he didn't desire to give up his work with the native Indian people. Would the government expect that of him? Would they see the natives as less important and demand he work solely with the whites?

Even if they tried to demand it, he wouldn't allow for it. People were people no matter the color of their skin or the place they lived. He'd give his all, so long as he had the ability to work.

But it wouldn't be easy. He knew that. He wasn't one of those men who could cast aside the truth and pretend that roses would pop up where turnips had been planted.

An idea took root. He needed help. Where could he find someone with enough of an adventurous spirit to abandon city life and a steady income to come here? During one of the worst economic times the country had ever seen?

The scent of spruce trees and the glittering powder of fresh-fallen snow greeted Gwyn as she exited the train at the tiny stop for their valley. Quiet. Serene. With nothing around. Finally, her world was right again. The meeting with the ARRC had been thrilling. To her father, at least. To her, it just meant change. The unknown. Between all the details and the rapid timeline, she found her thoughts spinning out of control. As they made the trek to their home on foot, she longed for space to mull it all over, and the place calling her right now was Nasnana's.

She kept pace with her father. "I'd like to go visit Nasnana and Sadzi, if that's all right with you."

Her father turned to her and patted her shoulder, his breath visible in little puffs. "That would be fine. We will definitely need their help preparing the newcomers for the next winter. Would you mind asking them for their assistance?" Without waiting for an answer, he continued, "I wonder if it would be prudent to move my clinic closer to the train. It would take a bit of effort, but maybe we should think of moving the cabin as well."

Gwyn wasn't sure she liked the direction her father's thoughts were taking. Change, change, change. Too much change. She felt her forehead crease with a frown.

Father turned back to her. "Goodness, there I go again. Don't mind me, Gwyn. You know how I think ahead. Don't worry about all that right now. It will all come in time." He gripped her shoulders and squeezed. "I need to write a letter, so I will be in my office."

Standing on tiptoe, she nodded and kissed her father's cheek before heading to her friends' home.

The solitude of the woods gave Gwyn the time she needed to corral her thoughts. The thick blanket of snow muted her steps. All was quiet. And peaceful. But how long would it stay that way? Her native friends would understand her feelings better than anyone.

How could she love the Lord, love people, love Alaska, and want to share it, and then *not* want to share it all at the same time? Her special little world seemed to be crumbling around her. Was she really that selfish?

Gwyn stopped in her tracks. Is that what had happened? Had she become selfish and uncaring? The thought horrified her—because those were traits she equated with her mother. Even though she loved the woman and still longed to know her mother's love in return, Gwyn had no desire to be like her. At all.

She crested a hill and poked her head through the trees. There in the distance, across the shining water of the Knik Arm, lay Susitna. The beautiful mountain rose up seemingly out of the water to bask in the sun's brief winter rays. The Sleeping Lady.

If only Gwyn could be like the native legend and lie down

to sleep one day. She could become a lush mountain and remain the same while the world changed around her. One day, Gwyn wanted to see if she could hike to the lovely lady and picnic at her base. But the legend behind the beloved mountain wasn't real. The changes to come *were*.

Soft munching to her right brought Gwyn's attention back to the moment. She smiled as she watched a young moose about twenty feet away stretch his neck to reach a shrub covered in snow. She giggled at his antics, but then mama moose appeared and stared straight at Gwyn. Time to move on.

It would have been smarter to grab her snowshoes before she headed this way, but she didn't mind the deep snow that slowed her steps—it gave her more time to think. How could she share all that was on her heart? Would the changes to come alter their relationships as well?

Sadzi greeted her outside the small cabin as she approached. Her friend's long black braid swung back and forth as Sadzi waved and then wrapped Gwyn in a tight hug. "It's so good to see you! Are you back from the meeting? What did they say?" Sadzi grabbed her hand and dragged her to the door.

Gwyn laughed in response. The only thing that could break through her barriers was one of Sadzi's hugs. They'd first met on Gwyn's sixth birthday. As the young native girl hugged Gwyn and played with her curly blond hair, she announced her birthday was the same day. Only she was a year younger. The two were fascinated with each other and had been best friends ever since. Gwyn always felt alive and real when she was with these precious people. "Yes, I have a lot of news. And I'm afraid it's a little scary."

Nasnana appeared at the entryway, dish towel in one hand,

iron skillet in the other. "The one scary thing on this earth is not knowing where you will spend eternity." She pointed the skillet at Gwyn. "The rest is just worry. And worry—"

"—is a sin."

"—is a sin."

Gwyn and Sadzi laughed as they chimed in together and followed the older woman back into the house.

"Ah, so you have been listening to this old woman after all."

"Only for the past sixteen years." Gwyn hugged the woman who'd been the only grandmother she'd ever known.

Sadzi went to the stove. "Tea?"

"Yes, please." Gwyn twisted her hands again and sat in a chair.

Nasnana sat next to her. "Now, what is this news?"

Two weathered hands covered Gwyn's. Taking a deep breath, she decided to just plunge in with every detail, starting from the time they waited in the large room of the government lodge up to the end of the train ride.

After she'd spilled out every fact and word she could remember, she watched her friends. Sadzi's eyes glowed—her excitement and anticipation palpable in the small room— while Nasnana's smile grew.

"Well?" Gwyn glanced from Sadzi to her grandmother. "What do you think?"

The crinkled lines around Nasnana's eyes increased. "I think this is exciting news. We all love this land, and God is using it as a way to rescue others from poverty and death."

Sadzi bounced on her toes in the kitchen. "And just think of all the fun we'll have teaching everyone about salmon and berries, and there will be children! Won't it be fun to have little feet around here? We can make cookies, and fireweed honey, and jellies . . ." Gwyn's friend twirled around the kitchen as she continued her list.

Nasnana gripped Gwyn's chin in her hand, forcing Gwyn to look at her. "You are afraid, precious one—I see it in your eyes. But there is no need to fear."

Before she could stop them, tears sprang into Gwyn's eyes. Their valley would change. "Oh, but there *is* . . ."

2

"You are hereby stripped of your medical license." The board chairman slammed his gavel down on the solid table as whispers permeated the room.

Jeremiah Vaughan swallowed. His worst fear had just come true. He straightened his shoulders, waiting for the chairman to continue.

"Your use of the new intravenous anesthesia without the consent of Mr. Brewster, and your reckless abandon have proven your ineptitude in the surgical arena—"

"Chairman, the patient's wounds were fatal. I was just trying—"

"Do *not* interrupt me, young man. We've all heard the facts of this unfortunate case. The decision is final." The chairman stood.

Feet shuffled. Papers rustled. For a brief moment, time stood still. Then everything sped up and blurred around him in the cacophony of voices and the pounding pulse in his head. Jeremiah turned to pick up his medical bag and several flashbulbs blinded him. Reporters. He was sure to be in every paper in the city in the coming days.

Pushed and shoved and interrogated as he made his way out of the building, Jeremiah took one last look back. Everything was gone with that final bang of the gavel. The new hospital. The hospital *he* was supposed to be heading up. All the years of training and the horrific hours he'd invested. All the people he'd fought to save.

All gone. In an instant. His dreams were dead now. He wasn't allowed to practice medicine anymore. At least not legally. What would he tell Sophia?

Thoughts of his beautiful fiancée shut out all the questions around him. Sophia Hillerman. Their wedding was to be the society event of the year. He'd just turned thirty-four, and he would be a distinguished hospital head, and she would be his bride.

But not anymore. All of that would change.

He'd better speak with her before she heard the news. She would be devastated, of course, but maybe they could start fresh in a new city. Maybe there was a way he could fight the medical board's decision. With Sophia at his side all would be right again. They shared such wonderful dreams.

Hope welled within him. Sophia's beautiful face and tender smile would surely heal his wounds.

He picked up his pace and headed to the historic mansion where Sophia lived with her mother and grandparents. The lavish wrought-iron gate opened to what would be a beautiful garden come spring. He took the front steps two at a time and knocked.

Leonard, the butler, opened the door and stepped to the side, his face grim.

"Good evening, Leonard. I'm here to see—"

"We know why you're here." Mrs. Hillerman's smooth voice echoed off the marble foyer around the silent butler. "It's best we speak privately in the parlor." She turned on her heel and headed to the first room on her right.

He nodded.

Leonard stood rigid, neither offering to take his coat nor acknowledging his presence at all. His future mother-in-law, who had always greeted him with such grace, often taking hold of his arm as they walked together, continued to walk away. Tonight, her cold demeanor and stiff gait sent a chill up his spine.

A sense of dread built in the pit of his stomach. Impending doom. Like the last nail in a coffin. The air around him threatened to suffocate him. Hadn't it already been a bad enough day? Maybe his imagination just ran wild.

His fiancée sat on the couch by the window. Mrs. Hillerman headed straight for Sophia and stood behind her. Sophia looked away from him. Her red-rimmed eyes and furrowed brow weren't much of an encouragement.

He loosened his collar. "I'm afraid I don't have very good news to share with you." Jeremiah held his hat in his hand.

Mrs. Hillerman's icy voice crushed the last shred of hope in his heart. "Mr. Brewster's secretary has already called to inform us of your action and the board's subsequent decision." She pointed her manicured finger at him. "How dare you drag my daughter down with you! I warned her of your type. You doctors. Always so selfish, so—"

"Mother, please." Sophia looked down and then straight into his eyes, her expression full of animosity.

In that moment, all the warmth seemed to leave his limbs. His heart constricted. Warning bells went off in his brain.

"You've ruined everything, Jeremiah. Everything. And now you've tarnished my name and my family's name along with yours. I can't believe you would embarrass me in such a ghastly manner. It is totally unacceptable for someone of my station." She reached up, locking her hand with her mother's. "We've already called the papers to announce that the engagement is off."

Jeremiah tried to swallow his shock. Who was this callous woman in front of him? Was it Sophia? The woman he loved? The one he wanted by his side? The unmistakable truth pierced his heart—she hated him. The haughty look on her face spoke volumes. This woman never cared about *him*. "Sophia . . ." He turned to his future mother-in-law. "Mrs. Hillerman, would you excuse us for a few moments?"

The tall woman stood straighter, placing both of her hands on her daughter's shoulders. "I most certainly will not."

Sophia dismissed him with a distasteful look and glanced away.

His temper began to build, pushing aside the dull ache in his chest. "I have the right to speak to my betrothed. Don't you care that I wasn't at fault?"

"She is no longer your betrothed. You have ruined our family name with your carelessness. I won't have you ruin Sophia's reputation as well." Mrs. Hillerman's eyes narrowed to slits. "I should have known better than to let a doctor worm his way into my daughter's affections. You have nothing. You are worthless."

His anger died in a rush of pain. What had he done to deserve such hatred? He hadn't done anything wrong! Had he really been this blind to how shallow women could be? "Sophia, don't you even care about me?"

The icy glare from her eyes froze his heart in place. "No, Jeremiah, I do not. How could I?"

A scalpel to his chest couldn't have done more damage. He opened his mouth but then slammed it shut. He clenched his teeth, allowing the rage within to burn. These conceited women didn't deserve a response.

Jeremiah turned on his heel. He wouldn't give anyone else the chance to humiliate him.

The walk home did nothing to clear his head. As he stood outside his apartment building, Jeremiah couldn't go in. His feet propelled him away from the city. Away from the hospital. Away from Sophia. Away from everything he knew.

The world around him muted. He bumped into a bum and knocked the man down, the man's words not reaching his ears. Everything seemed like a dream. More like a nightmare—and all he could do was watch. Jeremiah helped the bedraggled man up and then kept walking. Thoughts battled inside his head. Why hadn't God intervened? He could have saved Jeremiah from the humiliation. Could've saved Mrs. Brewster's life. But no. God betrayed him just like everyone else.

And he'd lost everything.

God couldn't be trusted. Jeremiah was done with Him.

His anger built with each step. The pain from Sophia was the worst. All the words of endearment, sweet smiles, and promises for the future were a lie. Her manipulative mother was just as bad. All fake. The façades of those two women crumbled at his feet, and he'd seen what they really were. How could he have been so fooled?

Females were not to be trusted. It was that simple. All they did was sink their claws in to get what they wanted. Vain, conceited, shallow creatures.

He was done with women.

He'd been under the impression he was in love. And his career was as good as gold.

But that was all a lie too. His world crashed in around him.

No more dreams. No goals. No hospital. No wedding. Nothing.

The sounds of the city finally blasted through his barriers. Jeremiah stopped and turned back toward his apartment. The cold seeped into his bones. He didn't know how long he'd been walking, but his hands and feet were numb. Anger had driven him, but now common sense reminded him of the threat of frostbite.

Warmth blasted him backward as he opened the door to the building that he called home. Maybe he'd gotten colder than he thought. His lips cracked and burned, his feet, legs, and arms prickled and were stiff.

He stopped in his tracks as his gaze hit the table. Piles of notes lay scattered. Notes from procedures, surgeries, tests, new ideas he'd had for the new intravenous anesthesia. Had it all been a waste? A lifetime of learning? Of research? Of love . . . for medicine, for helping people?

Memories washed over him from his childhood. Any injured creature he found, he'd brought to Dr. H. down the road. The prestigious doctor had always taken time out to teach him. Had fanned the flames within young Jeremiah to pursue a career in medicine.

Was it all for naught? In an instant, his arms swiped everything to the floor.

He flung his coat and gloves over a chair and tried to quell the unconstructive thoughts. He needed sleep. Maybe tomorrow would bring a glimmer of hope. And some answers.

A clanging down the street jolted Jeremiah from a hard sleep. He reached for the dark nightstand and checked his pocket watch—a gift from his grandfather when Jeremiah graduated from medical school. Three o'clock. As he sat up on the edge of the bed, his thoughts raced back to the events of yesterday. He rubbed his face. It couldn't be over. If only it had all been a bad dream.

Jeremiah couldn't give up medicine. It was like asking him to give up breathing. It was his passion. It surged through his veins.

But what could he do?

His resolve hardened. He would not go down without a fight. A new plan constructed in his mind. He would contest the board's decision. Howard, his cousin, was a lawyer. Howard could appeal it.

By nine o'clock in the morning Jeremiah was standing on the steps to his parents' home pondering how they would take the news. He'd already met with Howard and laid out his case. He wasn't sure they had any hope of beating Randolph Brewster and his rich cronies who ruled the medical community, but he had to at least try to be reinstated. It was a matter of honor. Brewster might be one of the wealthiest and strongest politicians in the state, but that wouldn't stop Jeremiah from fighting for his honor. Brewster knew him. That was the biggest problem. Jeremiah had willingly worked under the tutelage and guidance of that man for years. How could Brewster stab him in the back this way? Had he been nothing more than a scapegoat all along?

His mother greeted him at the door, eyes swollen. Her hug was brief and cool. "Your father is in his study." She wiped her nose with a hankie and walked away.

"Jeremiah? That you?" His father's deep, gruff voice echoed down the hallway.

"Yeah, Pop, it's me." A whiff of pipe tobacco brought back memories as Jeremiah entered the wood-paneled room. "Mother doesn't look too good."

The senior Vaughan looked down at his desk. "Well, you know your mother. She's worried about you. And worried what her friends will think. This news hasn't been easy on any of us."

The real crux of the matter. So that's how it would be. His own parents didn't believe in him. They believed what society told them. The blow was like a hammer to his stomach.

He cleared his throat so his voice wouldn't betray the pain. "I'm sorry you're having to endure so much."

"Don't take that tone with me, Jeremiah. We support you, but these are tough times. If the people can't trust the Vaughan name, we could go under as well." His father tapped more tobacco into his pipe. "But your cousin called this morning, and we're confident he'll get all this straightened out in no time."

If only Jeremiah could leap forward in time to that point.

"Your mother and I have a suggestion for you in the meantime."

"Oh?" This ought to be good. How was he supposed to save face at a time like this?

"We think you should leave town for a while." His father hesitated as he struck a match and lit the pipe. "Here." An envelope was shoved toward him. "Here's five hundred dollars. That should get you through for a spell."

Jeremiah's anger burned again, his fuse all too short these days. "You want me to leave town? How am I supposed to appeal and defend myself?"

"Howard will take care of all of that. He's already assured me there's no need for you to be present—"

"So you're saying you've discussed my leaving with him? And that's it? Decision made? I'm dismissed?" A horrible thought sank in, dispelling all the anger. Once the pride of his parents, he'd now turned into a black sheep they needed to distance themselves from. He fought the clenching of his gut as it all became clear.

His loving parents were too embarrassed to have their disgraced son remain in Chicago.

3

The man allowed a deep chuckle to leave his lips as he read an article from the front page. This reporter was so idiotic. As the paper crinkled in his left hand, he reached for the china coffee cup with his right. It was a good thing he hadn't used his real name in Chicago. No one was the wiser. And he'd like to keep it that way.

The waiter was at his elbow. Again. Did he need anything? No.

The draped towel over the man's arm almost touched the table as he bowed and left.

He must admit, he liked being waited on, but when people knew you had money, the cloying attention became claustrophobic.

The headline on the front page caught his attention again and he smiled: *Pinkerton Agents Search for Mastermind Behind First National Robbery.*

He had to give the snot-nosed reporter a little credit—at least he acknowledged the mastery behind the theft.

The Pinkertons had their work cut out for them. The article

suggested they *guessed* it might be an inside job. Little did they know. No need to worry, though—they'd never figure it out. He was clean as a whistle.

And he was rich.

A beautiful dame sashayed by, her bright red fingernails tapping their way along the linen tablecloth. The not-so-subtle glance she threw over her shoulder made him forget all about the papers. Too bad she was only after his money.

He took a long drink from his water goblet and stood. There was more than one beautiful dame in this outrageously expensive hotel.

Tucking the folded paper under his arm, he headed toward the marble foyer.

There'd be plenty of time to read the news later.

Matanuska Valley, Alaska Territory

Even though the temperature had warmed up into the double digits in the past week, two feet of snow still covered the ground and probably would for several more weeks. Gwyn stoked the fires in the upstairs fireplace, the stove, and the living room fireplace. Trying to keep their cabin warm in the depths of winter was always an undertaking. She loved their home with its huge log walls and giant windows. But the enormity of it for just the two of them overwhelmed her at times. She understood that her father had built it to her mother's grand expectations because he loved her and wanted her to be happy. But after Mother and Sophia left, it seemed to mock the Hillermans who remained. The emptiness often engulfed Gwyn as she cleaned.

She slid two pans of bread into the oven and surveyed the kitchen. She had plenty of time for it to bake. The long toll of winter the past year and the government's new project propelled her out of doors. Gwyn walked down the path to the barn and cast a glance at her spade. How she ached to start her garden! Each year it was the same. Her father would tease her about having "ants in your pants" to start digging in the dirt. Before her mother left them, she would scold her husband for using such undignified language for a young woman, but Gwyn never minded. He'd been saying it all her life and it endeared him even more to her heart.

Gwyn pushed on the gate to their fenced-in garden through the drifted snow. With a final shove, she moved it far enough to squeeze through. Kneeling down, she lifted her face to the sun. Spring couldn't come fast enough for her this year. Oh, she knew she'd have to contend with the moose and other critters trying to get to her garden, but she longed for it anyway. Gwyn pushed a gloved hand down through the snow. The ground was hard and frozen, but it didn't keep her from dreaming of spring. There was something about turning over the soil, the scent of it filling her head. Maybe it was that she loved watching things grow, or maybe she appreciated it all the more because the growing season was so short. She wasn't sure, but her heart never failed to anticipate the coming of spring with great joy. It was the waiting part she had trouble with.

Waiting.

Today she had to admit her anxiousness stemmed more from her father's absence than the long-awaited garden.

The gate to the garden clanged shut as Gwyn headed to the barn to check on the animals. The ARRC had once again summoned her father to Anchorage. And since patience truly wasn't Gwyn's virtue, she'd been flitting from one chore to another, glancing every ten seconds or so to the horizon.

Good heavens. It was ridiculous. The horses whinnied after her as she left the barn minutes after she'd entered it. Shouldn't Father be back by now? The wait was killing her. What would the board say this time? What news would there be from the president? Since they didn't have a newspaper yet in their little valley, she couldn't even read the delayed newswires.

Maybe she should have gone with him after all. This was silly. Pacing out in the snow while her sourdough baked.

One long step brought her crashing down as her foot sank into a snowdrift. The icy greeting to her leg brought a little sense back to her. Crawling out of the hole, she scolded herself for not watching where she was going. She might dearly love this land, but it could be harsh and unforgiving if ignored.

Gwyn brushed the snow off her pants and shoved her long underwear back into the fur-lined boots. Sadzi would be laughing hysterically if she saw Gwyn right now. The thought brought a smile to her face. She'd better get back to work.

In the cabin, the delicious smell of fresh bread wafted through the air. The scent always made Gwyn feel a sense of peace and home. She had read that many folks bought their bread in stores—some even bought it sliced. It all sounded ever so convenient, but Gwyn thought it a sad loss. Convenience had no inviting aroma. Convenience brought no sense of comfort. Would they *all* soon be buying sliced bread?

Depositing her coat and boots at the door, she tried not to let her heart be heavy. With a sigh, she gave the bread a quick check. It was done. She pulled out two round crusty loaves to cool and put two more into the oven. Taking up several pieces of wood, she added them to the stove in order to keep it hot.

The long blast of a distant train whistle pulled her attention from the bread. Father! He was finally home.

She rushed to get back into her boots and coat. Forgetting her worries, she hurried to meet him at the tracks.

He'd barely stepped from the train when Gwyn called out. She flung her right arm in the air and waved. "Father! You're back!"

He rubbed his hands together as he approached. "Here I thought it had been warming up, but my hands aren't agreeing with me on that point."

She wrapped an arm around his back and swallowed the million questions she wanted to ask as they walked toward home. "How was the trip?"

He glanced down at her, "You mean, what did they want and what information do I have to share?" The laughter in his eyes couldn't be missed.

He knew her so well. Ignoring his teasing, Gwyn feigned disinterest as they walked arm in arm toward the cabin. "Well, if you'd like to talk about it, I'm all ears, but if you're too tired, I'm sure it can wait."

Deep laughter filled the air. "Oh, you do my heart good, Gwyn."

She opened the door and the aroma of sourdough hit them both. Father smiled. "You've been baking bread. I hope you'll allow me to have a piece right out of the oven."

She tried to hide her smile. "Let me help you get your boots off first. Then I'll get you some coffee . . . and perhaps a piece of bread. Maybe that will help you to feel like . . . Well, maybe you'll feel warmer." He laughed and it momentarily helped to sweep away Gwyn's worries.

Finally seated with a cup between his hands and a hot

slice of bread on the table, Father didn't keep her waiting. "They've set aside another 180,000 acres. That makes a total of 260,000 acres, including all the land from the first home-steaders who didn't stay."

Gwyn remembered how many families had tried to home-stead in the valley when her family first came to Alaska. Only a quarter of them remained, Gwyn and her father included. She raised her eyebrows. "Are they expecting more people?" Would it fail like the first time?

"Not right now, but they want to be prepared. The choos-ing of the colonists is underway. The board has asked me to make medical supply lists and asked for your help as well in supplying information to the government, so they know what they need for this project." He took a long sip from his cup.

"You sound a little overwhelmed." The chair scraped the floor as Gwyn pulled it out and sat. "And you don't get over-whelmed very often."

"I want to do whatever I can to help, but I must admit that the task at hand boggles the mind." He looked up at her. "I understand their timing and the need for it, but I think we need to spend more time in prayer over this project. It feels so rushed. It's hard to believe that in the next month they'll start sending up construction workers and freight. And soon after that, the families."

"Will we be ready? I mean, is there any possible way every-thing can be in place by then?"

"I honestly don't know. But we've got to do our best to help." Her father exhaled a long sigh and took that oppor-tunity to sample the bread. After a long pause he picked up the conversation again. "I'm a bit concerned about the condition of all those folks coming up here. Who knows how many of them will get seasick, and with that number traveling together, there's bound to be a lot of sickness, especially among the children."

Gwyn's heart quickened. The thought of little children suffering was the worst. Maybe this idea wasn't so good after all. Maybe God was trying to get their attention—to tell them that the travel would be too risky, with too little health care, not enough time—so they could stop the project.

In an instant, guilt flooded her insides. All the discussions she'd had with her father since they found out about the colonization came rushing back. He'd dug up newspaper articles for her to read about the poverty and drought-stricken people. A lot of them had no work, no food, nothing.

In their private world in Alaska, away from the "real world," Gwyn and her father had been affected by the Depression as well, but not nearly as much as people in the States. A vivid memory crashed in of her father bringing the newspaper home a year or so ago that stated the New York City Welfare Council tallied 139 starvation or malnutrition-related deaths in 1933. And that was in just *one* city. How many more would suffer?

How could she tell her father she was scared to death? The whole project frightened her. But when it came down to it, it wasn't *really* the project. It was change. And all the new people. Could she tell her father the truth?

A glimpse of him answered her question. Even with all the added burdens, he was excited. It radiated from him.

She stood and walked to the window. Closing her eyes, she lifted a prayer heavenward, confessing her hesitation toward the project. *Oh, Lord, you know me. You understand me better than I understand myself. Help me, Father. I'm scared.*

Scared of change. Scared of all the new people and scared that I will fail to be a help to them, a light to them. But how do I reach people for Christ if I'm not around people? The thought lifted a smile to her face. *Give me the strength and courage to stand beside my father and help him. And please keep all those families safe on their long journey here.*

Sweet peace filled her. Even with all her fears, worries, and selfish pride, God was willing to use her. She needed to be ready. This land was plentiful. Hundreds of families could live off the land here and support their families for generations to come.

Gwyn straightened her shoulders and turned back to her father. "Well, if change and new people are coming to Alaska, what can I do to help?"

APRIL 1, 1935
CHICAGO, ILLINOIS

The radio in the corner of Jeremiah's apartment blared out the new song, *Alone*, for the second time that morning.

There must be someone waiting . . .

No. There wasn't.

Who feels the way I do . . .

No. There wouldn't be. Ever again.

Three brisk strides brought him to the table, and he turned the knob to silence the link to the outside world.

For three weeks, he'd holed up in his apartment. Not answering the door for anyone. Not answering messages from his parents. Not answering any mail.

Except for one letter.

A doctor he had idolized as a boy, Dr. H., lived in Alaska and asked if Jeremiah would be willing to come and help out as a doctor. His mentor apologized for the brief amount of time to prepare but raved about the land of Alaska and the incredible challenges. It was asking a lot of a promising young doctor like Jeremiah, but Dr. H. believed his one-time apprentice would thrive in the atmosphere, and that a long and full medical career could be had in the Matanuska valley. Dr. H.'s vision of building a hospital in the valley and his description of the Matanuska Project that was going to provide new lives for many who had suffered deprivation in the Stateside Depression excited Jeremiah.

Apparently the president's New Deal efforts had been put in motion, and hundreds of families were heading to the territory to colonize. Before the board's decision to revoke his license, Jeremiah wouldn't have given the proposition a second thought. After all, his former fiancée didn't even speak to her father. Sophia had whispered to him one night in tears, which he now assumed had been fake, that she hadn't spoken to her father or heard from him all these years. Edith and Sophia had attempted to poison Jeremiah's mind toward the man he'd admired as a youth. But now he saw things with clarity and eyes wide open, and his memories served him well.

Dr. H. had taken Jeremiah seriously as a child—what with his desire to become a doctor driving him with passion. Sophia tried to convince him that her father was eccentric and crazy in refusing to leave the territory of Alaska. She and Mrs. Hillerman refused to speak of the man in public. She'd also convinced him that the reason they were in Chicago was because of her ailing grandfather, but Jeremiah now understood all too well the real reasons: Mrs. Edith Hillerman had left her husband and older daughter to return to high society. That truth was all too clear. She wanted money, social prestige, and the comforts of her family's mansion. And in all honesty, Jeremiah had been close to falling into the same trap. He had been blinded by the temptation of gaining status, power, and money. What shallow relationships he'd forged!

With the clarity of the true emptiness of his life behind him, Jeremiah responded the same day to Dr. H.'s missive, hoping that news of his stripped license would never reach the northern territory. He didn't have the guts to tell his old mentor the truth. Yet. His only hope was the fact that Mrs. Hillerman never seemed to communicate with her husband in Alaska.

A new fear spread within him. What if Dr. H. found out? What if the man who'd taught him so much rejected him as well? That would be far worse than to be found practicing medicine without a license. Jeremiah realized that after all he'd lost, Dr. H.'s good opinion was something he didn't want to lose. It was really all he had left, and the fear of that being stripped away was more painful than Jeremiah wanted to admit.

President Roosevelt's words from his inaugural address rang in Jeremiah's mind: "*. . . let me assert my firm belief that the only thing we have to fear is fear itself—nameless, unreasoning, unjustified terror which paralyzes needed efforts to convert retreat into advance.*"

He wouldn't retreat. Not anymore.

He'd advance. And after reuniting with the man he respected more than anyone else, maybe then he'd work up the courage to tell him the truth. Maybe the good doctor could even help get him reinstated. Surely the restrictions in the Alaska Territory were fewer than in the States. No doubt the people there were desperate enough that any doctor, even one accused of accidentally killing his patient, would be considered useful.

Checking his pocket watch, his conscience pricked. There wasn't any time to say good-bye. But he'd planned it that way. No one knew where he was going. No one knew he was even leaving. His mother and father might be upset and say they had a right to know, but they'd slammed that door in his face when they asked him to leave.

Jeremiah would contact Howard when he was settled. His cousin already stated he would handle the appeal so Jeremiah could stay out of the spotlight. He'd let him.

The wall clock in the kitchen chimed the hour and urged him forward. Not much time left to make it to the train station. He surveyed his packing. A few more clothing items would fit in the trunk if he stuffed them in the nooks and crannies. The majority of the steamer held his papers and books, medical supplies and equipment he'd purchased over the years. Clothing wasn't as necessary. All the fine suits Sophia urged him to have tailored for his new position still hung in the closet. No need to bring any memories of what could've been. Her taste was far too fine for his liking anyway. He should've seen the signs earlier. Greedy, selfish, arrogant, vain—those were the words that described Sophia Hillerman. And he wanted no part of it. Ever again.

He'd had enough of women. His bitterness toward them had grown over the past weeks. First his fiancée and future mother-in-law had turned their backs on him and then his own mother. All because they worried about what people would think.

Angry thoughts propelled him forward.

The door thumped shut behind him as he made it to the street. Chicago dismissed him with a blast of icy cold wind. He had once loved this city. Would he ever return?

4

Nasnana kneaded the dough with her hands. Over the years, as her hands crinkled and withered, the process became more painful, but she'd always loved the feel of fresh dough between her fingers.

"Gwyn, would you mind stirring the soup?"

Thin and tall, blond-haired Gwyn reached for the spoon. The young woman had captured Nasnana's heart from the first time they'd met. Her deep gray eyes so like her father's gave away the yearning for a mother figure in her life. Even though her mother had been present for most of her upbringing, the aloof woman hadn't been a *real* mother to gentle-hearted Gwyn.

Nasnana shook her head at the thought, but her heart filled with pride as she watched the young woman bring a sample of soup to her mouth. She wasn't the bold beauty like her younger sister, Sophia, but her beauty went far beyond the younger Hillerman child. Gwyn held true beauty within her, and it radiated outward.

The one major flaw in the little six-year-old angel she'd taken under her wing so long ago was her tendency toward worry. Even with all of Nasnana's prayer and prodding, Gwyn could still work herself into a worried fit over the simplest of things.

"Let me take over for you." Gwyn's little shove brought her thoughts back to the present. "What's put that smile on your face?"

"Just remembering, my dear." Gone were the days she argued with the offer of help. Relinquishing the bread board, Nasnana patted the younger woman's shoulder.

"Remembering what?" Blond curls bobbed around her face as Gwyn worked the dough.

"You. As a child."

"Oh my. Maybe we should redirect your thoughts to something of greater import."

Another difference in the Hillerman girls: Gwyn always shifted the attention off of herself, where Sophia longed to be the center of attention, often forcing the matter. "You are of great importance and don't you forget it." Nasnana smacked the seat of Gwyn's pants with a wooden spoon.

"And you—" she grabbed the spoon—"should have all your wooden spoons taken away."

Sadzi entered the room laughing. "You two are very entertaining."

Nasnana watched Gwyn's ears turn red. "Don't be embarrassed, child. I've been trying to get you to speak your mind all these years."

"But that was very disrespectful, and I apologize." Gwyn ducked her head as she shaped the dough into round loaves. "I can't believe I sassed you." The slightest hint of a smile appeared.

"It's about time." Nasnana lowered herself into her rocking

chair. A bit of anger bubbled up inside her. "That mother of yours ran over you for so many years, and you just took it. I hated to watch as she squashed you over and over again"— tears threatened to choke her—"like a beautiful shell she crushed under her pretty patent leather shoes." Looking down, she realized her fists were gripping the arms of the chair until her knuckles turned white. *Lord, forgive me.* She breathed deeply and closed her eyes. "I'm sorry, girls. I should never—"

"Don't apologize." Gwyn turned, shoulders straight, chin lifted. "You said those words because you love me. Something I can't say my mother ever felt. I'm not a bold person like you and Sadzi, but I appreciate you both encouraging me to spread my wings."

Her granddaughter, Sadzi, hugged her friend close. "You are so amazing, Gwyn. Do you know that?"

"I agree." Nasnana motioned the girls to the table. "That's why as the bread rises, the passage I chose for today is Psalm 139." They were used to her abrupt ways. When she got down to business, they paid attention. "Why don't we pray."

Both girls nodded, sat, and bowed their heads.

"Father in heaven, hallowed be your name. We love you, Lord. We come to you with all our burdens, all our grief, and all our regrets. Guide us, Father. Teach us what you would have us learn today. And help us to be a blessing to all those around us. Amen."

"Amen."

"Now, Sadzi, would you read for us?"

"Yes, Grandmother." She flipped to the text and cleared her throat. "'O Lord, thou hast searched me, and known me. . . . There is not a word in my tongue, but lo, O Lord, thou knowest it altogether.'"

Sadzi let out a long sigh. "I wish He would sometimes *keep* my tongue from speaking."

Laughter rounded the table. Nasnana had worked for years on changing Sadzi's habit of "speak first, think later" to "think first, speak later." She cleared her throat. "Continue please, Sadzi."

Gwyn shot a grin to her.

Her granddaughter's bright voice continued as she read the entire passage, finishing with "'Search me, O God, and know my heart: try me, and know my thoughts: And see if there be any wicked way in me, and lead me in the way everlasting.'" Sadzi leaned back in her chair, a thoughtful look replacing the always-present smile.

"There's much in here that I'd like to discuss over the next week or so, but today, I want to talk to you both about who you are. Do you know you are fearfully and wonderfully made?" She glanced down at her Bible and read, "'I will praise thee; for I am fearfully and wonderfully made: marvelous are thy works.' Doesn't that just thrill you? Before you were born, God knew exactly who each of you would be, what your personality would be—and even everything you would ever go through in this life. He knew how many days you would live. More important, He understands—better than anyone—what it feels like to be rejected."

She reached a hand out to touch each girl. Gwyn's beautiful gray eyes filled with tears. "Gwyn, your mother's rejection is not a reflection of you. It doesn't define who you are. You are God's child. That's what really matters." Nasnana turned to look into Sadzi's dark brown eyes. "And Sadzi, the same is for you. I'm sorry my daughter ran off, but I won't apologize for the privilege I've had to raise you all these years." A knot formed in her throat. Her own husband had lived only two years after the birth of their daughter, Lahleli. Their headstrong daughter had brought much joy to Nasnana's life, but also much grief. Nasnana hadn't seen her since she left Sadzi all those years ago.

"When the missionaries came to my people over seventy years ago, I listened. I learned about Jesus, and I polished my English. Because I chose to follow their ways, most of my people rejected me. Their fear drove almost all of the tribe hundreds of miles away to get away from the white man and his ways, his sickness, and his alcohol." A deep sigh shook her frame.

"It's been a lonely time to be separated from my people, but think of all the wonderful things God has done through this. And look what He's doing now to bring all these hurting and suffering folks practically to our very doorstep." A stray tear rolled down her cheek. "What I'm trying to say is that we're all rejected. Jesus was rejected. But that shouldn't stop us from doing the job He's given us to do. Neither one of you give Jesus enough credit. You both have incredible gifts. So get up and use them."

"Even when we're afraid." Gwyn's words were a statement, not a question.

"Yes."

Gwyn bit her bottom lip. "For years, I've prayed for God's direction. If He wanted me to go to the mission field somewhere, or just further into the bush here in Alaska. I've always been afraid of change. You know that. But still I've prayed. What if . . . what if God is bringing the mission field to us? To help me overcome my fear?"

Nasnana warmed with the joy she felt. Precious Gwyn.

Putting one foot in front of her even though change scared her to the core.

"So why don't we come up with something we can do for each of the families?" Sadzi leaned forward, light shining in her eyes. "You know, something to welcome them, help make life easier?"

Gwyn's face lit up. "I think from what Father said the colonists will have to live in tent homes while their permanent homes are being built. Since they have a limited amount of goods they are allowed to bring, there will probably be many things they won't have."

Nasnana nodded and pondered this for a moment. "You're right. And each family might have a different need. So what is something they all could use?"

"We don't have enough time to make quilts—definitely not for two hundred families." Sadzi tapped her chin with her finger.

"You are correct, and that may be something that everyone will bring plenty of . . ."

Gwyn stood up and went to stir the soup. After several moments, she turned, spoon in hand. "What about some kind of foodstuff? Something they could eat right away that could help feed their families?"

Excitement built in Nasnana. "That's a great idea. I bet most of them aren't as familiar with sourdough as we are up here. . . ." She let her words trail off as the thought took root. "If we all multiplied our sourdough and kept feeding it and dividing it, we could have enough for all the families by the time they get here."

"But what will we put it in?" A frown creased Sadzi's face. "We'd have it bubbling over onto the floor."

"Oh my, that would be a mess." Gwyn made a face. "But Nasnana's idea is wonderful! Just think of it, the colonists would be able to make bread and pancakes immediately upon arrival. If we could just think of a way to store it."

New plans formed in Nasnana's mind. If only she'd thought of it sooner. It could be a possible link to bring the whites and native people together. If . . .

"What are you thinking?" Gwyn asked.

"Well . . . I need to bring that pot of soup to my friends at Eklutna. There's a few sick, and I'd like to help."

Sadzi cocked an eyebrow at her. "You're not planning on walking all that way alone, are you? That's halfway between here and Anchorage!"

Gwyn frowned her agreement.

Nasnana laughed at their protectiveness. She'd been walking back and forth to Eklutna for decades. There was no other way. These young girls had been spoiled by modern society and the train in their valley. "Of course not. I was going to take the sled, but you girls could go with me. We could ask the ones who still work with pottery to make a small crock for each family."

The invitation appeared to ease their scowls. "That's a lot of crocks, Grandmother."

"But there's got to be at least twenty people who could do it. That would only be ten each." The excitement built. This could work.

"Oh, let's do!" Gwyn clapped her hands together. "Let's go right now."

Laughter erupted.

Gwyn covered her mouth. "Oops. I guess we should wait until the bread is baked?"

Nasnana nodded.

Sadzi tugged on her sleeve and pulled her away from the table as Gwyn went to place the bread in the oven. Her granddaughter whispered in her ear, "Grandmother, aren't you worried about prejudice? You know how many of the white people still treat us."

"I know, my dear," she said, patting Sadzi's hand, "but we're going to leave this in the Lord's hands, all right?"

Gwyn reread the return address. Eagerness and dread waged a war in her stomach.

A letter.

From her mother.

The postmark read February 1. And here it was the middle of April!

It often took weeks for them to receive mail, but this letter must have traveled by way of China.

Gwyn removed her gloves and sat at the kitchen table. Did she want to read it now? To risk her feelings? As much as she longed for words of love or even the slightest affirmation, Gwyn knew there wouldn't be any in the missive. But there was always hope. Hope that her mother truly did care. Hope that circumstances would change and her mother would return to her family in Alaska.

Six years she'd been gone. Six. Years. And in that time, Gwyn had received five letters from her mother. Only five. None ever arrived for her father. Her heart broke a little more for him each time his eyes filled with expectation when a letter from Chicago arrived.

Gwyn would read the letter aloud, sharing all of Edith's

pieces of gossip and details of every event they'd attended. There would always be a sentence or two about Grandfather Titus and how weary Mother had become from all the toil she put forth in caring for him. But never a mention of missing Gwyn and her father. Never a personal note to the man she'd been married to for over twenty-five years.

Would this letter be any different?

No matter how hard she tried, Gwyn couldn't deny she longed for her mother's acceptance and love.

Hope always won out. Maybe this time would be different. Gwyn ripped the envelope open.

Dear Gwyneth,

I pray you are doing well in that ghastly little shack your father built in the middle of nowhere.

We are all doing incredibly well here. Although your grandfather Titus has weakened yet again. His illness has taken a toll on everyone, but in the midst of it all, we've found happiness. The lavish surroundings and kind servants soothe our minds and souls.

Your last letter asked if we would be returning soon. Gwyneth, you should know by now that I'm needed too much here to leave. You have your father to look after, so I'm sure you understand, even though his needs are nothing compared to Grandfather Titus's. There are many nights I've had to read to him for over an hour before he could rest comfortably—you must acknowledge how taxing that has been on me! Oh, and precious Sophia has a fiancé now. I couldn't possibly take her away from her intended. Our lives are here.

Why don't you come here for a visit? Your father has

kept you hidden from society long enough. There are parties and dances, shows and dinners—well, at least for the wealthy. And we are wealthy, Gwyneth, dear. It's time you made your grandparents proud and came back to the family home.

I must end. I'm already late for my hair appointment. There are such cute new styles now. I'm sure the butler will post this sometime soon. I'll let you know when the wedding is going to be so you can make arrangements to come.

Mother

That was it? She turned it over. Nothing more. Gwyn took the letter to her room and flopped herself onto her bed. The ceiling seemed to stare back. Why didn't she measure up to her mother? Did her mother even care? Her father was the most amazing man, and her mother just up and left him. For what? Grandfather Titus had a heart attack six years ago. He was still alive. And according to Mother there were plenty of servants to see to his needs. So why didn't she return home? Didn't her husband and daughter matter?

Nasnana's words from the other day came back. Gwyn was God's child. That's what mattered. Not the fact that Edith Hillerman had abandoned her husband and firstborn.

Gwyn rolled over and sobbed into her pillow. Was it Sophia's beauty that gained their mother's favor? Or her love of frivolous things? And now she was getting married. Her baby sister would marry before Gwyn did.

The letter lay crumpled next to her hand. Sitting up, she grabbed it and read it again.

It was just as bad the second time as the first.

Why did she torture herself? Gwyn wadded up the letter and determined not to write back this time. It was useless. Her mother didn't care.

Besides, Gwyn would have her hands full with all the preparations for the colony. Fear or not, she would move forward.

The world still turned, even if she wasn't in Edith Hillerman's good graces.

"Gwyn? Are you here?" Her father's voice jolted her into action.

"Coming!" Gwyn swiped at her cheeks and ran down the stairs.

"I've got to head down to the train station. Dr. Vaughan is supposed to arrive today, and I just heard the whistle."

She rounded the corner to the kitchen. "Who?"

Her father smacked his forehead, "I'm sorry. I completely forgot to tell you. I invited Jeremiah Vaughan to come—"

Another whistle from the train interrupted her father.

"I'll tell you all about it in a little bit."

As her father raced out the door, Gwyn gripped the balled-up letter in her hand.

Without another thought, she threw it into the fireplace. The paper blackened, shriveled, and then turned to ash.

No longer would she think of herself as Edith Hillerman's daughter. She didn't even want to acknowledge she had a mother.

Her identity was found in the Lord and no one else.

5

Never in his most vivid dreams could Jeremiah have imagined a more beautiful place. Compared to the dingy gray streets of Chicago, the massive mountains and pure white snow set against the backdrop of crystal-clear blue sky were almost unbelievable. And yet, here he stood.

In Alaska.

The train slowed to a stop at his new home. The Matanuska valley.

The long train ride across the country to the West Coast had put plenty of miles between Jeremiah and Chicago. Then boarding the boat in Seattle ensured that number would multiply. But after a rough voyage, he'd been ready to settle into any small hut he could find—as long as it was secured on dry land.

Now the final leg of his journey brought him to mountains surrounding a picturesque valley. A small flicker of hope awakened his dreams again.

A new life.

A fresh start.

And the chance to practice medicine for the rest of his

days. He would earn the people's trust with his skills and care. License or no license, he was called to heal.

Jeremiah grabbed his satchel and exited the train. Cold air greeted him. Not the windy, gritty cold of Chicago. This was a crisp, clean cold.

"Jeremiah!"

He knew that voice. As he turned, Jeremiah spotted the man he'd idolized as a young boy. "Dr. H.!" He couldn't help the smile that grew on his face. "Thank you for inviting me."

The older man gripped his shoulder. "I can't believe a promising young doctor like yourself would agree to come, but I'm so glad you did."

"It sounded like an adventure."

Dr. H. chuckled. "I can guarantee it will be that." He led Jeremiah to the small station. "Let's get your baggage and we'll head to the house for some dinner. It's a little bit of a jaunt from here, but I'm sure you're up to it." The older man winked at him. "After we get you fed, I'll show you the small office I have set up."

"Sounds good. I'm famished."

"I've got your sleeping quarters set up in the office for right now until your cabin is constructed. Everyone is so focused on the colony that there aren't any extra hands, but I hired some good men from a village well north of here to help. It should be done within the week."

Jeremiah hadn't expected that. "That's very generous, but I don't need you to go to all that trouble. I—"

"Already done." He patted Jeremiah on the shoulder. "And it's not any trouble. We've got bigger hurdles coming up, so I wanted you to feel as comfortable as possible before the chaos truly begins. Your cabin is between our home and the train lines here, so it will be closer to where I hope we'll eventually build a hospital. There are already plans for a town here. They've named it Palmer.

"I apologize. I'm overwhelming you with information. It's been so busy already that I hardly remember what day of the week it is." The older man laughed. "I even forgot to tell Gwyn that I'd invited you. I've spent so much time with the ARRC and all the plans for the colony, that I haven't filled her in on everything."

That was fine with Jeremiah. He wanted to avoid women as much as possible, and any sibling of Sophia was bound to be a high-hat Jane anyway. But it'd be best not to say anything to Dr. H. As far as Jeremiah knew, his mentor had no idea he'd ever been engaged to Sophia, much less had any interaction with his family.

They walked for about a quarter of an hour and arrived at Dr. H's home. The wonderful scent of fresh-baked bread floated out the door and caused Jeremiah's stomach to growl. How long had it been since he'd eaten?

"Come on in, Jeremiah. I'm sure Gwyn's got something that will cure what ails you."

"I doubt it," Jeremiah said under his breath.

"What was that?"

"Oh, nothing. I didn't realize how hungry I'd become. They offered us food in Anchorage when we switched trains, but I was too excited to get here to think about food."

The doctor took his coat, hat, and gloves. "Well, you can think about it now. Let's eat and we can discuss any questions you might have over dinner." He turned toward the kitchen. "Gwyn, is that stew about ready?"

A slim blonde with long curly hair stood with her back to

them. Not at all the curvaceous Sophia. She held a spoon up to her mouth as if she'd just tasted from the pot.

A quick turn and she placed her hand in front of her mouth. "Oh, excuse me. I was just sampling to see if it was done." Her cheeks tinged pink as her eyes darted around, never meeting his.

Not a flirtatious glance or anything.

"No need to stand on ceremony, Gwyn. We'll all be working together around the clock and in close conditions, so let me reintroduce you to Dr. Jeremiah Vaughan." Dr. H. looked at him with pride in his eyes. "May I present my eldest, Gwyn." The smile between father and daughter almost did Jeremiah in. "She is the finest nurse I've ever worked with, and I don't say that just because she's my daughter. It might take her a little while, but I'm sure she will learn your preferences as we go along and become your extra set of hands like she has been mine all these years. I realize she wasn't even in school yet when you last saw her, but perhaps you remember."

Jeremiah stuck out his hand. Not wanting to be rude to his benefactor, he attempted a smile. "Vaguely. Nice to meet you, Gwyn." No need to let them know that he remembered the little pigtailed waif who had followed him around. That flash of memory overtook him for a moment. Let's see, he was thirty-four, so that would make Gwyn around twenty-two or twenty-three.

The woman in front of him brought him back to the present. She lowered her brows a bit and seemed to study him as she shook his hand. "Welcome to Alaska." She made her way back to the stove and threw over her shoulder, "Go ahead and get cleaned up. Dinner's ready."

Jeremiah had a chance to study Gwyn as her father kissed

her cheek. She wore no cosmetics, and her dress reminded him of something from decades past. Not that it was old or frayed, but it was nothing like the provocative styles women were wearing in the city. The single word that came to mind to describe her was *simple*. He followed Dr. H. to the sink and washed his hands.

For some odd reason his heart jumped a little. He frowned. He couldn't allow himself to be attracted to *any* woman. Not to mention one he'd see every day who just happened to be Sophia's sister.

As they sat around the table, Dr. H. blessed the meal and peaceful silence surrounded Jeremiah. The enticing aroma pushed his rumbling stomach into overtime. He took two pieces of bread, buttered them, and downed the first one in three bites. The stew was delicious as well, but just about anything would taste good when he was this hungry.

Dr. H. filled his daughter in on the plans for the clinic and where Jeremiah would be staying. His hope was that, between the three of them, they'd be able to put forth a valiant effort in taking care of the two hundred families about to descend on the valley.

"It won't be easy. Although the government officials promised that the families chosen will know how to endure the cold winters and isolation, they really have no idea of what they're talking about."

"Why do you say that?" Jeremiah asked.

"Having lived both in the States and here, I can honestly say there is nothing to compare," Dr. H. replied. "People often think that because they have lived in a small town or in a place miles from a city, they will understand how it is to live in Alaska. But it's not the same. Here you have no big city close by. Anchorage is just a baby herself. There's no constant flow of supplies. Even transportation is limited. And when the weather turns bitter cold, there can be days, even weeks, when getting around is difficult to impossible."

"Those people coming here will surely realize their limitations. I imagine the government would have advised them," Jeremiah suggested.

"But that would require knowledge on the part of those government officials, most—if not all—of whom have never been to Alaska. You're old enough to remember that ten years ago we had a terrible diphtheria epidemic in Nome. Getting serum there to save lives was very nearly impossible, and only through the ingenuity of dog-sledding teams were we able to connect to those poor folks. Imagine other epidemics breaking out. Those newcomers will be used to picking up the phone and ordering what they need."

"True." Jeremiah considered the situation for a moment. "Perhaps that should be something that is addressed first thing. Perhaps we could hold some sort of forum to advise the colonists."

"They'll need to know about so much," Gwyn murmured. "The wildlife, the planting season, the weather signs, and many other things." She shook her head, as if disapproving of the entire undertaking, and Jeremiah couldn't help but wonder about her opinion. Perhaps she resented the idea of newcomers. Perhaps she even resented the idea of his being there.

Dr. H. continued speaking about the area and future plans for the colony. Gwyn nodded, seeming to listen to every word her father spoke. She had brief answers to each of his questions, and asked intelligent questions. Sophia certainly would never have had such sharp thoughts on the matters at hand.

Perhaps Gwyn was nothing like her sister. Jeremiah shook his head and refocused on his food. All women were alike.

He laid his spoon down, realizing he'd eaten two bowls of stew and five pieces of bread in a matter of minutes. The doctor and his daughter both still had dishes full in front of them.

Gwyn passed Jeremiah the bread basket again without even looking at him, and he took another slice. This piece, he took his time enjoying rather than inhaling. The tanginess of the bread mixed with the saltiness of the butter had to be one of the greatest things his taste buds had ever known. He could live off of it.

Dr. H. looked toward him. "I'd like to help you unpack your supplies after dinner." He took a bite of the stew. "Then I can show you everything in the office. Eventually, my dream is to see a hospital built here, but that will be sometime down the road."

Jeremiah took a sip of his coffee. "That sounds great." He realized his manners were lacking. In all his effort to avoid Gwyn, he'd been rude. "Compliments on the meal, Miss Hillerman. That was excellent. Was that beef?"

"Moose." A small smile lit her face. "And please, just call me Gwyn."

"Moose? I don't think I've ever had moose. Do you eat a lot of it up here?"

Gwyn stood and gathered plates.

Dr. H. answered his question. "We do. One moose will feed us all winter and then some."

A brief pounding at the door preceded the stomping of feet. A tiny girl with jet-black hair and dark eyes burst into the dining room. "Dr. Hillerman, they need you. Baby coming."

Jeremiah watched the scene unfold. Gwyn and Dr. H. moved into immediate action, working together without a word. In half a minute, they had supplies and were grabbing coats and boots.

"You can come along if you want, Jeremiah, but you have to come now."

The doctor's words spurred him out of his chair and into action as he trailed the trio out into the snow.

Jeremiah rolled over in bed. Exhausted, his body screamed for sleep, but his mind wasn't cooperating. All the events of the night kept replaying in his head.

His first glimpse of Gwyn. In those first few moments, he'd convinced himself she seemed plain and ordinary. But as the night wore on, he found himself drawn to her. What was it that fascinated him? He didn't even know her. But as she'd helped deliver that baby—her calm, quiet nature, her soothing spirit—he'd realized he'd never met anyone like her.

His thoughts drifted back to home. Chicago. And everything he'd ever known. All the women in his life had been concerned with finery, money, catching a man, and social status. Now that he thought about it, every woman he knew had manipulated him. Had manipulated the people around them.

He realized he'd been manipulated—used and managed— by everyone in his life. Randolph Brewster, Edith Hillerman, Sophia Hillerman, even his own mother and father.

Had his busy life been full of fake people? Had he been so focused on money and securing his future that he fell for it?

A picture of Gwyn darted through his mind again. Her simple appeal was powerful.

But maybe that was her way. Maybe she wasn't real either. He didn't want to be caught in another trap.

No. Gwyn's gentle spirit didn't seem false. But he couldn't allow himself to get close to her. The Alaska Hillermans didn't know the truth. Gwyn would despise him if she knew.

Then she would have something in common with her sister.

Jeremiah beat his fist against the pillow. How was it that a grown man could be so mistaken about life and the people in it? How was it that he could have gone through all his schooling and training to be a physician and not understand that most everyone lived behind a façade—a pretense of images and possessions?

He'd always seen his mother and father as simple people but nevertheless genuine. Now his heart ached at the thought that even *they* were driven by the opinions of others. It seemed ridiculous. It was 1935 after all. They had watched their investments and livelihood threatened in the stock market crash of '29. They'd lived through Prohibition and the government's attempt to force morality upon a people who clearly saw no purpose in being moral. They'd even lived through a worldwide war that threatened the very freedoms which allowed them to live their socially focused lives. How could they be so blind?

How could the medical board have been blind to the fact that medicine was far from a perfect science—that patients lived and died, often receiving precisely the same treatment. It wasn't an exact practice. There were far too many variables that entered into the picture. Even so, to not risk the new innovations, to ignore the modern inventions and medicines that were being created, was akin to hiding in the dark and hoping that the monsters would leave them alone. They were like silly children.

Jeremiah flopped over on his back and stared in the darkness at the ceiling. Why had this happened to him? What had he done wrong?

Gwyn watched as her father and Jeremiah hovered over a newer medical journal. Jeremiah talked about the innovative intravenous anesthesia, and her father sat fascinated, hanging on every word.

As she cleaned and sterilized the instruments they'd used on the last call, Gwyn thought about this new doctor. In fact, thoughts of him came far too often during the day. Brown-haired, hazel-eyed—she'd never met a more handsome man. And he was so sophisticated! What was a man like that doing in a remote place like this? Certainly someone of his caliber wouldn't have any reason to stick around for long.

Of course, her father was the best man she'd ever known, and he chose to serve here. Could it be possible for Jeremiah to have that same kind, generous heart?

Or was he more like the other city people she knew? They didn't care about other people. Only themselves. Like her mother.

She shook her head in an effort to rid herself of the negative thought. Jeremiah wasn't like that. Was he?

What if her father came to rely on him too much and one day Jeremiah just decided to up and leave? Father was so ecstatic to have him here. Looked at him as a godsend. It's all he'd talked about for days. Jeremiah this and Jeremiah that. Jeremiah showed him this great new technique. Jeremiah studied blah blah blah under so-and-so.

If this new doctor didn't treat her father right, she wouldn't be able to hold her tongue. Most people knew she was quiet and reserved, but what they didn't know was that she also had a temper.

And it began a slow burn. If this young city boy thought he could use her father and then turn around and hurt him, he'd better think twice. Maybe she needed to intervene.

Her father left the office for a moment. Yes, she needed to intervene. Now. Before she had time to lose her nerve.

"Dr. Vaughan, may I have a moment?"

"Sure. And please, call me Jeremiah." He washed his hands at the sink.

"What exactly are your plans?" She allowed the picture of her father being rejected and stranded again to rule her imagination. No matter how handsome the man who stood in front of her.

"Plans? For what?" His brow furrowed.

"Why did you come here?" Her voice squeaked on the last word. Why did she feel guilty for asking?

"What? I came to help your father. There are going to be thousands of people in this valley to care for." He dried his hands on a towel in a slow, methodical way. "What *exactly* are you asking?"

Gwyn placed her hands on her hips. She and the new doctor hadn't had much time to converse over the past week since he arrived. And she'd had way too many daydreams with him in it. That and visions of her father being abandoned didn't help her temper. "I'm just asking what your intentions are. Not many doctors from the big city would want to venture to a place like this. So I'll just say it plain and simple. I don't want my father to trust you only to have you abandon him at a time when he needs you the most."

There. She'd said it. Her shoulders lifted with a huge breath of relief.

A frown deepened on his face. "I won't abandon him."

"How do I know that's the truth?" Gwyn pushed. "My father is a wonderful man who's given up his entire life to serve the people here. He loves medicine. And he loves people."

"I won't abandon him, Gwyn." Jeremiah swiped a hand down his face. "Look, I think it's wonderful that you are so protective of him, but you hardly know me. Your father does. And he trusts me."

She deflated in an instant. He was right. Her father *did* trust him. But her father had also trusted her mother. Was there any way possible to protect Father? Her anger abated. "Please don't hurt him. He's a good man. And he's all I've got." She rushed out the door, tears threatening to pour from her eyes. Why was change so difficult for her to accept?

Tears stung her cheeks as she hit the frigid air outside. Stomping around in the melting snow, she tried to sort out her thoughts. But Jeremiah Vaughan was doing things to her brain. She loved that her father had help. She knew the heavy load would be impossible for the two of them to bear alone, but she also hadn't expected to be attracted to the young doctor, or to worry about his abandoning them. The jumble of her thoughts wasn't helping matters. She needed to calm down. Think it through. And give it time.

Her father headed out the door and straight for her. "Gwyn, what are you doing out here without your coat? It's freezing."

She clapped her hands together. "Oh, just getting some fresh air." She watched her father's eyebrows rise and turned on her heel before he could respond. "We've got lots to do before those workers arrive." She cringed and slipped past the older man. Her father would know something was up. Hopefully he wouldn't ask. *Hopefully* he would realize she didn't want to talk about it.

Blessed warmth greeted her inside the small office. Avoiding Jeremiah, she went right back to the stack of instruments she'd been cleaning and sorting. She felt guilty for having said anything to him. He'd done nothing to earn her distrust. Her suspicious tendencies served no good and only made her look petty. Good heavens, would she ever give up her worrisome ways?

"Jeremiah," her father stated, "I've got a little project I need some help with. Word has come from the ARRC that the first group of transient workers will begin their journey in a couple days. I didn't realize how little time we have left."

Jeremiah grabbed his coat. "Sure, I'll do whatever I can. Although I can't guarantee how good it will be if it includes knitting or cooking." His smile aimed her way seemed genuine enough. Albeit cool. It never reached his eyes when he looked at her.

Her father laughed. "No knitting or cooking. This time." He turned back to the door then looked at her. "Gwyn, why don't you take some time for yourself today, since I've got Jeremiah to help me? You never take any time off." Another smile directed at her.

And then they were gone.

Gwyn stood with scalpels and scissors in her hands. She stared at the door. Should she be offended that her father had replaced her? Well, maybe not replaced her, but it sure felt that way.

When her father had a project to do, he always needed *her*

70

help. They'd been a duo for so long that Gwyn forgot what it was like to be alone. That niggling worry worked its way up her spine again. No. She wouldn't allow it. "*Humph*. I won't." A stomp of her foot and a nod of her head. No need to worry. Nope. A little time to herself sounded wonderful, but then her thoughts turned back to handsome Jeremiah. She wanted to trust him, wanted to hope that he would stick around—she'd really like to know him.

Maybe being alone wasn't such a good idea. Too much time to let her thoughts wander, which also meant she'd have time to worry.

Not a good combination.

"Of course, it's silly for me to presume anything about him," she said aloud. "He might hail from Chicago, but that doesn't mean he's like Mother. Father obviously thinks highly of him." But her father had also thought highly of her mother, and that had proven unfounded.

Thinking of her mother caused the age-old sadness to stir in her heart. She had always known there was a wall of sorts separating her from her mother. They had little in common and she had always seemed an irritation to her mother. She could remember times when she'd tried to show Mother some new plant she'd found or a craft she'd learned. Mother was never impressed or even interested. She always chided Gwyn, telling her that one day all of this would be nothing more than a memory. Even then she had her plans for leaving Alaska behind. Gwyn wondered if her mother realized the emptiness she'd also left behind in her parting.

A knock sounded on the door of the office. Gwyn laid the instruments down. "Come in."

Lilly McLaughlin hopped in on one foot. "Hey, Gwyn."

Her friend from Anchorage came every year to work with the experimental station where the University of Alaska planted and grew crops of enormous size in their fertile valley soil.

"Hey there." She scratched her head. "What on earth are you doing? You're not hurt, are you?"

"*Pbbft*, no." Lilly continued her strange hopping, wiggling off a boot at the same time. Her bobbed red hair stuck to the sides of her freckled face. "A big mound of dripping snow fell off the roof as I walked around the corner, and now I've got a boot full of slush" She looked up and winked. "Have I told you how much I hate wet socks?"

Gwyn giggled with her friend. She'd always wanted Lilly's petite size and cuteness. "Don't we all." She went back to putting everything away. "But I hate to tell you this—we live in Alaska. And the snow's not gone yet."

"Ugh. I know. Every time I think it's warming up, we have another cold snap. But at least it *is* finally melting." She shook out her boot, and Gwyn threw her a towel. "Thanks."

"So what's brought you over here today?"

"Do you have time to help me over at the experimental station? With all these people coming, we're going to have to plant about five times as much as we usually do. You're so good with growing things, and . . . I'm behind. The green-house is overflowing, and I've got much more to plant." Lilly replaced her boot and clasped her hands in front of her face. "Please?"

Lilly's pixie face with her lip jutted out caused Gwyn to laugh even harder. "Of course I'll come help. And you don't ever have to beg, unless, of course, I'm with a patient. But you are in luck. I'm free for the afternoon. As long as we're not planting Brussels sprouts. I hate them."

"Swell! I promise, no Brussels sprouts. You *are* the best, Gwyn."

Well, Lilly thought that. But it wasn't true. Gwyn pulled on her boots and coat. Because if it were, then a handsome young doctor would be plagued by her as much as she was by him.

6

"Tony"—the weasel of a man twisted his hat—"we got a real situation on our hands. And I ain't goin' to prison."

The idiot rambled on and on about what facts the coppers had on the robbery. While the information was good to have, he didn't need a sniveling rat raving like a lunatic for the whole world to hear. "What are you saying, Simms? You're going to squeal?" He leaned forward across the table. All business.

The weasel's face went white. "No, I would never do that to ya, but those Pinkertons are gettin' closer. I got a tail. I just know it. They're sendin' stuff to the cops, and I can't go back to Chicago."

He drummed his fingers on the silk-covered tabletop, the diamond-studded gold ring on his pinky adding an extra thump. The man in front of him had been useful, yes, but now he appeared to be more of a liability than a help. If he was right and someone was on his tail, the stupid man could lead the authorities right to him here in Boston. That was a completely unacceptable thought. He'd worked too hard to plan things out and wasn't about to let it all fall apart now.

"Simms, I think you're right. You can't go back to Chicago. It wouldn't be prudent."

The flunky nodded. "I knew you'd see the problem right away, boss."

"I do see the problem." And it sat across the table. The thorn in his side. He looked Simms in the eyes. "And as you know, I'm very good at eliminating problems."

Simms looked around him in an anxious matter. "So you got a plan?"

"I do indeed." A plan to pin it all on Simms. After all, even dead guys could be convicted.

He straightened his tie. A change of scenery was in order. Somewhere out of the country, off the map. Not easily accessible.

Yes. Maybe it was time to go see his brother for a while.

He allowed a slow smile and tapped his breast pocket. What had seemed a stupid letter earlier about family members being chosen for a fresh start now held more merit. Just needed to clean up a few things here first. "Simms, I've got an idea. We need to relocate you—get you somewhere you can lay low. I know the perfect place. Let's take a drive."

"Aw, thanks, Tony. I knew you'd understand. Can we pick up my girl too? We're supposed to get married, and I wouldn't want to leave her behind."

"Of course. I wouldn't want her wondering what had happened to you." The smile widened. Two for the price of one and there'd be no one left who could identify him. A perfect setup.

May 1935
Matanuska Valley

Gwyn sifted through the small stack of mail in her hands in front of the station. The fresh air of spring was finally upon them, and she so enjoyed the warmth from the sun. Daylight increased by several minutes a day at this time of year, and she wanted to spend as much time out of doors as possible. Especially if it was in the garden. She loved to help things grow.

Her shoulders slumped as she spied a return address. Another letter from her mother. She couldn't remember the last time she'd received two letters in the span of a year. Had she . . . ever? Gwyn stood and debated whether to open it now or not. Could it be urgent? Could something have happened to Grandfather?

The snow had melted this first week of May, but it would take time for the ground to absorb all the moisture. Gwyn lifted each boot to relieve it from the mud's suction. Taking a step forward, she chewed on her lip. It wouldn't do any good to wait, so she might as well open it.

The perfect penmanship reminded her of the time she'd seen a copy of the Declaration of Independence firsthand. The calligrapher had done an immaculate job.

Her mother demanded the same perfection.

Dear Gwyneth,

It is apparent that you do not care about your family anymore. Since you have decided not to respond to my last letter, I've decided that I don't have time to wait for your letters or news. Not that you ever have any in that horrible little country. I should have known that your childish selfishness in wanting to stay with your father was an indicator of your attitude toward me. All those years I raised you in less than adequate circumstances and this is the thanks I receive in return? Well, young lady, I have much better things to do with my time. Your sister, Sophia, is loving and gracious. Even though she is the prize so many men seek after, she tells me how often she worries about leaving me alone. She wants to serve me as long as she can. That is what a true daughter's heart should be—and that is exactly why I am here with my own dear father.

Your grandfather is still weak, but the doctors will be trying a new treatment next week, hoping to help him rally. Sophia called off her engagement—the man was hideous and a liar. She deserves so much more than a simple doctor anyway. As much as your beloved sister and grandparents would have loved to see you, there's no need for you to come now. Stay in your precious little Alaska. I don't have time to worry about your future any longer. I have my hands full with our many social obligations and the constant care of your Grandfather Titus.

If you care to check on any of us, you know the address, but I won't promise the reply will be speedy.

Mother

Gwyn's temper flared. Her mother was the queen when it came to making Gwyn feel guilty. Words fashioned in such a way that she would stagger under the weight of them until she was convinced she'd committed whatever "crime" her mother charged. Why did it always work? And the comment about the "simple doctor" was unneeded. In fact, it was downright hateful!

It was true Gwyn had just received the letter a couple weeks prior, and she *did* decide not to respond. How could her mother have known?

Was she a horrible daughter because of that? Gwyn couldn't remember one time she'd ever done anything right in her mother's eyes. Not one. And now she was the bad daughter for not following her mother back to her snobby family.

"And what about loyalty to *my* father? Mother can see validity in forsaking her own family to care for Grandfather Titus but sees only betrayal in my staying here to assist Father." There were clearly two sets of standards being applied, but wasn't that always the way with people like her mother's family? The socialites and moneymakers of the world had only one consideration, and that was one of self. As far as Gwyn knew, her grandfather had never cared about anything as much as he did his bank account and investments.

More guilt pooled in her stomach. She shouldn't think such nasty thoughts about her relatives, but Mother's family only cared about their mansion, how many motorcars they owned, and which friends had the most money and influence. They lived daily to see their name mentioned in some positive manner in the society pages of the newspaper. They placed value not on people, but on their bank balances, on how much they could acquire while the rest of the country suffered in hunger and poverty.

Gwyn thought back to the first years of the Depression after Mother went back to Chicago. Her early letters had been filled with derogatory comments about the poor, and how she hoped they'd all get shipped off somewhere so they wouldn't mar her beautiful city any longer. The begging got on her nerves.

Grandfather Titus had lost relatively little compared to the fortune he still hoarded away, yet the doctors believed the market crash had caused his heart attack. Losing two nickels was enough to send him into a rage. Gwyn remembered hiding behind her father's coat as a small child when the butler had asked Grandfather for a raise. Grandfather flew into such a fit about the man's ungratefulness that he smashed a vase against a wall, sending the butler running for the door.

And then Gwyn made the mistake a couple years ago of asking why her family didn't help the poor and unemployed, since they had more than enough. Mother informed her that Grandfather underwent a horrible relapse after hearing his granddaughter's inconsiderate words in the letter. She was commanded to never ask such a thing again. Didn't she know how long he'd worked to amass the family name and fortune? If people like the Vanderbilts and Rockefellers could build an empire out of nothing, then anyone could. If the poor lacked vision or drive to see such success, why was that the fault of the wealthy? It served no purpose to hand out money to those who didn't care enough to fend for themselves. After all, once the handouts started, the impoverished would soon come to depend upon them. Such dependence would in turn be the ruin of those who'd spent a lifetime building their fortunes. Didn't Gwyn understand this? Didn't she care about the family's survival?

Survival? They lived in the wealthiest part of Chicago! With servants and enough food to feed hundreds every day. Gwyn huffed at the rock she kicked. Why did her family infuriate her so?

Persuasion, one of her favorite Jane Austen novels, came to mind. As Gwyn walked home, her anger grew. Just like the snobbish Elliot family in the book, Gwyn's family wouldn't help those less fortunate because they were looking out for themselves. Willing to go only so far in giving up their way of living and appearance. The Elliots had gone so far as to accrue mountains of debt to keep living the same way. The 1929 crash proved that many had done likewise in America. The battle to keep up appearances had brought about the collapse of more than one fine family.

The story similarities didn't end there. Gwyn had never thought about the likeness between herself and the heroine, Anne Elliot, until today. Anne was quiet and sensible and surrounded by a snobbish family. She was also unappreciated and forgotten, almost abandoned.

Abandoned. That was how Gwyn had always felt. While she had a father who loved and adored her, provided her with stability and consistency, her mother deserted her. The woman poured everything into Sophia. Always. Gwyn never measured up. She was always too dirty, too ordinary, too clumsy, too . . . too Gwyn. And that wasn't good enough for Edith Hillerman. Ever.

A train whistle sounded in the distance. Her heart raced. The first contingent of transient workers was supposed to arrive today, which meant she'd better hurry. Her depressing thoughts weren't going anywhere. Gwyn wadded up the letter in her hand and shoved it into her pocket. Her swift and steady stride brought her home in a jiffy.

Nasnana waited for her outside. "You look like a storm is brewing in that head of yours."

In uncharacteristic fashion, Gwyn threw the balled-up letter at the woman who'd cared more for her than her mother had. Tears sprang to her eyes and rushed down her cheeks. "You don't want to be around me right now." Pushing through the door, Gwyn ripped off her boots and jacket. The anger and hurt inside felt like a volcano ready to explode.

Nasnana walked in, her stride steady and slow. She placed the mud-covered paper on the table in front of Gwyn. "Sit down." Her cane thumped on the floor with each word. "Now."

The older woman never scolded Gwyn unless there was good reason. Her little temper tantrum provided the perfect one. Gwyn bit her lip. "I'm sorry."

"I know you are." Nasnana sat across the table from her.

The flow of tears down her face rivaled the river after the spring breakup. "Why does she hate me?"

"Who?"

"My mother." Gwyn tapped the letter. "Read it."

"I don't need to read it, child. I can see the fury written all over your face."

"I just don't understand. All these years, I've longed for her approval. I've worried about what she thinks of me. Even dreamed of the day she would return and find that I was grown and trained as a nurse—"

"You want your mother to be proud of you."

"Of course. What child doesn't?"

Nasnana fingered the shawl around her shoulders. "But your mother will never be proud of you that way. Her pride is in money and things. Not people."

"She's proud of Sophia."

"Only because she's raised someone more conceited than herself." The older woman grabbed Gwyn's hand. "Your mother and I had one heated discussion after another over you and finally agreed to disagree so she would allow you to spend time with Sadzi and me. She hated this place. Hated your father for bringing her here. She kept up appearances only because of her pride. She didn't understand you, child.

Couldn't understand why you would enjoy it here, or why you would want to learn how to help people. To her that seemed a betrayal.

"Her heart is a large, empty place. Instead of filling it with God and His love, she tried to fill it with pride. Take away her money, her family name, her social engagements, and you'd have a shell. Hollow." A single tear slipped down Nasnana's cheek. "As much as that woman angered me, I knew God was asking me to pray for her. And to be there for you. You were a casualty of that war and I'm sorry. But I'm going to ask you to do the same thing. Have you been praying for your mother?"

"Of course." The emotion of the older woman she respected so much reached deep inside. "I pray for her every day."

"But do you pray for her heart? That she would know God?"

Gwyn knew a momentary twinge of guilt. "No. I don't." A small ache started in Gwyn's chest. "All this time, I've prayed she would write, come home . . . love me. But I've had no idea what condition her heart is in—where she would spend eternity if she died." Gwyn stood and walked around the table. "I've been so selfish."

"Yes, you have." Nasnana winked at Gwyn, tempering the honesty. "But now you know how to fix it."

"Do you believe that Mother could change?"

Nasnana smiled. "I believe with God all things are possible. I thought you believed that as well."

"I do. Honestly, I do." Gwyn wrestled with her conscience for a moment. "I want to be a better person. I want to care more about Mother's soul than my broken heart, but I can't say that it doesn't matter. Even in my selfishness, I feel entitled to feel this way."

"Ah, and so you are. You are entitled to feel all the bitterness and hatred you were taught. You are entitled to carry with you the pain and sorrow, the longing and disappointment. They will happily accompany you through life. Claim them if you will, but remember they are greedy, and their demands are many. You must be ready to pay the price they require."

"The price?"

Nasnana sobered and nodded. "Yes. There is always a price. Little by little these companions will steal away your joy, your peace of mind, your contentment. They will take your very heart and turn it to stone."

Jeremiah raced to scrub his hands. The train had just arrived with the second group of transient workers and word came to him and Dr. H. that there were many sick aboard. Most likely a lot of seasickness, but he couldn't be too careful. An epidemic would destroy this community before it began.

The chaos of spring in Alaska was crazy enough—what with the long hours of daylight and short growing season— but add to that a new colony project, and his head felt in a constant spin. He'd just moved into his small cabin but didn't think he'd be spending much time there in the near future. At least the busyness helped to keep his mind off his past failings. Shortly after his arrival he'd written to his cousin Howard, asking about his progress with the appeal. There had been no reply. Nothing. Not a single word of encouragement. It left Jeremiah feeling completely forsaken. Maybe the news was so bad that the lawyer couldn't bear to share it. Maybe

Randolph Brewster had gone through with his threat to have Jeremiah charged with murder. The thought left him cold.

If Brewster had found a way to put the authorities on him, then Jeremiah was a fugitive. Not only would he be practicing medicine without a license, not all that big of an offense in Alaska, but he'd be wanted for killing a patient.

"But I didn't kill her," he muttered. Mrs. Brewster had been too far gone by the time he attempted to save her. It wasn't his fault and it wasn't the fault of the anesthetic. But apparently that hadn't mattered—at least not to the medical board and perhaps not to the authorities. Brewster was a powerful man with powerful friends. Jeremiah could only hope Brewster had let the matter drop, but he didn't count on it.

And this thought only served to cause him further guilt and grief. He'd not found a way in all his time in Alaska to be honest with Dr. H. He owed the man an explanation— especially since he'd been engaged to his younger daughter. But where to begin? And how could he do it now, after so much time had passed?

"I should have told him first thing." Jeremiah quickly dried his hands and tried to reason away his guilt. It wouldn't have helped anything. Dr. H. needed the help—he needed to believe in his associate. Jeremiah frowned. "Why should he? I don't even believe in myself." The entire Chicago mess had left him with a great deal of doubt.

But even in his guilt, Jeremiah found it somewhat easy to put aside his thoughts of the past. The pace of preparation kept them working around the clock and left little time for much pondering about former mistakes.

Everyone was in a frenzy to get the tents erected, supplies unloaded, and ground ready for planting. The experimental station run by the University of Alaska was in high gear, preparing to grow a record crop to help feed all the new people. And the ARRC planned to have the first set of colonists arrive in three days. The poor people had already been waiting on the ship in Seward because they beat the workers to Alaska. There was no telling what condition they'd be in when they finally made it to the colony.

And, despite those things he'd hidden away, Jeremiah had never felt so fulfilled. Granted, the mud was atrocious and slowed everyone and everything down, and the mosquitoes were a downright pain, but he loved working side by side with the man he respected most: Dr. Hillerman. His admiration continued to grow as time passed. The man was a rock. Always capable. Always considerate. Always caring.

These were traits every doctor needed. He vowed to work on them himself.

He caught a glimpse of Gwyn as she comforted a young worker who hadn't kept anything down since his arrival yesterday. That kid wouldn't want to get back on a train for a long time.

Gwyn's eyes shot up to his. "Dr. Vaughan, did you need something?"

"Uh, no. I'm heading to help with the new arrivals."

"All right." She looked back to her patient and helped him sip some water.

And then there was Dr. Hillerman's elder daughter. So unlike her sister, Sophia, so gentle and patient, so unconcerned with how she looked. Even now with new people arriving every day, Gwyn wore her nearly floor-length skirts and well-weathered blouses. Her long hair was pinned up and out of her way, but done so in a very simple manner. Appearances were of no matter to her, and Jeremiah found this so refreshing. It drew him.

He stole another quick glance before heading out. She really wasn't anything like Sophia. Gwyn herself had stated this one evening as they shared supper. Her father had commented on how different his two daughters were, and Gwyn quickly agreed.

"Sophia has always looked at the world in her own way. I wish we could have been closer, but we shared so few common interests." Her words had been spoken with an edge of sadness that touched Jeremiah's heart.

There were other conversations and examples that had touched him as well, although Jeremiah fought long and hard to ignore those feelings. He'd done a good job so far of keeping Gwyn at a distance. They'd been busy enough. But every chance he got, he found himself looking for her. As if a glimpse of her curly blond hair would cure what ailed him. Jeremiah shook his head and picked up the pace. Those thoughts would get him nowhere. How could he trust another woman?

But Gwyn wasn't like any woman he'd ever met. Even though every guy he knew said that about the woman he was in love with. Whoa! He wasn't in love. Not even close. He'd better get a handle on his feelings right away. Trusting a woman would be fatal. He'd already lost everything. He wouldn't do it again.

The secret that had brought him to Alaska twisted like a knife in his heart. Would his lie of omission ruin his future here as well? Would Dr. H. send him packing if he found out? It wasn't just the matter with the board and practicing medicine without a license. It was the implication that he had, with full intention, thrown caution and good medical wisdom to the wind in order to make a name for himself. It was also the matter of having been engaged to Sophia. The web tangled just a bit more with each passing day.

A photographer blocked his path. How he hated the press. This once quiet area of the world now teemed with them. Everyone wanted to know about FDR's new project. The world was fascinated with Alaska's brave new pioneers. And many, sadly, just wanted to watch America fail.

Sidestepping the brash young man, Jeremiah pulled his hat lower over his brow. Maybe they would go away as soon as all the colonists arrived. Or at least the press's attention would be steered toward them. It had to die down at some point. He just needed to hold out long enough. Keep his head down and his nose clean.

When the ARRC hired its own photographer for the project and asked to take a picture of the clinic, Jeremiah asked Dr. H. to excuse him. His mentor had given him an odd look but didn't push the subject.

One day Jeremiah would tell him the truth.

One day.

7

Sixty-seven families comprised the first set of enrollees in the Matanuska Project that arrived on the cool spring day, May 10. Harold placed his hands on his hips as he surveyed the tent city. Children—cooped up for weeks on trains and ships—now expelled their energy running through the mud "streets" of the city.

Chaos was too tame a word for his surroundings. The ARRC rushed to record all the families as they arrived and assign them a tent. After weeks of travel and then days forced to stay on the ship until their final train ride to what was now being called Palmer, Alaska, it was no wonder the colonists just wanted to unpack and do normal tasks. People milled about, unpacking crates and boxes. Women worked to get some sense of order in their new "homes," and many were still sick from the voyage.

One of the most difficult parts came in understanding how the caseworkers had chosen some of these people. One man had been committed to a mental hospital before he even arrived, another man arrived crippled and hobbling on a wooden leg, and eight people had full-blown cases of tuberculosis.

Harold couldn't imagine where they would be if he didn't have Gwyn and Jeremiah. Not all the people had arrived yet, but already his hands were overly full. He'd better step up his prayers for the colony. Not only did these people need the hope of a fresh start, but first they needed to survive.

He looked down the long neat rows of square white tents. What did God have in store for these people?

The cry of a small child brought him back to his work. Dehydration was a dangerous threat in these little ones.

As he turned and walked back to the clinic, he caught sight of Sadzi and Nasnana pulling a cart toward the tent city. They waved, and he returned the greeting. Gwyn had mentioned something about a project the three of them had been working on, but he hadn't paid much attention. His daughter left the clinic and joined them.

Whatever they had planned, it had to bring some smiles and encouragement to the weary travelers.

Jeremiah met him at the door. "Why don't you go with Gwyn and the ladies. You need the fresh air, and I've got everything under control in here." He handed Harold his jacket before he could say no.

"Are you sure?" Harold straightened his tie and put on his coat. "There's a lot to do."

"Not a problem. I'm sure you'll be back before long, and then I can take a break." Jeremiah seemed in a hurry to close the door.

Harold turned around and almost slammed into the ARRC photographer.

"Hey, Doc. Mind if I tag along?"

He cast a backward glance at the closed door and frowned momentarily before turning back to the man with a smile.

"Not at all." Harold straightened his jacket and caught up with the women.

Gwyn whispered in his ear, "We were wondering if you could explain to everyone what we're doing. I think it might sound better coming from you."

"You just don't want to speak in public."

She smiled up at him. "Exactly."

"Okay, I'll do it."

She squeezed his arm.

"But first, I need to know what it is."

Gwyn laughed and explained all the work they'd put into the gifts for the families. As they neared the tent city, many of the people had already stopped and were watching them approach.

He sent a brief prayer heavenward.

The photographer set a large crate in front of him to stand on. Others gathered the remaining tent families.

Harold stepped up onto the crate. "Ladies and gentlemen, welcome again to the Matanuska valley and your new home. Most of you know I'm Dr. Hillerman, and I've been asked to explain a special gift these women have prepared for you.

"My daughter Gwyn and two of her dear friends, Nasnana and Sadzi, are here to deliver a small gift to your home that will help you in your fresh start here. As you probably know, we have many different native peoples in this great land of Alaska— people who have lived on these lands for centuries. They've spent many hours helping with this project." He nodded to Gwyn.

Gwyn lifted the blankets covering the crates that sat on the cart.

A few delighted gasps were heard in the crowd. Several of the women moved forward.

Harold was relieved at their enthusiasm. "These are hand-crafted pottery containers made by the natives in Eklutna. Each one includes sourdough starter, which will make it possible for you to make bread and pancakes today, if you would like. Gwyn and the ladies have prepared recipes for you as well, if you are unfamiliar with it."

More women moved forward, smiles lighting their faces. Gwyn greeted each one, handed them a crock and paper, and introduced them to Nasnana and Sadzi.

But Harold noticed a couple of women move away. They followed a larger woman with graying hair, and she looked angry. As the volume of her voice grew, Harold picked up some of the words. "Indians." "Massacre." "Can't trust 'em."

The rest of the group seemed content enough with Gwyn, so he pursued the stragglers. "Ladies, is there some way I can assist you?"

The vocal one narrowed her eyes at him. "Yes. You can tell those Indians to leave. I didn't come all this way and leave everything behind to be murdered in my bed."

"I assure you, ma'am, you will not be murdered in your bed."

"Gertrude," a smaller woman said as she took the arm of her angry cohort, "maybe we should listen to the doctor. He's lived here a long time."

Gertrude raised her voice. "I will *not* listen to him." She turned around to ensure she had everyone's attention. "Maybe you are all too young to remember trouble with Indians, but my mother watched her parents get butchered by them when she was a little girl. They were all warm and kind at first, and then when my family least expected it, those savages came in and stole everything and killed for the fun of it."

Gwyn looked to him, her eyes wide. Nasnana and Sadzi stood still, heads bowed. Harold needed to nip this in the bud and fast. "Ma'am, I understand where your fears come from, but these people are native Alaskans. It's offensive to hear such prejudiced words. They haven't attacked anyone. We've lived in peace—"

"I don't care what you say." She wrapped an arm around another lady. "We just got here. We've already lost our homes and land, and we come here to live in tents? Then you want us to accept a bunch of Indians? How much are we supposed to take? We're the colonists, selected for President Roosevelt's project, I might add. They have no business here." The large woman raised her chin, a defiant, angry expression crinkling her face.

"When was this massacre, Gertrude?" one of the women in the back questioned. "That sure does sound like a long time ago."

Another woman started crying. Several others stood in shock, looking from one woman to another.

Harold straightened. "This community will not be built on prejudice. I understand your fears, but they are unfounded here." A reporter wrote furiously on his notepad, flipping page after page. *Oh, Lord—this won't make it into all the papers, will it?* "We need steady minds and tempers right now. There's a lot to be done if everyone wants to be prepared for winter. These women gave of their time and hearts to help provide for your families. They're giving you the means to make your own bread. It's a very important step toward survival."

The woman stuck her nose in the air. "I'll get my bread from the store."

"What store would that be?" He knew there were plans for amenities of every kind, although some seemed like nothing more than a pipe dream. "Do you suppose we have the luxury of store-bought bread here? Anytime you want or need it? This starter will take the place of yeast—something you also will have difficulty getting at first. My daughter and her friends are happy to share with you, as well as teach you how to use this Alaskan staple."

"Dr. Hillerman"—a wiry woman in the back raised her hand—"if you trust these . . . native women, then I will too. I'm sure we could all use a helping hand. Especially given that it won't be as easy to get supplies as it was back home. Besides, we live in the twentieth century, don't we? It'd be ridiculous to worry about pettiness and prejudice now." She walked forward, took the gift, and thanked the ladies.

Harold watched Gertrude shoot an angry glare at her dissenter. "They could be using this to poison us."

Gwyn dipped her finger into one of the crocks and then put her finger in her mouth. "There, satisfied? This is a gift, not an act of violence. Goodness, but you see us as murderers rather than as what we are—good neighbors reaching out in Christian charity."

The demonstration seemed to put most of the women at ease. After murmuring among themselves for a few moments, most of the women moved forward to accept the gift. Gertrude, however, continued to hang back. The photographer and reporter waited with the rest of the crowd to see what she would do.

Nasnana moved forward, but Gwyn held her back. Taking a crock to Gertrude, the same one she'd sampled, Gwyn offered it without a word.

The woman raised it in the air as if to smash it—

"Doctor! Come quick!" A filthy little boy ran toward them, his little legs pumping.

Harold jumped off the crate. "What happened?"

"It's Charlie. He just wanted to pet the baby . . ." The child sobbed and fell to the ground.

Gwyn rushed to the child's side and picked him up.

Harold hoped it wasn't a bear. He gripped the boy's shoulders. "Calm down. Just tell us what happened. Where is Charlie?"

The child pointed. "Over there. The mama came out of nowhere and stepped on him pretty bad."

Gwyn set the child down. "You need to show us the way." She looked at her father.

They took off at a run, a small crowd following.

Harold shot another prayer heavenward. Putting two and two together, he didn't have much hope for the child. Not many people survived being trampled by a moose.

After all the luxuries of the cities, he wasn't sure he'd enjoy living in this minuscule excuse for a settlement with its muddy roads and filthy people. But it would be the perfect place to hide. Especially with all the chaos. A pleasant surprise to be sure. Chaos always aided his cause. However, it was the press that surprised him most. There had to be more than a dozen reporters and their faithful photographers doing their best to give top exposure to the colony. It would spell trouble for him if his picture were to become part of some Associated Press release. If he could just avoid the pesky photographers, he'd be fine.

He'd arrived an hour earlier but had already scoped out the tent city in the chaos. Apparently the first colonists arrived only days before. Wasn't much to look at, but several of the poorly dressed women sent him flirty little smiles. He hadn't expected such a warm welcome, so his time in Alaska might be more fun than he'd hoped.

Rounding the corner, he spotted a blond woman. Now, she was a nice little dish. Looked innocent too. She was carrying a basket and passing something out to the children. She had a Lillian Gish sort of sweetness to her expression with a Carole Lombard grace in her walk. A white pinafore apron covered her dress. Not at all the style of Chicago or New York, but she made it look good anyway. The rubber boots on her feet made her appear a bit childish, but considering the mud, he'd overlook it.

She laughed at one of the kids, and her blond curls bounced. Her presence could make his exile in Alaska even enjoyable. He'd have to pour on the charm. No doubt a few stories of life in luxury would turn her head. He hadn't met the dame yet who didn't want to swim in diamonds and furs. He couldn't keep the grin off his face. This was a game he knew quite well.

As she turned and headed his way, he straightened his coat and looked around.

She passed right by without so much as a glance. Maybe he was losing his touch.

"Uh, miss?" He put on his best smile.

"Yes?" She turned, hesitation shimmering in her gray eyes.

"I'm afraid I'm a bit lost." He scanned the tents. "I'm looking for my brother and his family. Perhaps you could help me?"

"Sure." Her quiet voice barely reached him. "What are their names?"

"William and Suzanne Novak. I was told they were already here." His charm wasn't working like he'd hoped. She wouldn't even look at him.

"Oh yes. Beautiful family. Just follow me." Her boots made an awful squishing noise as she walked at a brisk pace to the third row of large tents. "Suzanne?" she called into the tent. "You have a visitor." With that, she started to walk away.

He reached out and touched her arm. "Thank you, miss . . . ?"

"You're welcome." Then she was gone.

"Why, Clarence!" His sister-in-law's high-pitched voice grated on his nerves. "What in the world are you doing here?"

He'd really have to pour on the charm now. "Suzanne, you're growing more beautiful by the day."

"Why, thank you"—she put a hand to her throat—"but I must say, I'm shocked to see you. Does William know you're here?"

"Not yet."

"Uncle Clarence. Uncle Clarence!" Little voices rushed toward him.

He couldn't stand children, and his brother had too many. "Well, look at all of you. Aren't you just so grown up." He turned to Suzanne. "So . . . where is my little brother?"

"Right here." William smiled at him from the tent's makeshift door. "I'm surprised to see you here, Clarence."

"Well, I was so excited when I received your letter that I thought I should come see Alaska and my family."

William's eyebrows rose. He looked to his wife. "We don't have a lot of room, but you are welcome to stay."

"Oh, would that be asking too much? I don't want to put you all out."

Suzanne came forward and wrapped her arm around her

husband. "It's not a problem. We so rarely get to see you. We can make room. I'm sure William will be glad for the help."

"Help . . . Oh, of course. I'd love to help," Clarence lied. "I want to see you all make a go of it. I've even got some money I could pitch in—"

"No, no. We can't take your money."

William's stubborn pride was still intact as he hugged his wife. Just as Clarence had hoped.

"We're just thankful for some hope for the future. The farm in Wisconsin failed fast."

"I'm so sorry to hear that. These have been tough times for everyone." Except for him. But he'd have to keep that a secret. He patted one of the kids' heads. "I'm so glad to see you all."

Hours later he had reached his limit of pleasantries. He needed air. All the disgusting humility he'd spewed out began to sour his stomach. How did people live like this?

Plunging his hands into his pockets, he found his gold ring. He'd better hide it before one of the kids caught sight of it. Couldn't allow his family to know the extent of his wealth. At least they'd been gullible enough to take him in. And they couldn't even afford a house or enough food to feed all those mouths. Clarence shook his head. They didn't have any sense at all. Didn't they know how the world turned?

He strolled through the tent city, hoping for a glimpse of that pretty blonde he'd talked to earlier. Suzanne told him her name was Gwyn and she was the daughter of Dr. Hillerman. They'd lived in this little nowhere town for many years. Maybe if he played his cards right, he could woo her with his money. He bet all dolled up she was a real looker. And he needed a new conquest, or at least a distraction.

She wasn't anywhere in the mud-crusted city. Children ran in every direction imaginable. Clarence caught one by the collar. "Do you happen to know where the clinic is?"

"Sure, mister. Just walk down that road for a few minutes. You'll find it."

Exasperated at the wiggly fellow's lack of detail, Clarence turned the boy loose. Road? They called this a road? What century were they in? The Dark Ages?

His handmade leather shoes would no doubt be ruined after this little excursion. But maybe the dame would be worth it. Maybe.

Outside the little building marked *Clinic*, Clarence spotted the blonde talking to a man. They both had serious expressions, and their heads were close. She nodded. An older gentleman exited the building, wiping his hands on a towel. His shoulders were slumped. The older man wrapped an arm around Gwyn's shoulders. Her father, perhaps?

Clarence watched from a distance, sticking to the tree line. What were they talking about?

And who was that younger man? Gwyn Hillerman certainly seemed comfortable with him.

Bits and pieces of the conversation floated toward him.

". . . we may need to do another surgery on the boy's . . ."

". . . it's the head injury I'm worried about the most."

Then Gwyn's lyrical voice caught his attention. She placed a hand on the other man's arm. "But if we can convince Charlie to fight, show him how much he's loved, maybe he'll have the will to fully wake up."

Clarence didn't like the camaraderie between the two

younger people. Not one bit. Then the younger man turned. It couldn't be! Clarence's luck had just changed. He'd recognize that face anywhere. Brewster had ensured that anyone in Chicago would recognize the face of one Dr. Jeremiah Vaughan. *Former* doctor.

The little group went back into the clinic, nodding and somber. Clarence decided to head back to his family's tent. Tapping his chin, a new plan formed as he trudged down the rutted road. This was valuable information. Hadn't the young doctor's license been stripped? He filed away the little tidbit. One always needed a plan to eliminate the competition.

8

Little Charlie Sirven shivered under the mound of blankets. Nasnana wiped his brow and prayed. *Oh, Father, heal your precious child if it be your will.*

Dr. Hillerman and Dr. Vaughan had worked long into the night trying to save the boy's life. Then in the past three days, they'd performed three different surgeries to stop the bleeding. Charlie hadn't awakened since the accident. They said the blow to the child's head was the worst. Mama moose could be deadly when protecting their young. And this poor child had been trampled trying to pet the little baby. Charlie's legs were in casts and his face was black and blue. He hadn't been in Alaska long enough to learn about the native creatures. And what child could resist the gangly, awkward-looking young animals?

Charlie moaned in his sleep. More than anything, Nasnana hated to see children suffer. She always came to see him in the wee hours of the morning so as not to upset anyone. Gertrude Albany had done her best to instill fear in some of the newcomers about Indians. But many of the women reached out to Nasnana anyway. Several of them came looking for her daily—seeking guidance on berries, edible plants, productive gardening, and sourdough uses. It might be 1935—the twentieth century—but the women who understood they were living as pioneers would be the ones to survive, along with their families.

It did her heart good to be able to be a part of the lives of the new people here. The community atmosphere seemed healthy except for a few negative souls.

Charlie's mother, Cora, slept on a cot in the corner. The poor woman tried her best to be there as often as possible. She told Nasnana she wanted to be there when he awoke, but with three other children who were younger than Charlie, the young mother was exhausted. The boy's father had disappeared after the accident, no doubt hunting the "killer" moose. They all prayed for his safe return soon. The boy needed his father.

Sadzi appeared at Nasnana's side, causing her to gasp. "Child, you've got to stop sneaking up on me."

"Sorry, Grandmother. I didn't want to wake anyone."

"I know. It just never ceases to amaze me how you can step so lightly." She rose to her feet, letting all her joints work the kinks out. Getting older had not been fun, but she thanked God each day for another day to live for Him.

"Gwyn brought us an early breakfast. She asked if the three of us could pray together before everyone else wakes."

"That sounds wonderful." She took Sadzi's arm and walked with the precious child God had given her the privilege to raise. "I'm starved."

"You should be. You fasted and prayed all day yesterday." Sadzi kissed her cheek.

"That's right. I'd forgotten. No wonder I'm so hungry." She giggled with her granddaughter.

Gwyn laid out a small feast on the tiny table by Dr. Hillerman's desk. "There's not a lot of room, but at least here we'll be able to hear any of the patients should they need us."

After prayer, the girls chatted about the children who'd already stolen their hearts. There were so many families it was hard to keep them all straight, but Gwyn and Sadzi seemed to know everyone's name already. How blessed Nasnana was to have these young women in her life.

"How are things at the experimental station?" Sadzi asked as she grabbed another piece of toast.

Gwyn's gray eyes lit up. "I can't believe how much we'll be growing this year. Lilly is doing a great job, but she will be very busy. I just keep praying there will be enough food to sustain all the people."

"The enrollees will be planting gardens as well, so I'm sure the Lord will provide." Nasnana hated to think of anyone going hungry during a winter in Alaska. Supplies couldn't always be guaranteed to arrive on time, if at all.

"Grandmother's right, and there's plenty of hunting in the winter and fishing in the summer."

They all nodded together. Gwyn set her coffee cup down. "There is a little bit of dissent going on in the tent city, though— a lot of the men are concerned that the houses won't be built fast enough. Two hundred homes is a lot to build in a short amount of time."

"Especially when many of the men will need to clear a good portion of their land and try to plant crops as well." Sadzi leaned forward. "They won't be able to draw for the lots until the rest of the men arrive in a few days. June will be upon us before we know it. It's understandable the colony men are worried. The women too."

Nasnana reached into her pocket for a pencil. "Hand me a sheet of paper, Gwyn. Rather than gossiping and worrying, I think we need to start a prayer list of all these concerns. It might seem like an insurmountable mountain of tasks for us humans, but I know God can handle it."

Gwyn blushed. "You're right. As always. I continue to let worry take over my thoughts."

"Me too." Her granddaughter fidgeted with her napkin. "I'm sorry."

"Everything is best left in God's hands. Everything." A shadowy figure passed by the window. The hairs on Nasnana's neck prickled. "Girls, there's something else I would like to mention." The shadow moved on.

Gwyn's brow furrowed. "What is it?"

"That new fellow—visiting his brother?"

Gwyn's expression turned into a scowl. She crossed her arms across her chest. "Clarence Novak."

"Yes, that's the one. Something about him doesn't sit right with me. He's too sneaky—like a snake slithering in and out of the rocks. Almost . . ."

"Slimy," Sadzi threw in and giggled.

Gwyn laughed with Sadzi. "*Eww.* That's a great word for him. He makes me feel like I've got bugs running up and down my skin every time he talks to me."

"Well, I don't think he can be trusted, and you know I do not say so without thought." Nasnana quirked an eyebrow. "There is something . . . well . . . he seems . . ." She struggled to remember the English word. "*Beghejashla qilan.*"

Gwyn nodded. "He's dangerous. I agree. There are in fact several other workers who seem the same. I think we need to be aware of the dangers."

"Knowing them is only part of the problem. You must promise me you will stay far away from him."

Gwyn quickly complied. "I promise."

"I—" Footsteps sounded. Sadzi stood up, "Good morning, Dr. Vaughan. Do you need us to move?"

"Not at all, ladies. I just need to grab some medication, and I will be out of the way." The young doctor's smile didn't quite reach his eyes, but Nasnana watched him take a brief second glance at Gwyn when she wasn't looking.

After Jeremiah left, Sadzi elbowed Nasnana. "Grandmother, I think Dr. Vaughan would be a nice man for Gwyn. Don't you agree?"

Red crept up Gwyn's neck and ears. "I . . . I . . ."

"I'm sorry, I couldn't help but tease. Every once in a while, I catch him watching you. Has he shown any interest? Do you even like him?" Sadzi propped her chin on her hand.

Quiet Gwyn stood and wrung her hands. "I don't know. He sure is handsome. And I find myself thinking about him a lot. But he's often so quiet—so indifferent toward me. Father says he has a great deal on his mind, and I heard him pray for Jeremiah and ask God to help him with his burden, but I don't know what that burden is. I'm not sure Father does either."

Nasnana listened with interest. She'd have to keep a close eye on Jeremiah Vaughan if he were to be worthy of precious Gwyn's heart. She had an inkling the young man was hiding something. Perhaps that was a part of the burden for which Dr. Hillerman had prayed. She would pray for him as well. He *seemed* to have a heart of gold and she liked him. He was hardworking and quick to lend a hand. But could he be trusted?

The shadow passed by the window once more.

A foreboding sensation replaced the prickling she'd felt earlier. She sensed an evil had entered their valley. She stood and walked to the window. The air felt heavy and weighed on her like a wet blanket.

"What is it, Grandmother?"

"I don't know. But we need to pray."

Mud oozed through the knees of her pants, but Gwyn didn't care. The rain the past couple of days couldn't quench her love for being outside after the winter snow. And the planting needed to get done, mud or not. If they waited for the soil to dry out, there wouldn't be enough growing season left.

She'd been on her knees in the garden for hours, but this was one of her favorite things. The soil didn't talk back. It just allowed her to work it while she worked through her thoughts.

Sitting back on her heels, she stretched. The mountains surrounding the valley were majestic and snowcapped. She never tired of looking at them. The brilliance of the blue sky peeking through the puffy gray clouds took her breath away. How amazing of God to allow her to live in such a place. She'd always been happy here.

As she stabbed her trowel back into the ground, her thoughts turned back to Jeremiah. No matter how hard she tried, the handsome young doctor inevitably came to mind. The other morning he'd arrived with his hair sticking out all over the place. Not that she minded. It was an adorable sight—and considering he'd maybe gotten about an hour of sleep after setting a broken arm, she didn't think he cared about combing his hair. But she often wondered if these thoughts were healthy. She kept praying about it. Asked God to take away her feelings if they were inappropriate. Yet day after day, she'd see Jeremiah and her insides would melt into a puddle.

Once in a while, they'd have a chance to talk alone about a patient or a project she could help with, and she felt as if they were getting to know each other. Then other times, his treatment of her was cool—standoffish—as if knowing her as his nurse was the single purpose. Why would a sophisticated doctor from the city care about a simple girl from Alaska?

The conflict this created in her emotions made her want to cry. She threw a clump of mud across the garden and made a decision: no more second-guessing the doctor's motives. Gwyn would be herself and continue on as normal. If Jeremiah Vaughan wanted to get to know her, he'd have to pursue her. All these frivolous daydreams weren't going anywhere, and she certainly didn't have time to waste. It's not like they had time for anything extra right now anyway. The next few months would be a blur of activity and hard work.

She dug through the thick layer of mud again and reached into the luscious soil of the valley. She allowed seeds to fall from her other hand as she worked along the row, digging and planting.

Her nose itched. As she reached up to scratch it, she noticed a pair of boots in front of her and fell back on her rear.

"Hello, Gwyn."

She put a hand to her heart. "Jeremiah, you scared me."

"I'm sorry. That wasn't my intention." His smile reached up and crinkled the corners of his eyes. Was this the first real smile she'd seen from him? It didn't matter. It just made him more handsome.

"That's all right." Gwyn looked down. Good grief. Was

it possible for her to be covered in more mud? "I probably scared you just as much with my muddy appearance."

He laughed. A deep, warm laugh that she knew for certain she hadn't heard before. She liked it. A lot.

"I admit I've never seen a woman work in a garden." The smile lingered on his face.

Meaning he'd never seen a woman covered in mud. "Really?" She shoved her trowel back into the ground. She'd better avoid looking at him or the butterflies in her stomach would work themselves into a frenzy.

"Well, you know, growing up in the city. My parents hired help to do everything for them, or we just bought it."

"Oh, I see." Did she? Wasn't that what her mother always complained about? Not having hired help in Alaska? Just another reminder that Jeremiah came from a different world than she did. Gwyn had a few memories of childhood in Chicago, but they all revolved around her father and their backyard. It had been her sanctuary, and Mother had sent her there often.

Jeremiah shoved his hands into his pockets and paced the outskirts of her garden plot. "I needed some air this morning. We've had so much work that I thought it was a good time to clear my head."

She nodded. How was she supposed to respond to that?

"I forgot to tell you—Charlie said a couple of words today. Now that he's fully awake, we're confident he will continue his progress."

"That's wonderful news!" She'd been present when Charlie woke for the first time, but his eyes hadn't been clear. He spent most of his days asleep, but yesterday, he'd woken three times during the day, and they'd all been hopeful.

"It is. I know you stayed by his side a lot. Thank you. You're a great nurse, Gwyn."

She felt her neck and cheeks heat up under his praise. "Thank you."

Several moments passed. She continued to work and heard his steps squishing through the mud.

He stopped by the fence. "Why such a high fence around the garden?"

"The moose love to get into gardens. Just when you think everything is ripe and ready to harvest, the moose get in and eat up your winter's food." Gwyn looked up and removed her gloves to relieve an itch. "We lost our entire garden one year, and Father built the fence the next day."

Jeremiah chuckled. "I can imagine." He looked toward their cabin. "Your father built a beautiful home here. It's so large."

"Mother didn't think so. She always called it a shack. He certainly tried to please her. I admit I love the house, but I love people and what's outside of the house even more." She replaced her soiled gloves and pointed her trowel at the panoramic view.

"Alaska is like nothing I've ever seen before. I should've come here sooner." His voice turned melancholy, serious. "We always see the past clearer looking back from the future, don't we?"

Gwyn went back to her digging again. His eyes held depths of emotion she wasn't ready to question. She pulled out a big rock she hit with her trowel. This was the first time they'd discussed anything outside of the clinic. And she hated to ruin it. "I guess that's how we learn from our mistakes. If we always knew the correct path to take, we wouldn't learn as much." She threw the rock out of the garden. "But constantly looking back isn't healthy, and dwelling on past mistakes only manages to keep our eyes off the finish line." She dared a look up at him.

He looked off into the distance, his expression hard. "You make a good point, but what if what you thought was the finish line really wasn't?"

She shrugged her shoulders and dug back into the dirt. Might as well be honest. He *did* ask. "Then you weren't focused on the *real* finish line, and God is trying to get you back on track."

"I'm not real happy with the way God handled things. He could've spared a lot of pain and heartache if . . ."

Gwyn leaned back and looked up at him again. "If?"

He clamped his lips shut. "It doesn't matter."

The train's whistle sounded in the distance. That meant the rest of the colony men were arriving, and the ARRC could commence with the drawing of the tracts of land.

"Look—" she stood and shook some of the mud and dirt off her pants—"I've lived with and worried about the 'what-ifs' all my life—"

"Gwyn, it doesn't matter." He held a hand up in front of him, his smile not reaching his eyes again. Now that she'd seen the real thing, she knew this one was forced. "Thanks for trying, but I shouldn't have bothered you." He turned and walked away.

As Gwyn watched him, her heart ached. For a moment, she'd hoped the real Jeremiah would open up. But why would he do that? She didn't fit into his world.

The whistle sounded again. She'd better get cleaned up.

The colonists had been waiting for this day—to know

where they would be living for the next thirty or so years. Excitement had built in all the families already in the valley. It was happening—their new start.

Maybe she needed to pray for her own new start.

The street was muddy and rain drizzled down on the crowd huddled around the Federal Emergency Relief Administration's Stewart Campbell, but it didn't dampen anyone's spirit. May 23 would be a day in the history books for the Matanuska valley. Gwyn watched in joyful anticipation. There wasn't a need for a grand ceremony or parade. Just simple slips of paper and a man from each household.

Arthur Hack drew the first tract of land. Gwyn clapped with the others and smiled at the faces around her. The men who'd just disembarked the train were still a little green and weary from traveling, but the others who had been there almost two weeks were bouncing on their toes, looking eager to get started. It looked like half of these men had enough balled-up energy to go build their house that very day. Even in the rain.

She smiled at the thought. The excitement was catching.

Watching a few of the newcomers, Gwyn felt a little sorry for them. Their families weren't with them yet and wouldn't get to see the historic land drawing. But at least they'd all made it to Alaska. The train only had room for the men so that the draw for the land could move forward. Time was of the essence. Their families would follow on the next trains.

This latest bunch couldn't take their eyes off the landscape around them. No one seemed to care about the rain or the mud. Or even the rows of white tents with children running in every direction. This was their new home. And what a beautiful home it was.

Gwyn had lived here most of her life, yet the scenery still took her breath away. Granted, the tent city and its chaos did mar the valley a bit—the land's pristine and rugged features now cradling the hundreds of tents and its pioneer occupants—but all one had to do was look up. Above the noise. Above the white tents. And there . . . the grandeur of the snow-covered peaks in vast array, too numerous to count, towered in sentry over them. The lush green of the spruce and the crystal waters caused many to be speechless on first sight.

Gwyn walked through the crowd for a while, listening and watching as each man drew for his family. Several of the children standing on the outskirts waved at her, while others played in the mud. She had to admit the children livened up the settlement. She loved seeing Alaska through their eyes. There was always such wonder and delight when something new came to light.

Supplies and machinery arrived every day for the commissary. All the colonists were given three-thousand-dollar loans to help them get started. And even though they'd be toughing it out in tent homes for a while, most of the people didn't mind. They had a roof over their heads. Food to eat. Promise and hope for the future.

Charlie's mother walked up to her, a baby on her left hip. "Thank you, Miss Hillerman, for all your care for my boy."

"You're welcome, Cora." Gwyn tweaked the baby's nose. "And please, call me Gwyn. I hear Charlie's talking now?"

"Yes, and he recognized us. We just came from visiting him. Doc says we can bring him home tomorrow, but we wanted to be out here for the draw." She shifted the baby to the other hip.

"I'm so happy for you. You keep us informed as to how he's doing, okay?"

The woman nodded and rushed into the crowd. She must be thankful her husband had returned before the land draw.

A man approached Gwyn and held out his hand. "Hello, Miss Hillerman. I'm Arville Schaleben from the *Milwaukee Journal*. I was wondering if I might ask you some questions."

Ah. So this was the one reporter who would stay here and live in a tent side by side with the colonists. "Nice to meet you, Mr. Schaleben. But I don't know if I have anything of import to say." She began to walk again.

"Oh, but you do. I hear you have lived here for many years."

"Yes, most of my life." Gwyn glanced at the newspaperman. He seemed nice enough. And anyone willing to live in these conditions rather than travel back and forth to Anchorage like the other press must at least have a spirit of adventure.

"It's a beautiful area."

"Yes, it is. I love it."

"How do you think the colonists will fare?" He poised his pencil over a small notepad.

Gwyn thought for a moment. "I think if they have positive attitudes and don't mind working hard, they will do very well here."

He nodded. "That's a splendid answer, Miss Hillerman. Did you know that the *Milwaukee Journal* is the only paper that guaranteed exclusive day-by-day coverage?"

"I did not. But thank you for sharing." Maybe the man was a little proud of his job. Gwyn wished Sadzi were there to hear the conversation.

"This is an exciting time for our country. I'm thrilled to be a part of it."

"Oh, so will you stay long term, like the colonists?"

He laughed. "Well, I'm not sure about that, but I'd love the chance to speak with you again as everyone settles in."

She stopped and turned to face him. "It's very kind of you to ask my opinion, Mr. Schaleben, but I'm very busy with the clinic." Hoping the conversation was done, she started walking again.

"Thank you."

The cheers from families made Gwyn smile as she left Arville Schaleben behind. It would take some time to finish, so she might as well get some more work done in the clinic. Her long steady steps took her to the office her father had run for almost two decades. A good jaunt from the tent city and the train stop, they would need to move it closer to the colony soon, but oh, how she loved this place. Hopefully the people here would appreciate what he'd sacrificed to stay here. And maybe they would love this land too.

Little Charlie waved at her as she walked in the door. Removing her light jacket, she went straight to his side. "Hi, Charlie."

"Hi."

"I'm so glad to see those big blue eyes of yours."

The little boy reached up and touched one of her curls. "I like your hair."

"Thank you, kind sir. Would you like a drink of water?"

He nodded.

"And how about a story?"

"Yes, please."

Gwyn went to a shelf in the back and grabbed a small

children's book. A soft snore caused her to jump. As she looked around the corner, she spied Jeremiah sitting in a chair, fast asleep.

Their earlier conversation came to mind. Should she try to talk to him again? In this day and age, she knew that women were bolder than they'd ever been, but she wasn't one of those women.

A shock of brown hair covered one of his eyes. She fought the longing to reach over and brush it away from his face. Maybe these feelings were all wrong. It could just be that she'd never been attracted to a man before. Being isolated shaped her world in a different light. Besides, he wasn't attracted to her.

Jeremiah was a doctor. From Chicago. He'd probably had the opportunity to have any beautiful girl on his arm that he wanted.

Gwyn needed to stop these foolish thoughts.

She turned and brought the book back to Charlie and read to him while he drifted back to sleep. Small snores joined Jeremiah's in harmony.

The door banged behind her father. He flicked rainwater off his black coat. "Gwyn, have you got it all under control in here?" he asked quietly.

"Sure. And Jeremiah's in the back if I need him. Why?"

"Well, it took three hours for them to finish the draw, and some of the tracts were so bad that they granted some men another draw. A few of them even demanded to trade. But it's done. That Stewart Campbell got it done. He's the FERA administrator. Everyone's in a hurry to get closer to their land, so they're moving the tents to separate camps, where they can be closer to their lots."

"That makes sense." She laid another blanket over Charlie.

"But I think I need to go along. Some of them are in a big hurry, and I don't want anyone getting hurt."

"All right." She hugged him. "I'm sure that's a wise plan. It will be a mess, that's for sure. I'll be here if you need me."

He headed back out into the rain.

Gwyn longed to go back and look in on Jeremiah but made herself stop those thoughts. It wouldn't do any good.

A young woman burst through the clinic's door with her baby in her arms, thrusting her toward Gwyn. "Please help me. She's burning up with fever."

Any tidying up could wait. Another child needed her.

9

CHICAGO, ILLINOIS

He'd missed something important.

Frank Rhoads tapped his pen in rapid succession on his desk. If he could just put his finger on it, he knew he could crack this case.

Twenty years he'd worked for the Pinkertons. And he'd never had an unsolved case. Never.

Frank scanned all the papers in front of him. Where had this Tony Griffin fellow gone? The man had an exemplary record with the bank. Not one sick day in all his years there. So why . . . only three weeks after the largest heist in the history of First National Bank, did the manager go missing? It just didn't add up. And the story he got was that the man had become seriously ill and left the state for treatment. But no doctor had any record of that. Nor any hospital. Just the word of the two bank employees under the manager.

There was nothing on Tony Griffin. Maybe Frank was just chasing his tail. Wouldn't be the first time. He dropped the stack in a heap and threw his pen at the wall. What *was* he missing?

He stood and stretched and walked around his desk. The answers had to be there. Somewhere.

Frank sat back down and shuffled through the papers again. Another name caught his attention.

Gregory Simms. Now, there was a fella who was always in trouble. Petty stuff but trouble nonetheless.

For years, Chicago had been a prisoner of the mafia and gangs. Prohibition had increased the crime rate in his city. Over seven hundred gang murders had been directly related to the liquor trade.

Even after Capone and all the others they'd locked up, there were plenty of men in the lawbreaking business. And they liked it.

Frank chewed on a toothpick. Simms wasn't a mastermind. But Frank bet the man knew something about it.

Maybe it was time to track Gregory down. But what could he bring him in on? "Connor!" Frank yelled out his door.

"Yeah, boss?" The short man leaned in.

"I need you to find this guy for me. And fast."

"Got it." Connor grabbed the paper and ran back out to the hallway.

The papers slid around his desk like a deck of cards. What was he *missing*? It was here. He knew it. The toothpick cracked in his teeth as he chomped down.

Jeannette, one of the secretaries, sauntered up to his desk. "John thought you'd want to see this, Frank." She let the packet drop and sashayed her way back out.

Frank opened the envelope and looked at the pictures. Dropping them to his desk, he cursed under his breath. His gut had been right. Simms definitely had something to do with it.

"Connor!"

The new agent ran back to Frank's desk, sucking in air. "Sir?" He bent at the waist and put his hands on his knees.

"Go pack a bag. We're going to New York."

"Sir?"

"We just found Gregory Simms." He pointed to the pictures—a man and woman lying at odd angles with bullet holes in their foreheads, holding bank bags with *First National Bank* imprinted on them. "And he's dead."

JUNE 1935

It was gradual, but guilt ate him alive. Every day that passed and Jeremiah didn't tell Dr. H. the truth felt like another day past the point of no return. May had come and gone like a thief in the night. How could he tell his mentor now? They had hundreds of people to care for, and chaos reigned in the Matanuska Project. As he worked side by side at the clinic-now-hospital with Harold, Jeremiah passed iodine to the doctor. Would there ever be a good time to tell the truth? And if he did tell the truth, what would Dr. H. think of him? Would he shrug it off in his casual style or would he feel betrayed and demand Jeremiah leave? Shaking his head, Jeremiah realized he'd become just like the very people he despised—worried about what others thought of him, dishonest, and selfish.

Another measles case had come in that morning. If they didn't do something soon, one of these sicknesses could turn into an epidemic. That was a fear no one wanted to voice. But it hung in the air. And it was another excuse to keep from telling the truth. Would Dr. H. care that his license was revoked? Or would he still value Jeremiah for his skill? Lots of people practiced medicine without a license in remote areas. But did they carry the title *Doctor*?

And there was the entire matter of his former engagement to Sophia. Another secret. One that weighed him down the longer he was around Gwyn.

Jeremiah washed his hands for what seemed like the hundredth time that morning. His skin cracked from all the cleaning. For now, it was best to focus on what he could do to help. And forget about his troubles.

Gwyn walked in the door and swiped at her brow. "Good morning, Father, Jeremiah." Without even pausing, she moved to a cabinet, opened it, and pulled out a jar. She handed it to Jeremiah. "Here. Nasnana makes it for us."

He recognized the tub. He'd seen Dr. H. slathering the cream on his hands on many occasions. "Thanks."

"It'll help with the cracking until your skin gets used to the dry air." Gwyn moved over to her father, pushing her blond curls out of her face. "They've set the first log for the construction office."

"Good, it's about time." Harold washed his hands and reached for the cream. "That should build some excitement and momentum."

"It is." She nodded. "Now if they could just get the supplies shipped properly. The whole last shipment of perishables was spoiled when it arrived."

Jeremiah watched the exchange, rubbing the thick cream into all the cracks on his hands. He hadn't wanted to admit it, but Gwyn wasn't anything like other women he'd met. She was amazing. Even though he tried not to, he watched her as much as possible. She seemed genuine in her love for everyone around her. And she was good at *everything*. The rest of the world might have plenty of amenities to make life easier, but Gwyn was perfectly comfortable doing for herself. She didn't seem to mind the labor that went into simple tasks. All the other women he'd known were spoiled and selfish. Not wanting to get their painted fingernails dirty. But not Gwyn.

As a nurse, she was finer than any he'd worked with in Chicago. She could also teach and counsel—always making the other person feel as though they could accomplish anything.

Gwyn cocked her head as she listened to her father. Her often quiet ways hid a lot of the strength and knowledge within—she was like a buried treasure. Didn't know what was there until he dug deep enough.

Jeremiah watched her walk around the room. None of the women he knew would be caught dead in the dress she had on. It was at least a decade behind the fashions of the city. But its simplicity and modesty caught his eye more than the flashy, provocative styles women pranced around in nowadays. And when it came down to it, she was comfortable in a pair of overalls or pants, covered in mud in the garden.

He leaned back against the cupboards. No denying it. Gwyn Hillerman had worked her way into his heart. Only problem was, he couldn't do anything about it. Because as soon as she learned the truth, she'd kick him clear into the Bering Sea.

And then there was Clarence. The man was slick, he'd give him that. But did he always have to appear whenever Jeremiah managed to get a moment alone with Gwyn? The man's manners might be impeccable, but Jeremiah had looked at his hands. Clarence had never done manual labor a day in his life. So what was he doing up here? And why couldn't he leave Gwyn alone?

"Jeremiah—" Dr. H. cleared his throat. "Jeremiah, did you hear a word I said? Are you feeling okay?"

Just a little lovesick. "Sorry, Harold. Would you mind repeating it?"

"There's a reporter and a photographer out front. They've been hounding me for days for a quote or two and a picture. Would you mind joining me?"

All the blood seemed to rush from his head to his feet. With the way the country was watching with baited breath to hear any and every tidbit they could about the colony, there was no way Jeremiah's presence here could go unnoticed if his picture was in the papers.

"Jeremiah?" Harold reached out. "You don't look so good."

He put a hand to his mouth. "I'm sorry. I think I might be sick."

Gwyn rushed to his side. "Let me get you a cool cloth."

"No!" He pushed toward the back door. "No, please. I don't want to vomit on anyone."

"Rose," Gwyn whispered. "Rose, honey, wake up."

The young widow's face was pale and drawn. It had been three weeks since her husband's death, and Gwyn's father was very worried. He'd asked her to go spend the day with Rose and see what she could do to bring the young woman some encouragement about life.

Long black lashes blinked against her cheeks as Rose opened her eyes. Tears formed before she spoke. "I can't believe he left me." Sobs shook the young woman in her bed.

A soft cry rose from a box beside the stove. The tent homes were sturdy enough, but when the winds decided to blow, it was sometimes hard to stay warm. At least Rose had the presence of mind to keep the baby's bed by the warm stove.

Gwyn went to pick up the seven-month-old baby, who was entirely too tiny for his age. His little lips moved in motion to feed. "Hi there, little one. You must be hungry. Let me bring you to your mommy."

Cuddling the baby close, she took the little guy to Rose. Couldn't she find the will to live at least for her son? "Rose, I think he needs to nurse. Would you like me to help you sit up?"

The young widow worked to stop her tears. "Yes, please."

After helping Rose and giving her a moment's privacy, Gwyn decided it was best to get Rose talking. There had to be some way to bring the woman out of her shell of grief. "Rose, I don't know your baby's name."

"Daniel."

"That's a good strong name."

"Yes, he's named after his father." A few fresh tears ran down her cheeks.

"Daniel. It suits him." Gwyn swallowed. "I heard they started on your house first. That will be a blessing, won't it?"

Rose looked out the tent flap toward the mountains. "I don't know what to think anymore. Daniel was so excited about this land. We were going to raise our family here." She sucked in a gulp of air. "I can't believe he didn't tell me about his sickness. Why didn't he tell me?"

Gwyn reached over and wrapped her arms around Rose and baby Daniel. Mr. Benson died of tuberculosis just three short days after the tract drawing. Apparently, he'd wanted to keep his illness a secret so that he could provide a future for his wife and son. "I don't know, Rose. I don't know."

The baby settled down and began to nurse in earnest.

Gwyn wanted desperately to help ease the young mother's pain but knew she had no experience in this area. She'd never had a husband or child, so how could she possibly relate to the misery and loss this woman was feeling?

"Just talk to her," Father had urged. "Just help her to keep focused on what's important."

But what was important to this devastated young widow?

"Were you excited to come here, Rose?" Gwyn asked. Anxious for something to set her hand to, she reached into a basket of freshly laundered diapers and began to fold them.

"I was." She stared off into space, not even seeing Gwyn. "Daniel's excitement was contagious. He told me our life was going to be so much better than what we'd had. He promised we'd be happy here."

"It's a wonderful place to live. There's purity and peace that can be had here," Gwyn said without thinking and immediately regretted her reference to peace. "I was so surprised to hear about the colony at first. I have to admit I felt rather guarded about my home." Rose said nothing, so Gwyn continued.

"Alaska has always been such a blessing to me. I love the people here and the beauty. It's a good place to raise children," she said, nodding toward the baby. "You certainly don't have to worry about all the problems they suffer down in the States. Life here is much simpler, although it does require a strong back and a will to survive."

Rose looked at her blankly. "I haven't got that will."

"Oh, but you must. Look at little Daniel. He needs you to have that will. And God can give you that will. He provides all of our needs."

Rose pulled back and gave Gwyn a strange look. "Do you know what Daniel's last words were to me?"

Gwyn shook her head.

"'God has provided.'" She sobbed. "Those were his last words. And then he died."

God has provided. How could she tell a woman—going through horrendous grief after her husband's death, in a territory thousands of miles from her home—that those words were true? *Lord, give me the words to say . . . please. . . . I don't want her to give up, and I'm so weak.*

Rose collapsed in Gwyn's arms. Her sobs shook all of them as they huddled on the bed. "I hate God. He took Daniel away from me. What am I going to do?"

The words hung in the air and mixed with the baby's cries.

God has provided.

Gwyn walked back to the clinic. She hadn't had the right words to give Rose. Had she failed? What good had she been?

Clarence Novak stood in the road, waiting . . . for her?

Just what she needed. He was the most annoying man she'd ever met.

"Good morning, Miss Hillerman." His smile was all too white, his suit all too clean. "May I walk with you?"

"Oh, I'm not on a walk. I'm on my way back to the clinic. If you'll excuse me." She picked up her pace.

He didn't take the hint and stepped in beside her. "It's a lovely day. If only we had a grand restaurant here, I'd love to ask you to dine with me."

Maybe he'd get the hint if she didn't respond.

"But since we don't have anything like that right now, and I'm spending all my spare time helping my brother, perhaps you'd agree to a picnic sometime?"

The words were all too smooth. As if she couldn't have a reason to refuse him. She looked out to the trees. How could she get rid of him? "That's awfully kind of you to offer, Mr. Novak—"

"Please, call me Clarence."

"Uh, that's a nice offer, Mr. Novak, but I'm really quite busy, and I don't think it's wise to take time for frivolous things right now when all these families need to get ready for winter."

"Oh, but a picnic isn't frivolous, and besides, winter is a long ways off."

"Not by Alaskan standards. There's a great deal that needs to be accomplished in these brief summer months," Gwyn countered with an air of authority.

"But everyone needs some time off now and again."

"That may be true, but as a nurse here, and as someone who's lived here for many years, I know how difficult it can be, so I have a responsibility—"

His all-too-soft finger covered her lips. "Gwyn, you work entirely too hard."

"If it's all the same—" she removed his hand and stepped back several paces—"I'd prefer you call me *Miss Hillerman*."

"Come now, don't be such a little mouse. You must know that my intentions are pure. I've been attracted to you since the moment I stepped off the train." He stepped forward and closed the distance between them. "I think you've felt something similar for me."

Gwyn stepped back again. "Mr. Novak, I'm not sure what kind of women you are used to being around and associating with, but that is a bit too forward for my liking." She walked away as fast as her legs could carry her.

But he caught up. Wouldn't this man ever take a hint? "I apologize. I'm sorry if I've overstepped my bounds. How about I just walk you the rest of the way to the clinic?"

Did she have any choice? "Apology accepted. But I am in quite a hurry, so I won't be much for company."

"I don't mind."

But *she* did. Didn't he understand that? Maybe she hadn't been bold enough in her words. Were women these days *more* forward than men? She had no idea. All she wanted was to conduct herself in a manner worthy of the Lord. All those crazy social rules were above and beyond her knowledge.

"The clearing of the land is coming along quite nicely, if I do say so myself. William is a bit lazy, but I've put in lots of labor to help the family out." His chest appeared to puff out with each word.

He couldn't be serious. He actually wanted her to believe that? Not only was he forward, he was a liar. His hands were smoother than any person's she'd ever seen. If he'd ever picked up a hammer or saw she would have been surprised. This man made her feel so uncomfortable.

"You should come out and see it sometime. I imagine myself building my own cottage one day. Just a vacation home, you see. I'd still like to return to the city and all the luxuries there." He looked over at her.

She avoided his gaze and kept walking. "That's very nice." If only he knew how his words repulsed her . . .

"But this is a wonderful adventure. I'm glad I can be of service to those less fortunate."

Less fortunate? What was he implying? Here he was, mooching off his family that had little to nothing. He slept in their tent. He ate their food. Gwyn bit her tongue so her temper wouldn't get the best of her.

The clinic was in sight now. Clarence tugged on her arm and stopped her. "I enjoyed our walk, Miss Hillerman. Maybe we can do it again sometime?"

"It was very gracious of you to accompany me." She pulled her arm out of his grasp. "I hope you have a nice day." With that, she turned on her heel and half walked, half ran the rest of the way to the clinic door.

Sadzi was right. *Slimy* described Clarence Novak to a tee. And now she felt like she needed a bath.

Gwyn yanked open the door with a little too much force. She had allowed Clarence to irritate her, and that hadn't helped her mood. She ran straight into Jeremiah's back. "Oh, I'm sorry, Jeremiah."

He turned, a frown on his face. "Did you have a nice *walk*?"

"I just came back from checking on Rose Benson," she huffed. Why did she feel so defensive? He must've seen her with Clarence. Could the day get any worse? "Father and I are really worried about her and the baby."

His expression softened. "How is she?"

"Distraught, discouraged. I don't think she's eating much, and the baby is weak."

"You're upset."

"Yes, I'm upset." Gwyn grabbed a clean apron. "I'm sorry, but I don't think I can talk about it." She cinched the knot a little too tight.

"I hear they started her cabin. It was the first one?"

Was he trying to make small talk? Calm her down? "Yes, I just wish there was some way to encourage her."

"I'm sure you did everything you could."

She nodded. But it wasn't true. Once again, she hadn't measured up. She'd failed. Rose had looked no more encouraged by the end of their visit than she had when Gwyn first arrived.

"For some reason I don't think you believe that."

She met his gaze and could see he seemed sincerely concerned about her. "I suppose I don't."

"But why?" His voice was gentle and soothing.

"I don't know what it is to lose a husband that way, or any way, for that matter. I've never been married. Never been in love, and I certainly don't know what it is to be a mother. I said what I could and tried to offer solace, but my own experiences are limited."

"Have you never suffered a loss?"

"Of course I have," she replied.

"Loss of any kind shares similar tendencies. Pain, betrayal, anger, shock. Those are all things you've felt before."

Gwyn felt her anger calming. "Yes. That much is true." She felt her heart skip a beat as Jeremiah offered her a smile.

"It's all about reaching a person where they hurt."

For a moment Gwyn lost herself in his gaze and found herself wondering what it would be like just to put her head on his shoulder. He seemed such a pillar of strength. But as quickly as the thought came to mind, Gwyn pushed it away. What in the world was wrong with her? She turned away, anxious to busy herself with something else.

"Did you hear about the new visitor?"

His words helped her shift gears. "What? No. I haven't heard much news lately. Is everything okay?" She busied herself with the pretense of counting bandages, knowing that if she looked into his greenish eyes she'd never hear another word.

"Yes, the president sent up a man named Eugene Carr. Seems like a nice enough fellow. He's here to calm down all the complainers."

"Oh. I'm sure that will be a fun job." She felt a pang of guilt. "Sorry for the sarcasm. I'm not good company right now. I suppose I'm not feeling very gracious either. Those people knew coming here wouldn't be easy. They knew there would be a great deal of work to do. It's not like they didn't have—"

"Gwyn!" Nasnana burst through the door, her cane clattering to the floor. "Can you come with me?"

"What's happened?" Gwyn went quickly to pick up the old woman's cane.

Nasnana took the piece and steadied herself. "It's the river. It's flooding Matanuska. The people need help getting away from the water."

"Matanuska?" Jeremiah moved closer. "I thought we were in Matanuska."

Gwyn tore off the apron she'd just tied and grabbed the rubber waders. "We're in the Matanuska valley, yes, but there's a small village of native people right on the river. It's called Matanuska as well, named after the river." She grabbed her father's rain slicker. "Father, are you here? I'm going with Nasnana. I'm wearing your gear."

"I heard." He appeared beside Jeremiah, wiping iodine off his hands. "Nasnana, are there any injuries? Should Jeremiah or I accompany you?"

The clinic was packed. They'd had their hands full with TB patients and children who'd contracted measles. "If it's nothing serious, I can do it, Father. Why don't you send me with one of your medical bags? That way you and Dr. Vaughan can stay here."

Her father shook his head. "While I'm confident with your nursing abilities, Gwyn, I'd feel more comfortable if Jeremiah went along. I don't like the thought of you and Nasnana going alone."

"We'll be all right."

"I know you will, but Dr. Vaughan needs to be there, just in case. I'll be busy here, but you send word if you need me, all right?" As Jeremiah packed a bag, her father reached out to hug her. "I'm sorry things have been so busy lately." Her father pulled back and kissed her forehead. "Be careful. Don't take any chances. Floodwater can be very dangerous and unpredictable."

10

His rubber boots slipped on the terrain. Jeremiah followed Nasnana and Gwyn through the thick spruce but almost fell face first multiple times. The women made their way at a brisk pace. Why didn't they seem to be having difficulty? Was he that much of a lummox?

Gwyn glanced back at him but continued running through the thick undergrowth of the forest. Her face conveyed her fear.

Here he was, selfish thoughts invading his mind, when there were people out there whose lives and homes were in danger. What kind of a man had he become?

Not the man he wanted to be—that was for certain. Jeremiah shook his head and watched his steps. He could learn a thing or two from these brave Alaskan women and their giving hearts—willing to drop everything to help a neighbor. Not caring about what people thought or how much money they had. Another prick to his heart. Would he never be free of the past and its fierce grip? Everything he'd done . . . everything he'd been . . . everything he'd hoped for . . .

Well, he could be thankful he was here now. He would look forward to a better future. A future where he helped people, worked alongside them, and made a *real* difference.

A loud roar captured his attention. Jeremiah stopped and focused on the scene ahead. The scent of dirt and moisture surrounded him. Mist filled the air and dampened his face.

"Quick! Jeremiah, over here!" Gwyn waved him to a man on the ground. "He fell carrying their belongings. I think his leg might be broken."

Jeremiah knelt before the groaning man and examined the leg. "You're correct. It's broken, but it appears to be a clean break. Let's get it splinted and move him to high ground."

Gwyn squatted down and placed a stick between the man's teeth. She nodded to Jeremiah.

With a pull and a snap, he realigned the bones. "What happened to cause this?" He jerked his head toward the river. "Does it occur every year?"

She shook her head. "No, just a combination of an abundance of snow this year, especially in the mountains, and our warm weather lately." She sniffed. "I've never seen it this bad."

She didn't even look at him. Disappointment washed over him, but Jeremiah couldn't think about that just now.

"Just relax and we'll get you to safety," she told the old man.

"My things," the man moaned. "They all we have. You bring them?"

"Of course," Gwyn assured him.

"Dr. Vaughan!" Nasnana drew his attention. "Over here!"

Jeremiah retrieved his bag and glanced down one more time. "Will you be all right? Can you splint it without me?"

"Yes, I'll finish and get someone to help carry him up the hill."

Two bags lay by the man. All his belongings? Yet another prick to his heart. As the feelings churned and took up residence, Jeremiah realized one thing: To be a different man, his perspective had to change. Permanently.

He moved toward Nasnana.

And he'd have to tell the truth. Otherwise, he was just as bad as Randolph Brewster, Sophia, and her mother . . . and everyone else he'd despised for caring about what others thought.

The roar grew, and he looked over to the swollen river. The water rushed by, large chunks of ice floating on its surface. Several homes were already overtaken by the surge.

Nasnana reached for him as he approached a woman on the ground. "It doesn't look good. She's lost a lot of blood."

"What happened?"

"I don't know. . . ."

Blood oozed from the elderly woman's wrinkled and weathered forehead. A red puddle on the ground beside her prostrate form confirmed Nasnana's words. "Head wounds bleed a lot." He grabbed some gauze from his bag. "Hold this to the wound and apply pressure."

Nasnana did as instructed. "She's been a dear friend of mine all my life."

Jeremiah nodded. Even in the midst of grief and disaster, Nasnana remained calm.

In fact, everyone around him seemed quiet. They scurried about, hauling people and items up the hill, but there wasn't screaming or chaos. Just folks helping one another.

As he checked the woman for other injuries, Jeremiah couldn't get over the fact that all of this was having a profound effect on him. But would it make a difference? Or was he destined to fail?

"God's working on you, isn't He?" Nasnana patted his hand.

"What?" The comment took him off guard.

Her smile was the only reply.

He focused on stitching the wound.

A male voice shouting interrupted his work. "The river's crested the upper banks!"

A new sensation took over. Palpable fear settled in on the people. Jeremiah let his years of practice take over, and his fingers flew, but he had to know. "What does that mean?" He looked to Nasnana.

"It means that it's breached where the river bends and winds down here. We don't have much time. All of this will be underwater in a matter of minutes if that's true." She closed her eyes and her lips moved, though no words were voiced.

He threw his things into his bag and lifted the woman into his arms. Nasnana gathered other items off the ground.

"Lead the way, Nasnana."

When they reached a safe distance, Jeremiah laid the woman down and headed back down the hill. Dozens of people scurried from house to house, but the water had already risen to his knees by the time he made it back down. They didn't have minutes. They had dozens of seconds at most.

The roar intensified, filling his ears and his mind. Jeremiah's hair stuck to his head, the mist and spray from the water nearly drenching him. Where was Gwyn? He hadn't seen her since he'd left her splinting the man's leg.

Water rushed past, the current threatening to take him off his feet. Now it reached his waist. Where was she? He scanned all around him.

Several women carried what they could on top of their heads. A young father lifted a toddler up onto his shoulders.

"Gwyn!" Jeremiah looked back up the hill to Nasnana.

She shook her head.

"*Help!*" A child's scream split the air.

Across the river's new path, a small girl stood on top of a boulder. It must've been safe enough before the breach, but the raging water now threatened to overtake the rock. And there was no way to get to her. Except through the crashing river.

Jeremiah stripped off his coat and moved toward the girl. He could swim well, but he wasn't sure he was strong enough to battle this current for long. And the water was bitter cold. Hypothermia could set in before he reached her.

But he had to try.

Another scream and Jeremiah watched as water crested the rock and covered the girl's feet. The yardage between him and the rock had to be greater than fifty. Could he make it in time?

Lungs burning, he kept his head above the water and pumped his arms in a breaststroke motion.

Something bobbed in the water ahead of him.

He couldn't make it out.

But the child's screams increased in volume. There was no mistaking the fear. The water now reached her thighs.

As he pushed forward, Jeremiah began to feel numb. The frigid water attacked him. He fought back. Had to stay focused. Pushed. More. More.

He caught sight of the bobber again. The wet head in front of him had a few curls at the crown. *Gwyn!*

She was alive. And she reached the little girl.

Small arms wrapped around Gwyn's neck. The child climbed onto Gwyn's back.

But a surge of water crashed over them both, dunking them.

Jeremiah swam as fast as he could. One . . . two . . . three . . .

four . . . five . . . the seconds passed. Too slow. And no Gwyn. No little girl.

He pushed harder. Faster. Always looking to the last place he'd seen them. But the current would have carried them a good ways by now.

Allowing the current to propel him downstream, Jeremiah dove under the water's surface and opened his eyes. Nothing.

He needed air. As he broke the surface again, he spotted a tiny head. Where was Gwyn?

Another surge of water lifted him on a swell.

Crack!

Jeremiah turned his head to see a huge branch—more like the trunk of a tree—careening toward him. If he could just grab hold of it, maybe it would help him rescue the girl.

But there wasn't enough time. He couldn't reach it.

Water swirled around him.

"*Oomph!*" All the breath left him in a rush as the heavy wood slammed into his back. Debris pummeled his legs and torso.

Another swell and rush of water. If he could close his eyes for a moment . . .

No!

He had to fight it. Icy needles prickled his skin. Numbness took over.

Gwyn! His eyes flew open. Was she gone?

Kicking his legs, Jeremiah held on to the log. The water had moved him far from where he'd started. His body couldn't take much more. The doctor in him knew that time was short. Either he found them soon or he'd die trying.

Ahead, a long curve appeared in the rushing water. Maybe there was a chance to make it to the bank. But he had to find them.

A cry in front of him rang in his ears. The water pushed him up.

There! He caught sight of two heads. Faces pressed together, the two had their arms wound around each other.

But how could he reach them? They were approaching the curve and fast.

Lord, help.

Every part of her body had gone numb. Gwyn wrapped her arms tighter around the girl, hoping that her body heat could somehow help the child survive a little bit longer. At this point, Gwyn didn't have much hope they'd make it out alive. The lack of feeling would make it easier. The water moved too fast, and they were too cold. It was all she could do to stay afloat.

Lord, forgive me. There's so much I wanted to say, so much I wanted to do before I went home to be with you, but I know because of your Son that I can stand before you clean. Please help this child's family. Please help my father . . .

Water swirled in over her head and she closed her eyes.

"Mama! Mama! Look what I've found!" Ten-year-old Gwyn bounded into the house, her hands cupped to contain the small furry treasure. "It's a baby rabbit."

Mother turned with a glare of anger. "I've told you a hundred times never to bring those wretched creatures into my house. This isn't a barn or a stable." Her mother's exasperation spilled over to Sophia, who although a year younger than

Gwyn was quickly becoming an exact replica of their mother in looks and attitude.

"It's wretched!" Sophia mimicked.

Gwyn stopped and looked at the baby in her hands. "It is not. It's a baby. It lost its mother and is all alone."

"That is hardly our problem," Mother said, turning back to Sophia. It was only then that Gwyn realized her mother was marking the hem for yet another new dress for Sophia. "I don't know why I didn't just have that Indian woman do this."

"Her name is Nasnana," Gwyn said, "and she's not an Indian. She's Athabascan—Dena'ina to be exact."

"Do not speak that horrible pagan language, Gwyn. I've warned you about this before. I won't have you speaking that heathen tongue."

"Nasnana isn't a heathen, Mama. She loves Jesus and prays just like we do."

"Bah! Those people aren't capable of praying properly. Now, get that thing out of my house and leave me alone. Can't you see I'm busy?"

Gwyn turned away in dejection. She had thought her mother would surely understand the need to care for the baby rabbit. After all, he had no one else.

"He's just like me," Gwyn said with a sigh. "He's all alone."

"Hey there, Gwynie," her father called. "What do you have there?"

She looked up and smiled. She wasn't all alone. She did have her father, and he loved her dearly—even if Mama didn't care. "It's a baby rabbit. His mother left him."

Father smiled and took the animal from Gwyn's hands. "She probably didn't want to. Most likely something chose her for its dinner."

"How can we help him?" She knew her father would have the answer and didn't doubt for a minute he would help.

"He will require a great deal of care. Are you certain that you want the responsibility?"

"Oh yes," Gwyn declared. "I will do whatever it takes. I don't want him to die."

Her father nodded. "Then come with me. We'll make him a little place where he can stay warm and safe."

Warm and safe. The words echoed in Gwyn's head. Warm and safe. How she longed to feel warm and safe. She thought of her mother's harsh words and dared a question her father would probably not have an answer for.

"Why doesn't Mama love me like she loves Sophia?"

Her father turned and his expression was filled with sympathy. "Your Mama loves you in her own way, but she doesn't love this territory. Seeing that you . . . that we love it, as we do . . . well . . . I guess it makes her feel that we've reassigned our love for her. It's not true, of course."

Gwyn pulled and twisted her long blond braids. "Will Mama ever love Alaska?"

"I don't know, Gwynie. I just don't know. But you mustn't give up hope. God brought us here for a reason, and doing God's purpose comes with a price. He didn't promise it would be easy for us, but He did say He would always be with us."

Just then Nasnana appeared from around the corner of the small building Father called his clinic. Her face broke into a broad smile when she spied Gwyn. "Oh, how wonderful to see you today," she declared.

Gwyn ran to the woman's outstretched arms. "Yagheli ilan du?" *Are you fine?* She asked in Nasnana's native tongue.

"Yes, little one. I am fine and so happy to hear you speak my language. You will soon be able to converse like my people."

The approval and joy in the older woman's tone helped Gwyn to push aside the void left by her mother.

"Gwyn!" It was Father calling.

She looked to Nasnana. "Come see. I found a baby rabbit." The dark-eyed woman smiled, but her image began to fade. Gwyn frowned. "Come back. Come back." She turned to see her father, but he too faded into a mist of darkness.

11

"Gwyn."

Voices hovered over her. But she couldn't make them out. Maybe if she tried a little harder.

"Gwyn . . ."

She recognized that voice. Her father.

"Gwyn. It's time to wake up."

Why did it feel like glue held her eyelids shut? "*Hmm . . . I'm awake.*" She lifted a hand to rub one of her eyes. "I think."

Father's deep laughter rolled over her like a blanket. Warm. Caring. Loving. "Good to hear your voice again."

"Am I late?"

"Late? For what?"

"Isn't that why you're waking me up?" She cracked open one eye and then the other.

"No, you're not late for anything. Just had me a little concerned. You've been asleep since Jeremiah rescued you yesterday."

Rescued? In a rush, all the events of the flood crashed into her memory. "How's the girl?"

"She's fine. Already left with her parents."

"What happened?"

"You suffered from hypothermia. You rescued the girl from the rock in the middle of the river, but it took you both far downstream. Jeremiah said a tree plowed into him from the back and pushed him into the two of you. He doesn't remember much after that, but the little girl's parents found you all clinging to roots in a huge curve of the river."

Gwyn worked to sit up in the bed. Her head pounded. "*Ow*. That hurts." She placed a hand over her eyes. "How's Jeremiah?"

"He's doing okay. It took some time to convince him that you were all right, but he's up and around."

"I'd like to thank him."

"Don't worry. I already did. About a hundred times. Wasn't ready to lose my girl."

"I'm so tired." She burrowed back under the blankets. "And cold."

Father patted her head like he had when she was little. "Get some rest. I'll throw another quilt over you."

"Do you remember when I found that baby rabbit?"

Her father laughed. "Which time?"

Gwyn smiled and nodded. "I guess there were quite a few times, weren't there? I was dreaming before you woke me. It was the time when I was a little girl and I asked you . . . well . . . we talked about Mother and why she didn't love me like she did Sophia."

Her father's expression sobered, and he sat down beside her on the bed. "That was such a hard time for me." He reached out and pushed back a blond curl. "I didn't know what to say. I wasn't about to shame either of us and lie. But what can you tell a child about such things?"

Gwyn reached out to take hold of her father's hand. "I

just want you to know that you did the right thing. You told me that Mother didn't love Alaska and because we did . . . , well, it made her feel bad. I think I understand now. I think she felt so displaced, and Sophia was the only part of the past she could hold on to."

"A past she loved more than she loved you and me," he said sadly.

"In all these years I've selfishly considered how hard that loss was on me. I knew it had hurt you, but I never truly thought of how it must have been for you. You lost both a wife and a daughter."

"And you a mother and sister."

Gwyn nodded. "But we've always had each other . . . and God. Nasnana told me God would fill the empty places in our hearts, and you know . . . I think He has."

Father squeezed her hand. "I know He has. Sometimes we can't see what's right in front of us."

Jeremiah's thoughts drifted back to Gwyn. For the hundredth time that day. What would he have done if she'd died in the flood?

Those thoughts weren't productive, but they pressed anyway. Before the flood, his biggest concern had been what she had been doing walking with Clarence.

Clarence. Couldn't she see the man was a no-good heel?

Dr. H. came up behind him. "Jeremiah, I think we're going to have to bring Mr. Ellis here. His wife just called from the commissary. I don't think she can handle the care anymore. Would you mind going out to camp eight and checking on him?"

"Sure." That would give him some fresh air but too much time to think. Thankfully, they had phone service in the clinic and the commissary, but that only helped speed up getting word to them. It didn't help with the travel time. The camps were spread out over a large region. They needed a vehicle for the clinic. A phone in each camp would be even better.

"I don't understand what all these people were thinking, coming here with these illnesses. Didn't they realize how difficult the journey would be for them?" Harold shook his head. "And how difficult it would be to obtain care?"

"I know. It's hard to fathom how desperate people could be. Things were bad in the States, but I don't think Alaska has proven to be any perfect answer for them."

"No. Certainly not."

"Still, it gave them hope of a new start." Jeremiah thought of himself and the secret he continued to keep. He squared his shoulders. Maybe it was time to just get all things hidden into the open.

"Well, I'll never understand endangering their lives further, as well as the lives of others, by making this journey with disease as part of their baggage." Harold turned to refocus on some papers he'd left on the desk. "I suppose they thought it would be a solution to their problems. As if we can just cast off our troubles in one location and not have them follow us to another."

Jeremiah drew in a deep breath, but the words stuck in his throat. How could he explain his own decision to cast aside the troubles of one location in hopes they wouldn't follow him to the next? Maybe it *was* time to tell the truth. But no. he chickened out and changed the subject. "How is Gwyn?"

"Much better. Once she rested and warmed up, the headaches left. You'd better get a move on," Dr. H. declared. "We'll have plenty to keep us busy once you get back."

But his conscience pricked. He needed to explain. Needed to tell the truth. Should've done it a long time ago.

For a moment Jeremiah hesitated and then the decision was made. Again to take the coward's road. "I'll be back as fast as I can." He grabbed his medical bag and headed out to camp eight.

Dr. H.'s words continued to haunt him. Why had so many people agreed to come when they were ill? They weren't just putting themselves in danger, they were putting their families and the rest of the colony in danger as well. Then he thought about being in the same position. If he had a family to provide for, a failing farm and no job, wouldn't he do the same?

An overwhelming sense of selfishness filled his gut. At least these people had honorable intentions. *He'd* come here to escape. To hide and hope no one discovered the truth.

"But the truth must come out," he whispered to himself. There had been so many times when Jeremiah feared he'd been found out—when reporters had given him a second glance, when members of the colony eyed him a little longer than necessary.

Gwyn's face came to mind. What would she think of him when she found out? As much as he tried to ignore his growing feelings for her, they were still there. Stronger than ever. When he saw her with Clarence the morning of the flood, jealousy reared its ugly head. As much as he tried to convince himself that he couldn't have a chance with her—he *really* didn't want Clarence to have a chance. Gwyn deserved much better.

And then when he almost lost her . . . that fear could have devastated him.

Maybe if he cleared the air with everyone and told them the truth—maybe Gwyn would understand and be compassionate. That was one of her greatest strengths. She was so forgiving. Could it be possible to pursue her affections?

And then there was the matter of her younger sister. A memory of Sophia's stinging last words haunted him. No. He didn't have a chance. Even if Gwyn could forgive his deception, it was unlikely she'd want to take up with her sister's rejected suitor. Once she knew the truth, Jeremiah wouldn't stand a chance of convincing her of his heart. She might even believe he'd come here purposefully on the rebound—to get even with Sophia.

Clarence Novak appeared on the road in front of him. Did the man just stroll around all day? Didn't he claim he was there to help his family?

Jeremiah caught up to him in several long strides. "Hello, Clarence."

"*Dr.* Vaughan." The man's unusual emphasis on the title was interesting. "Out for a break?"

"No, Clarence, I need to check on Mr. Ellis. His wife is concerned he's getting worse." He tried to outstep the man, but Clarence was quick.

"How long are you planning on staying at the colony?"

Jeremiah pulled out his pocket watch, hoping Novak could take a hint. "I hadn't planned on leaving." The question made him pause. What was Clarence digging for?

"Nice watch. Family heirloom?"

"A gift from my grandfather." No matter how fast Jeremiah walked, Clarence kept the pace. And he was entirely too nosy. "How about yourself?" Jeremiah said. "I hear you are quite the traveler." Hopefully his travels would take him far away. Soon.

"Oh, I've got my eyes on some new prospects. But I quite enjoy myself here. Besides, Miss Hillerman and I would like to see more of each other. I wouldn't want to leave before I pursued our feelings for each other."

"Oh." Jeremiah swallowed. He couldn't be telling the truth. Gwyn? With him? "That sounds like a good plan. Does Gw— uh, Miss Hillerman share your love of traveling?"

Clarence chuckled. "Of course. What woman doesn't? She's been locked away in this hole for so long, she deserves to be spoiled like a real woman."

Hole? Did Clarence just refer to this beautiful valley as a hole? Many of the colonists even called it heaven on earth and looked forward to their homes being situated in God's most majestic little corner of the world. "I wouldn't think she'd want to leave. She loves Alaska."

"There's a lot you don't know about Miss Hillerman." The man stopped and turned to him. "I pray Mr. Ellis will be all right. Have a good afternoon, *Doctor*."

There was that tone again. What was he implying?

The fact of the matter was simple: Clarence Novak was a creep. And if Jeremiah had anything to do about it, he'd make sure Novak didn't get any closer to Gwyn.

The evening unfolded dim and gray, not at all like the bright sunny days they'd enjoyed recently.

Jeremiah sat at his desk making notes on the last two calls he'd made. His brain was weary and didn't want to focus on medicine. It wanted to focus on Gwyn. *He* wanted to focus on her.

It amazed him that when he'd first arrived, his bitterness had caused him to think of her as plain. Sophia had been beautiful, yes, but on the outside. When he found out how cold and dark she was inside, it tainted any beauty he'd appreciated. But as he grew to know Gwyn, *her* beauty only increased. Her mind was sharp, her wit quick, and her heart large. These were things that meant much more than a pretty façade.

But then there was another problem. Gwyn *was* pretty. Very pretty. Those golden curls that she refused to cut into the fashionable bobs of the day were unruly and fascinating. And her eyes . . . a gray that changed with the intensity of her mood. Sometimes as light as silver, and other times, deep and stormy. He longed to stare into them.

Jeremiah shook his head. The reports wouldn't write themselves. Besides, he couldn't afford to feel anything for the lovely Gwyn Hillerman.

The wood floor creaked.

The very subject of his thoughts stood in the doorway, dripping, wrangling with her rubber boots.

Jeremiah jumped up and grabbed a couple of towels. "What are you doing up? You're drenched."

She shivered and took one of the offered towels. "Rain will do that." Her tone belied her furrowed brow.

"It's raining?" How had he missed that?

"I take it you've been lost in thought—" she glanced down at his work—"or those reports."

He ran a hand down his face. "You've pretty much summed it up." He stood and walked her to the fire. "You look chilled to the bone."

"I usually don't mind the rain. But now, I must admit, I feel frozen almost like it's winter." Gwyn peered around the clinic. "Have you seen my father? I thought he'd still be here."

"He left a couple minutes ago to grab something to eat at the house. I'm sure he'll be right back." He touched her elbow. "And it's no wonder, it's not good for you to get a chill so soon after—"

"Nonsense." She sat in a chair by the stove, towel-drying her hair. "You need help, don't you?"

Stubborn woman. It fascinated him that she hated to have any attention on herself. "It's been a long day and yes." Jeremiah glanced at all the notes in front of him. "The sooner we get more help: doctors, nurses, supplies, more phones, sanitary conditions, and a vehicle would be nice—" he paused to grab a breath, hoping he hadn't overwhelmed her—"the sooner we can wipe out some of these sicknesses." His words gave him a thought. "But if I can't even get the nurse we have to follow instructions, how can I hope that the people will?"

Gwyn gave him a weak smile. "You're right, I should have stayed in bed. Then again, I'm tougher than you give me credit for."

She put the towel aside, and her long blond curls tumbled down her back in a most alluring fashion. Jeremiah couldn't help but wonder what it would be like to run his fingers through that beautiful tangled mass. His thoughts were interrupted, however, as Gwyn continued to speak.

"There's so much we need to help all these people, but I fear it's going to be a while before your list comes to fruition." She looked weary and stood up, rubbing her hands together. "I've lived here most of my life. It's home. And I love it. But it's hard to watch these people suffer. Especially the children."

"Does that mean you plan on staying?"

Her eyebrows rose. "In Alaska? Of course! Why would you think differently?"

Jeremiah tried to keep his smile to himself. "Uh . . . no reason. You're just young and beautiful, and I thought maybe you'd like to travel and explore the world." After the words were out, he realized what he'd said. He wished he could snatch them back. The risk was far too great.

"No. I have no desire to travel or explore." Her brow furrowed, a frown etched her lips. "I'm staying right here." Gwyn slid her boots back on and headed out the door.

He stood and went to the window and watched her walk away. Had he upset her? He thought back to Clarence's comments. He was the one who didn't know everything about Miss Hillerman.

Despite his concern that Gwyn was miffed with him, Jeremiah couldn't help but feel he'd won some sort of victory. Gwyn had no desire to leave Alaska. Not on her own, and certainly not with Clarence.

Her old wooden rocking chair creaked and groaned as she leaned back, waiting for the girls to return. Nasnana held an old worn Bible in her lap. There was an undercurrent in the colony that didn't bode well. She'd spent the last hour praying for all the people. A little more than a month had passed since the colonists had drawn for their land tracts.

And she'd stayed away as much as possible. That Gertrude woman always did a good job stirring up the pot about "Indians" and their massacres, but time would heal wounds. *Time* would be the deciding factor. And over time, as Nasnana and some of the other native people showed them love and kindness, maybe she'd win them over.

Sadzi wasn't as patient. She wanted to help all the time, wanted to teach the women about all the unique berries and plants, wanted to play with the children, wanted to mingle with other young women close to her age. But Nasnana held her back. Something in her spirit told her that patience would have to be used in abundance.

Sweet laughter drifted to her through the open window. She hadn't heard the girls laugh together for some time. Especially after Gwyn's near-drowning. And then life started moving forward at a rapid pace. Nasnana had been so busy helping the families that had been displaced by the flood that she'd hardly been able to do much more than offer Gwyn a hug in passing.

Gwyn and Sadzi walked in the door, smiles on both of their faces.

"Good morning, Grandmother."

"Good morning, Nasnana." Gwyn leaned down and kissed her cheek. "How was your prayer time?"

"Very productive." She grabbed Gwyn's hand and squeezed. "How have you been doing, my dear? You look thin and pale."

"Well, I'm always pale, but I must admit, I often forget to eat." She pulled the pins out of her curls, ran her fingers through her hair, and began to pin it back up. "Father is constantly on me about it—even more so since the flood—but he's just as bad. We've been too busy to take time to eat. They're planning on moving the clinic soon."

"It makes me appreciate even more that you still make time to come for our Bible studies." Nasnana patted the sweet girl's arm. "Our journey through Psalm 139 has been precious to me."

"Me too." Gwyn sat across from her.

Sadzi brought a teapot from the stove. "Gwyn, catch us up on all the news in the town."

"There's so much going on. I think I told you that there's been all kinds of mix-ups with shipments. Some of the construction workers they sent up don't know what they're doing, but I guess they were so desperate for jobs that they lied about their skills. One of the colonist's homes has been torn down and restarted three times."

"Oh dear." Nasnana understood the people's desperation, but the consequences for everyone involved were always difficult to bear.

"But many of the others are going at a rapid pace. It will take a lot to get everyone in a home by winter, though. Things have been very rough, but the majority of the people understand that pioneering is just that . . . *rough*. The reporters and photographers are often a nuisance. They want to chronicle every little thing that happens and every dispute, stating that 'the American people want to know!'" Gwyn waved one of her hands in the air and rolled her eyes. "I don't mind Mr. Schaleben too much. He seems to genuinely want the best for the people. And the children love posing for his photographs. Since he lives among them, he truly understands. The others, well, they come and go in their fancy suits with their fancy newsreels and cameras. And they like to focus on the naysayers."

"I didn't think there were many complaints. Most of the people I've met are happy to be here."

"Oh, there are complainers all right. In fact, the latest is a group of a few that have been stirring the pot, so to speak. They wanted their complaints to be taken to the White House, even sent a telegram to Washington. So the president sent up Eugene Carr, who's supposed to be the troubleshooter for the Federal Emergency Relief Administration. He's the man that arrived the day the river flooded."

"A troubleshooter?" Nasnana questioned. "What a title. A man who will shoot at troubles."

"More like a man who will be shot at with complaints," Gwyn countered.

"Complaints about what?" Sadzi chimed in.

"Oh, the prices at the commissary, the shortage of supplies, and the sickness. Most of the colonists want the agitators ousted. They don't want to be ridiculed for coming to this country, for volunteering to pioneer. But even among those, there are people who are worried that some of the children might die."

"Is it that bad?" Nasnana leaned forward, her heart aching.

Gwyn hesitated before she answered. "Yes, I'm afraid some of the cases are pretty severe. And there's only so much we can do without adequate medical supplies. We need a hospital, desperately."

"Well then, I will add that to our prayer list." Nasnana wrote on a paper she kept tucked in her Bible.

"Grandmother, while you are at it, could you pray that Clarence would disappear and leave Gwyn alone?"

Nasnana looked up and caught Sadzi giving a wink to Gwyn. Her cheeks tinged pink.

"Sadzi, I told you that in private!" the blonde spit out through clenched teeth. "There are much more important things to pray for."

"You want him to disappear? Is that a prayer request?" She poised her pencil over the paper, teasing Gwyn.

Both hands covered Gwyn's face. When she let them down, her face was an even deeper shade of pink. "He annoys me to no end. Follows me whenever he gets the chance. Keeps asking me to go on a picnic with him. All he talks about is money and traveling and big cities and luxuries and how I should have all of it. It's disgusting."

"You mean, *he's* disgusting," Sadzi threw in behind her hand.

Nasnana tossed a scolding glance to Sadzi and then couldn't help but laugh. Clarence Novak *was* disgusting. "I'm sorry, Gwyn. We shouldn't be laughing about this."

"I was hoping he'd get the hint at some point. I haven't encouraged him. I don't even like being around him. He seems so . . . shady."

"What do you mean?" Nasnana's own senses had been heightened around the man, but she wondered what Gwyn had observed.

"Have you ever noticed that he's always completely clean? And yet, he talks nonstop about how much work he's doing to help his family." Gwyn held out her hands and turned them over. "And his hands. Not a callous or a splinter anywhere. His look more like women's hands than mine do!"

Sadzi poured more tea for all of them. "I haven't met his family. Are they nice people?"

"That's another thing. Suzanne is a sweet Christian lady. But I never see her anymore. I never see William either."

"That's odd." Sadzi bit into a cookie.

"And the worst part? I've seen Clarence talking with Gertrude Albany on several occasions. And she's always on a rampage about Indians. Clarence knows how close I am to you, and yet I've seen him nodding and whispering to her."

A disquiet grew in the pit of Nasnana's stomach. She needed to temper this discussion. "It's one thing to tell us why he's bothering you, Gwyn, but entirely another to be gossiping. I'm not worried about Gertrude or her rumors. She has plenty of reason not to trust us, just as my people have reason to doubt the newcomers. But I'm willing to be patient. Please let it take the time that's needed to build relationships of trust. Everything is new and overwhelming to these poor souls."

"I'm sorry, Nasnana." Gwyn bowed her head. "I'm just afraid he's up to something. I don't trust him."

"I don't either, dear. So maybe we need to add him to the prayer list."

"That he would disappear?" Sadzi giggled and grabbed Gwyn's hand.

She couldn't help but smile. "Well, we'll leave that in God's hands. But we should at least pray for his soul."

"Yes, ma'am." The girls replied in unison.

"Now, how are your father and Dr. Vaughan?"

Pink flooded Gwyn's cheeks again. She glanced at Sadzi. Apparently the two had already discussed the handsome young doctor. "Father is doing well, but I can tell he's wearing thin. I don't think he sleeps more than a couple hours at a time. Jeremiah as well. They both are working around the clock, it seems."

Nasnana knew there was more. So she waited. Then prodded. "And?"

The young blonde peeked up through her curls. "And . . . he called me beautiful the other day but hasn't said a word to me since. I'm so confused."

The rumble of a truck nearing the cabin brought all three

women to their feet. Nasnana peered out the window and watched one of the construction trucks barrel toward her front door. It came to an abrupt stop, and Jeremiah jumped out, leaving it running.

Something was terribly wrong.

"Gwyn! Gwyn!" Jeremiah yelled and banged on the door.

Nasnana opened it and welcomed him in.

"Please, there's no time. I need all of you to come with me now."

"What is it?" Gwyn voiced the question she assumed they all had on their minds.

"It's Rose. She begged me to come get you. Dr. H. is with her right now."

"Is she all right?" Nasnana put on her shoes and waved the girls to the door.

"It's little Daniel. I don't know if he's going to make it."

12

There had to be some way to get Gwyn's attention. He'd been subtle so far, but maybe it was time to make more of a move. Granted, it was a small community, but Clarence needed to *do* something. To stand out.

And not manual labor. Suzanne kept nagging him about helping in the community garden, and clearing the land, and helping build the house. Didn't she know who he was? Maybe if he threw a little money at her that would shut her up.

William was willing to ignore him for the most part. They left together each morning to work, and then Clarence found a way to leave every day in the middle of the chaos. William would keep his mouth shut if he knew what was good for him.

Besides, Clarence wasn't one of the original colonists. He didn't receive all the handouts everyone else did, so he shouldn't be required to do the work they were doing. It wasn't like he had any sort of investment here. Not in this barren little shoddy no-name town.

He walked through camp four and enjoyed watching all the women. They were all married, and dirty, but there were a few pretty faces in the group. Some even wore pants and low-cut blouses. That was what he liked to see. Modern women. What would it take to get Gwyn dressed up in a little number?

Wouldn't he love to have her on his arm as they cruised the world, spending all they wanted on rich foods and ritzy hotels? How much longer would he need to wait before he could return to the real world? The isolation of this territory weighed heavily on him. Why, he couldn't even get decent liquor. It was appalling.

"Clarence," a nasal voice accosted him. "I need to speak with you."

Gertrude. The woman might be useful at some point, but at the moment she was grating on his nerves. "Yes, Gertrude. What can I do for you?"

"Didn't you say you are adept at math?"

"Yes?"

"My oldest is wantin' to go to college, and he's a bit behind in math. Would you mind helping him?"

It would be the right thing to do. Even though he didn't want to. Maybe this could help get him into Gwyn's good graces. Besides, he needed an excuse to get closer to Gertrude. The woman was an absolute treasure of information. "Why, of course, I'd love to help."

"It would have to be after all his chores are finished, but I'm sure you've got plenty of time in the evenings."

Her insinuation rubbed him the wrong way. "Of course. We can start with once a week. How does that sound?"

"That will be acceptable. Thank you, Clarence." She raised her nose in the air and headed toward her tent.

Clarence stood in the road for a moment as a new idea emerged. It was a bit risky, but it would provide a solution.

"Good morning, Mr. Novak." One of the young teen girls from the camp smiled up at him and giggled.

"Good morning to you too." He gave her his best smile. Even though he hated children, he knew how important it was to have them on his side. And he needed everyone on his side.

The young girl went back to digging in the dirt. Didn't these people have any ambition? They seemed content to just farm and survive.

Depression or no Depression, Clarence had a far different life in mind.

And he intended to get it.

Gwyn looked at her father. She could tell by his expression that Daniel's condition was grave. "What can I do?" she asked.

"I'm not sure there's anything we can do," he said, keeping his voice low. It didn't do any good, however.

"What do you mean? What are you saying?" Rose asked. She cradled her tiny son even closer to her breast. "You have to make him well. He's all I've got."

Gwyn knelt down beside the woman. "Rose, we will do everything we can. Did I ever tell you how I used to nurse baby animals back to health when I was a girl?" She wanted desperately to get the woman's mind off her woes, if only for a few moments. "Father said I had quite a touch. We'll just have to apply that hard work to Daniel."

She glanced up to find her father frowning. She'd been warned in the past about not giving false hope to patients. Her father was a firm believer in being completely honest with people. He felt that to do otherwise bordered on cruelty.

"He's all I've got," Rose said again, as if to make certain Gwyn understood her desperation.

"You've got God as well, Rose. He loves you," she said softly. "Don't forget that. God created Daniel's life, and He alone numbers Daniel's days. But He loves you both."

"God isn't loving. He took Daniel's father," Rose said, reminding Gwyn of their previous discussion. "That's not love. You don't give somebody something and then just rip it away if you love them."

Gwyn couldn't help but think of her own mother. She had once claimed to love Gwyn, had said she loved her husband too. But then she'd gone away, as if the words meant nothing, as if they were only a lie.

Nasnana put her hand on Gwyn's shoulder. "I sent Sadzi for one of the Matanuska village women who recently had a baby. I doubt Rose here is getting enough nourishment to feed little Daniel. We'll have this woman help in feeding him. Maybe that will restore his strength."

Gwyn smiled and nodded at Rose. "That's a wonderful idea."

In her mind she could hear the echoing words of Rose's husband. *"God has provided."*

July 1935

Too many cases and not enough hands. If only they had a hospital built *now*. Not that Harold wanted to complain to the government. It was an incredible undertaking to build a colony like this, and many Alaskans were ecstatic that their territory was getting attention and growing. But to rush hundreds of people up here and not have all the pieces in place wasn't the smartest of moves. Harold would continue to do his best, but he was growing weary. Fast.

The monumental task would've been impossible without Jeremiah. He was so thankful the younger man had decided to come. He hoped he would stay. Could it really be the beginning of July already? Where had all the time gone? How would they be ready for winter?

And with all the tuberculosis cases and sanitation problems, how were they supposed to keep everyone well? Granted, most of the cases were common—measles, mumps, chicken pox, pinkeye—but there were so many. They were in desperate need of a vehicle for the doctors to get around to everyone in the valley, but all the vehicles were designated for the construction workers.

He was behind in his notes on all the cases, and they needed another shipment of medication. He'd called Anchorage earlier to see if they could ship up what they could spare on the next train, but they hadn't received a restocking yet either. More medications were scheduled to arrive on the next ship, which was supposed to dock tomorrow in Seward, but Harold didn't want to put all his hopes on that.

A knock sounded on the door behind him. "Come in."

Eugene Carr entered. "I'm sorry to bother you, Harold. But I'd like to discuss a few things."

"Not a problem. What can I do to help?" Everyone knew Eugene was there by order of the president of the United States. He didn't want to see the colony fail.

"Well, you know why I'm here. The newspaper reports were beginning to slant toward negativity, and then we received the telegram from the colonists. What I need to know is how much of it is true. You've been here a long time. I'd like to ask for your perspective."

"Certainly. But how much of *what* is true?"

Eugene held out a piece of paper. "This is the telegram received in Washington. I'd like your thoughts."

Harold took the paper and put on his glasses to read. The message bore no punctuation. Not even a break or the traditional "stop" between thoughts. Harold studied the message a moment to unscramble the words.

June 18

Six weeks passed nothing done no houses wells roads Inadequate machinery tools Government food undelivered Commissary prices exorbitant Educational facilities for season doubtful Apparently men sent to pick political plums Irwin and Washington officials OK hands tied Colonists cooperating Request immediate investigation

Patrick J Hemmer Mrs IM Sandvik
Colonists Representatives

"It has only been a few weeks. Sounds like some people are complaining just to complain."

"True, but do you see any merit to the complaints?"

"Mr. Carr, I know how difficult it can be to get the correct supplies up here. Things take time. This is Alaska, not New York City. Let the people settle in; I'm sure it will calm down."

"I hope so." Mr. Carr then handed him a newspaper. "But this was Arville's article the next day."

The headline on the front page read:

Colonists Appeal to Roosevelt for Aid

Harold skimmed the article. His heart sank a little. "This states that they are demanding better medical facilities as well."

"Yes, that's why I'm coming to you." Eugene leaned forward, his elbows on his knees. "The government thought when they first started the colonization that people could go to Anchorage if they needed medical care. But that's still a good distance. Over forty miles. I know you've been here for many years, but your clinic isn't in the town, and you already had a load of patient care from the settlers and natives who were previously here."

A sigh escaped his lips as he glanced out the window. "We don't have enough medical care. We don't even have enough supplies." Harold looked Eugene Carr—troubleshooter for the president—in the eye. "I need to level with you. I would never want to induce a panic in the people here, and that's why I haven't said anything, but with all the sicknesses, and so many children in close quarters, I'm concerned. If something started and spread, we could have an epidemic before we knew what hit us."

Eugene nodded and made a few notes on a piece of paper.

"When we do have sickness, it's almost impossible to quarantine the ill. We've done our best, but we've already seen cases of measles, mumps, chicken pox, and scarlet fever. I have children who aren't getting proper nutrition, and an infant who's failing to thrive. God help us if one of the new arrivals introduces polio or we get a diphtheria epidemic." Harold barely paused to breathe.

"Not only that, but as I've mentioned prior to this, we've had cases of TB. It's very contagious—especially to the children and the natives. Then there are the injuries. I can barely keep up with the broken bones and lacerations. And we don't have a vehicle, so just getting to and from the camps is difficult."

"I can see where this could be quite serious." Mr. Carr stood and shook Harold's hand. "Thank you, Doctor. Your information has been invaluable."

"The information won't matter if it doesn't reach the proper authorities and get the proper attention. I think the colony was a good idea overall, but it was poorly planned and badly supplied. The people in Washington didn't seem to think this through. Construction should have taken place before anyone came up here. A hospital and proper staffing should have been established, not to mention schools and regular supply shipments."

"Hindsight, eh, Doctor?"

"More like no sight," Harold countered. "Someone came up with the idea that doing anything was better than doing nothing. They couldn't have been more wrong."

Harold watched the man leave. Eugene Carr had quite the burden to carry, and no doubt Harold had just added to it. But the truth had to be said. Not only was Carr responsible now for the well-being of thousands of people, but the president and the rest of the country would be watching. And no doubt many a finger would be waiting to point out the failures and assign blame, while all these people headed unprepared into an Alaska winter.

The door closed, and Harold stood for a moment with his hand on the knob. Weariness overtook him. His mind kept going over everything they needed to make it all work.

Then there was Gwyn. Guilt grew in his mind. Had he been neglecting her these past few weeks? He couldn't even remember the last time they'd had a decent conversation. She was a great nurse, but she was also trying to keep their own garden going and helping with the co-op's experimental station that the university had been working on for years. There were a lot of mouths to feed this winter.

The weight on his shoulders seemed to grow. Was he doing the best thing for his daughter? Good grief, he'd nearly lost her just a month earlier. If it hadn't been for Jeremiah's determination to reach Gwyn and the little native girl . . . they both might have been killed.

Thoughts of Jeremiah weighed on him as well. The young man was an incredible physician. He was so thankful that he'd been able to work with him as a young boy and see him today as a man who loved medicine as much as Harold did. But Jeremiah was also very troubled.

Harold had hoped that perhaps his daughter and the young doctor would hit it off, but as he watched the two of them, he wasn't sure. There seemed to be an attraction, but Jeremiah kept his heart guarded in such a way that suggested real trouble to Harold. If only he'd just sit down and talk about it. Harold was certain there was nothing they couldn't deal with.

As weariness took over, his mind automatically went back to Edith. He'd loved her. Poured his heart into her. But it wasn't enough. Before the colony, there'd been many days he felt so alone, his heart ached to be ripped from his chest. And as he cried out to God, he wondered what could come from his broken marriage. But the Lord had been doing a work in his heart.

Harold wanted to forgive Edith. He knew now she would never return to Alaska. The papers were hidden away, and he kept the secret from Gwyn. He supposed he'd known it all along, but for his older daughter's sake he wanted to have hope. Maybe that had been foolishness on his part. His eyes clouded with unshed tears. He missed his wife more than he liked to admit. Sophia too. She had always been such a dainty little girl. He could almost see her dancing around the room, pretending to be at a grand ball.

Wiping his eyes, Harold shook his head. This was serving no good purpose. It wouldn't help the problems at hand. Forgiveness was what he would focus on. His forgiveness of Edith and a prayer that she would offer the same for him.

Maybe someday.

Gwyn called out at Rose's tent and waited just a moment before pushing the flap open. "Rose? I've brought you some soup."

The room was lit only by the sunlight that came in behind Gwyn. Since the day was warm, Gwyn put the soup on the table and tied back the flap to allow some fresh air into the musty room.

Rose sat on the edge of her cot rocking back and forth while holding Daniel securely to her breast. She hummed a song— nothing Gwyn recognized. Even so, it made Gwyn smile.

"It's good to see you up. Nasnana and I thought you might like some soup. It has a good, heavy meat broth with vegetables. I think you'll like it. Nasnana is coming to visit as well. She's gone to get the woman to nurse Daniel."

Rose said nothing, but Gwyn didn't mind. The woman had been through more than anyone should ever have to endure. Gwyn searched the tent for a spoon and finally found one. Bringing the soup to Rose, she smiled. "It's probably not as hot as it could be. If you'd rather, I could warm it on your stove."

A quick glance over her shoulder and Gwyn could see that the stove door was open. It appeared there hadn't been a fire going for some time. "I suppose it would take too long." She looked back at the humming mother. "Why don't I take Daniel while you eat?"

Still Rose said nothing. Gwyn frowned.

"Rose?"

The young woman didn't acknowledge Gwyn in any way. She continued to rock and hum, lost in her own world. A sense of dread washed over Gwyn. She returned the bowl of soup to the small table and approached the cot with empty hands.

"Rose, let me have Daniel."

The woman didn't move, neither did she fight when Gwyn took the baby from her arms. Pushing back the cover, Gwyn touched the soft pale cheek of the infant. He was cold and the body was stiff. She bit her lower lip to keep from crying out. Daniel had died sometime in the night.

"Well, I see you're enjoying the fresh air," Nasnana said as she entered the tent with a small dark-haired woman at her side.

Gwyn turned with the baby in her arms. She couldn't hide the shock and when she opened her mouth nothing came out. Nasnana seemed to understand immediately. She whispered something to the young woman, who turned and left the tent.

"Let me have him," Nasnana said.

The images in Gwyn's mind swirled. She played out everything they'd done in the days since her father had first sent her to visit Rose. She saw Nasnana and Sadzi helping her feed Rose and care for Daniel. She remembered the native woman nursing Daniel and how he appeared eager to feed.

Why hadn't it been enough? Why hadn't Daniel lived? She'd

done her best. She'd given it her all, and yet she'd failed. The baby was dead.

"Poor little one. He was just too weak to live," Nasnana said, re-wrapping the blanket around his tiny frame.

"It's all my fault," Gwyn finally said.

"Nonsense, child. These things happen far too often. Life is a fragile balance, and we cannot determine who will live and who will die."

Gwyn looked back at Rose, who hardly seemed cognizant of the situation. She was still rocking and humming. Feeling the overwhelming urge to scream, Gwyn ran from the tent, only to ram headlong into the tall, well-muscled frame of Jeremiah Vaughan.

He took hold of her. "Easy there."

"Let me go. It's my fault. I failed her."

He shook his head. "What are you talking about?"

Gwyn tried to pull away. "I failed Rose. Daniel is dead. He's dead. He died in the night, and no one was here to save him."

Jeremiah held fast her left arm while taking hold of her chin. "Stop this," he said, forcing her to look him in the eye. "This isn't your fault. You didn't fail anyone."

She slammed her head and then her hands into his chest. She fisted his jacket and wailed. "He'd barely started his life. And Rose . . ." She couldn't even finish the thought. It was all she could do to breathe.

Jeremiah wrapped his arms around her shoulders. "*Shh, it's all right.*"

"It's not all right," she protested and sobbed. "It's not all right that babies die—that husbands die. It's not all right to love someone so much only to lose them. I tried so hard." She stopped fighting and just rested in his arms.

"You did everything possible, Gwyn." His voice was low and tender. "You aren't to blame for any of this. Sometimes we lose patients. I've lost them myself. It's never easy, and we always try to second-guess our actions, but I know the care you offered Rose and Daniel. Your father knows it as well. You didn't fail." He stroked her head as if she were a child. "You're the finest nurse I've ever known—the finest woman. I've never known anyone with more love and consideration for the people around her."

Gwyn looked up, surprised to find their faces so close together. Stunned by the nearness, she pushed away and stared at Jeremiah for a moment. Her heart seemed to beat so fast—so hard. The breath caught in her throat, and rational thought fled. She missed the feel of Jeremiah's arms around her—the strength that they represented.

Then the reality of what had taken place in the tent crashed in. Shaking her head, Gwyn sidestepped Jeremiah. "I . . . need . . . I must . . . tell Father."

Tony Griffin had been there, all right. Frank chewed on his toothpick. The trail came to an abrupt stop in New York, but he had plenty of leads to follow the trail backward.

One of the biggest was Gregory Simms and his girlfriend. Even though they were both dead, there had been incriminating evidence on the bodies and in the hotel room. Everything pointed to Simms pulling off the First National heist. But it didn't add up. Simms was no mastermind.

So why was Tony Griffin, an exemplary bank manager, hanging out with Simms, a man with a criminal record in New York City? Frank couldn't prove it yet, but there was no way it was a coincidence. Maybe Simms had something on Griffin. Maybe he'd somehow forced Griffin to help him rob the bank. But Simms didn't have enough creative thought to come up with such a scheme. He was a know-nothing hood who did well to steal enough to keep himself fed.

Frank looked over all his notes. What if this was just the tip of the iceberg? What if Simms was working for someone else? What if they'd taken Griffin hostage? There were just too many variables. Not only that, but there was evidence that pointed to Griffin showing up in several other locations. If he was a hostage to a gang of thieves, why hadn't they just let him go . . . or killed him?

Looked like Frank needed to do some more digging and traveling. Seven states in all. And Tony Griffin had been in all of them. Everything in his gut told him that Tony was involved—that this had been an inside job from the start. But why couldn't Frank find him? He had to crack this case.

Wasn't it bad enough that the country was suffering through the worst economy ever? And then some idiot decides he's gonna rob a bank and live high and mighty while the rest of the world starved.

But what got to Frank the most? This wasn't just any bank. A bank the feds hadn't been able to touch in years, even though they knew that some of its clients were questionable. So why would anyone be stupid enough to steal from the mafia?

The toothpick snapped in his mouth. There was more to this robbery.

He pushed out of the lobby of the hotel and grabbed a paper. More headlines about the colony in Alaska. No doubt another exercise in futility. Well, that was great, but he had a case to crack.

He tucked the paper into his briefcase and headed to the station. He needed to catch the next train back to Chicago.

———

The tears wouldn't stop. Gwyn sat with Sadzi on her bed, just like they had done as little girls. Only now the weight of loss threatened to drown them both.

Her sadness for Rose multiplied every time she thought of precious baby Daniel. How could she pass on God's hope to someone who didn't believe there was a God? Gwyn herself didn't even understand why God would take first Rose's husband and then that beautiful little boy.

Sadzi wrapped her arms around her again. "Gwyn, I'm so sorry. Is there anything I can do? Anything?"

Gwyn sniffed and wiped the tears again. Her handkerchief was soaked through. "No. Thanks for being here, but I'm just so tired. And I'm confused." She thought again of Jeremiah and the way she had felt in his arms a couple days ago. The memories startled her, making it impossible to think clearly.

"You should get some sleep. You know what my grandmother says, 'Things always look better on the backside of a good rest.'"

"But things won't look better this time. Daniel will still be dead and I won't have any answers for Rose."

"Maybe it's not your job to have answers," Sadzi replied. "Grandmother has stayed with her around the clock and hasn't said much either. She reminded me last night that only God has the answers. And only He can show them to Rose in her heart. We need to surround Rose with love, encourage her, and leave the rest up to our heavenly Father."

Gwyn climbed off her bed and went to wash her face. She

was exhausted. She couldn't think clearly when she was this tired. And she just wanted to help. She hated to think that she had failed a sister in Christ.

"Gwyn, are you still going to the July Fourth festivities tomorrow?"

With everything going on, Gwyn hadn't thought about the date.

Even though Alaska was only a territory, it was still owned by the United States, and all the new colonists were U.S. citizens as well. Everyone could use a much needed break. The planning had been brief, but it had been exciting to think about—at least until now.

Gwyn dried her face. With all the newspaper reporters here, as well as the men who filmed the newsreels, the entire world would be able to hear and see how the Matanuska colonists celebrated the Fourth of July. The president and everyone who'd supported this experiment would want to show the world how happy and well settled the colonists were—whether that was true or not. She thought it rather funny the way the reporters told their stories to suit whatever slant they preferred.

She sucked in a breath as she thought of Rose. The woman appeared to have lost her mind. There would be no celebration for her. How could they rejoice with so much sorrow all around them? Then again—how could they not? They could, as her father once said, focus on the sad and painful details of their fallen world. They could allow themselves to concentrate only on the bad—or they could remember that Jesus had said there would be trouble in this world, but He had overcome, and because of that, they could as well.

The tears had to stop at some point. "You know, I *am* going to the celebration. I think we all need to go."

"There are some pretty handsome men among all those workers."

Sadzi, dear Sadzi. Nothing could keep her down for long. Her zest for life bubbled out of her. And she was a hopeless romantic. Gwyn couldn't help but grin. "You always make me smile."

"And laugh."

"Yes, and laugh." Gwyn reached over and hugged her friend. "Thank you."

Sadzi pulled back and wrinkled up her nose. "Is it rude to hope that Clarence won't be there?"

Gwyn marveled at how quickly Sadzi could change subjects. "Ugh. Clarence. I can't stand that man." She slapped a hand over her mouth. "I'm sorry. I shouldn't have said that out loud."

"It's okay. You were thinking it. I saw it on your face."

"I'm just so tired of him always appearing. He's like one of our mosquitoes—big and annoying."

"And you'd like to swat him."

Gwyn gasped. "I never said I wanted to hit him!"

"Hey, I was just referring to your comparison of Clarence with a mosquito." Sadzi held her hands up. She mumbled under her breath, "Not that a little *splat* wouldn't do him good."

"What was that?" Gwyn giggled at her friend's comment.

"Oh, nothing. I wasn't saying anything about squashing an annoying bug. I was being the perfect lady. I promise." Sadzi's long black hair shimmered.

Gwyn reached up to her own curls. She'd always wanted straight hair, even found herself jealous of Nasnana's and Sadzi's beautiful straight-as-a-board hair.

Her best friend of almost two decades went to her bureau and started digging through her clothes. "Now, I know there is someone worthy of dressing up for."

"What?"

"Don't deny it, Gwyn. Dr. Jeremiah Vaughan is probably the most handsome man I have ever laid eyes on. I know you've noticed. And he's noticed you."

Gwyn couldn't help but remember how he'd stroked her hair and offered her comfort. He had been so kind, so gentle. But that was just an act of consolation. He knew she was grieving and in shock. It wasn't as though he cared for her.

"No he hasn't." She twisted one of her curls. "Jeremiah's a very nice man, but he's much too busy to worry about . . . well . . . to notice me."

"Only because he's fighting it. He's probably doing that out of respect for you and your father," Sadzi said over her shoulder as she pulled out Gwyn's best dress. "You haven't worn this in ages. I think it's high time we brought it out."

"I don't know. It seems too dressy. And short."

Her friend smiled at her. "And this is from several years ago. The styles are even shorter now. But this is well below your knee."

"Don't women care about modesty anymore?"

"Not much. Stop trying to change the subject. The dress is pretty and modest. You just want to make excuses." Sadzi stepped behind her and started playing with Gwyn's hair. "What kind of hairstyle do you want? What do you think Jeremiah would like?"

"I am not going to the celebration to impress Jeremiah. I'm going to be part of the community."

Sadzi huffed.

Gwyn ignored her. "Besides, he probably won't even be there. They've had their hands full at the clinic." She picked at a piece of lint on her pants.

"Gwyn! Is that jealousy I hear in your voice?"

Was it? Probably. Sadzi always had a way of getting right to the heart of a matter. "Father used to need me to assist him on everything. Now he has Jeremiah. They spend all their time together, and all these trusted looks pass between them. I hate feeling this way. My father has poured everything he has into that clinic."

"And you've always loved him for it." Sadzi leaned around her shoulder. "You've also been right there with him. You love it as much as he does."

Gwyn sighed. That was true.

"So I'm thinking it's more that you feel a little abandoned."

Abandoned. Now, there was a word she knew well.

Her friend walked around her and sat back on the bed. "And it feels like your mother all over again."

Tears pricked Gwyn's eyes once again. She nodded. "But I know it's different. Father's not unhappy. He's not angry and complaining about everything. And I know he's not going to leave. I know he loves me. It's just . . ."

The pause stretched between them.

"What?"

"He doesn't *need* me anymore."

It was Sadzi's turn to nod.

"My mother *never* needed me," Gwyn went on, "and then one day she didn't *want* me either. I just don't want to go through the same thing with my father. What if it turns into that?"

Once again, Sadzi hugged her. And then she thumped Gwyn

on the forehead with her finger. "Nasnana is right. You worry too much." She bounced off the bed and went right back to sorting through Gwyn's clothes.

Gwyn shook her head. If only things were solved as easily as Sadzi thought.

13

"Please, Nasnana." Gwyn clasped her hands in front of her the next morning and shot a conspiratorial look to Sadzi. "Will you please come with me?"

"I don't know, dear." The older woman shook her head. "I'm not sure if enough people are comfortable with us yet, and I only came home to get a change of clothes."

"But so many of the women love you. They've seen your kindness to Rose and to others."

"That may be true, Gwyn, but these things take time."

"But this is for the community. And you and Sadzi were part of this community before it even started." Her begging didn't seem to be working. Maybe she needed to try another tactic. "I'd appreciate the company as well. Maybe Clarence will leave me be if you come."

Sadzi winked at her. "Please, Grandmother. I want to go, yes, but I'd also like to be there to protect Gwyn. Clarence won't leave her alone."

Nasnana shot them both a scolding glance. "All right, all right. Your little plan worked. We'll all go to the celebration. But I will not promise to stay long, and I will be checking on Rose."

"Thank you." Sadzi escorted her grandmother into the other room to help her get ready.

Gwyn's heart did a little leap. Her one wish for the day was to have a chance to talk to Jeremiah. And she hoped it wouldn't be about patients or the clinic.

They arrived a little late, but people were milling about, chatting and smiling. The wooden post sign declaring *Welcome to Valley City* greeted everyone at the event. No one seemed bothered by Gwyn's guests. Her father approached, and she spotted a large group of men rushing the train. Some even climbed in the windows.

"What's going on, Father?"

He sighed. "Oh, seventy-five of the transient workers resigned and are heading back home."

"Seventy-five? How on earth will they get the houses and town buildings up in time?"

Her father patted her arm. "It will be all right. Not to worry. A lot of these men didn't have any idea what they were getting into, just like some of the colonists."

Her father's words were all too true. Once Mr. Carr arrived, he'd gotten an earful of complaints. She'd been there for the first meeting, but the complaints were from just a few people. A couple of the families complained that there wasn't any running water to the tents. Then another mother came forward and said she had just learned to conserve water. She even went on to tell Mr. Carr that she didn't mind all four of her boys using the same bath water once a week. At least she could be thankful that she could bathe them! Many other families had laughed along with her as they tried to stay positive. But there had been complaints from workers too. They'd had to go without baths for three weeks, until twelve showers were erected.

Gwyn realized her father was still talking.

"And it's been a lot of hard work. Don Irwin has assured everyone that they have more workers on the way and everything will be fine. We definitely don't want to dampen anyone's spirits on this special day." He leaned in and kissed her cheek. "I've got to get back to the patients but wanted to get some fresh air. I'm glad I caught you. I'm not sure if I'll see you again today."

As he walked back to the clinic, Gwyn's heart sank a little. If her father couldn't leave the patients for very long, then Jeremiah probably wouldn't be able to either. The thought depressed her. More than she would have liked. She wanted to prove to him that she was all right—that she was just as strong and capable as she had been before finding Daniel dead. Now, along with her thoughts of his gentle comfort, she felt ashamed for the way she'd reacted. Medical personnel should never be given over to such fits. Jeremiah would think her completely incompetent. She had to assure him that wasn't the truth.

Their little trio walked further into the crowds, and Gwyn spotted Don Irwin. The man the ARRC had put in charge as general manager over the project seemed to be handling things well. And if he said more help was on the way, then she wouldn't worry. They still had plenty of time before winter arrived. If everyone worked hard, they could do it.

The barbecue was well under way, and the colonists were gathered around makeshift picnic tables. Several of the community buildings had been started, and most of the people seemed content. As the train pulled out, Gwyn thought of how desperate the men must be to leave in such a rush. Had something else happened?

Sadzi tugged on her sleeve and whispered in her ear, "Look, it's Jeremiah. He seems to be looking for someone. I'll bet he's looking for you."

Gwyn felt her stomach flip. "If he needs to speak with me, he will." She felt rather nervous at the thought of the very encounter she had hoped for. She took hold of Sadzi's arm. "Come on. The food smells delicious."

"Oh, you aren't any fun at all," Sadzi whined. "Don't look now—he's watching you."

"Well, stop staring at him, you goose. He's probably just wondering why you are watching *him*." It sounded like a good argument, even to herself, but that didn't stop her heart from picking up its pace.

"Where did Grandmother go off to?"

They scanned the crowd. "I'm not sure. She hasn't said anything since we left your house."

"She's probably found someone who needed help, or she's with Rose. I'm sure we'll find her." Sadzi squeezed her arm again. "Oh, look. That man over there is *very* nice looking. So tall and muscular. Ooh, he has a mustache too."

"Would you stop it?" Gwyn giggled. "You're worse than most of the kids. I thought you were looking for Nasnana."

"I am."

"Good excuse. You forget that I know you all too well." Gwyn greeted some of the ladies who were carrying dirty plates toward one of the neat white tents. "*Hmm*, I'll bet Nasnana has found a way to pitch in. It'd be just like her to tackle a pile of dirty dishes so no one else has to do them."

"You're probably right. Grandmother always said idle hands were the devil's workshop. She'll probably come looking for us to help. Oh, look!" Sadzi pointed. "They're playing baseball. I think it's so much fun to watch that game. I don't know how all the rules work, but it looks like great fun."

"I suppose it does," Gwyn admitted. "I heard there will be fireworks tonight. I haven't seen any of those since I was very young. I always thought they were so pretty. But if they wait until it's dark, that will be the middle of the night." While she was used to the long daylight hours, she wondered if the men were planning to shoot off the fireworks while it was still light—which was almost all night long at this time of year.

"Come on, let's watch the game for a little while. We can help Grandmother later. Besides, maybe she's just visiting with someone."

———— ❧ ————

Jeremiah finally caught sight of Gwyn and made his way through the crowd. He hadn't had a chance to speak with her since the death of baby Daniel. He waited nearby until he saw Sadzi step away to get popcorn and then made his move.

"I thought I might never find you."

Gwyn looked up at him, her eyes wide in surprise. "I . . . uh . . . I didn't know you were looking for me. Is there a problem? Is someone hurt?"

"No problem. I just . . . I wanted to see how you were. I mean, the last time we spoke—"

She held up her hand. "Please, the last time we spoke, I was completely unprofessional. I have wanted to apologize for it ever since."

He frowned. "What do you mean?"

She waved her hands in a casual manner. "I mean the way I went on about Daniel's death and Rose. I didn't handle that well at all, and I'm afraid you bore the brunt of my . . . well . . . my fit."

"You were upset. You had a right to react. A baby had just died." He didn't understand why she was acting this way. He had rather enjoyed their time together, had enjoyed holding her in his arms and offering comfort.

"I know, but it's not like it's the first time I've seen someone die." Gwyn fixed him with a most serious expression. "I'm trained to help heal people. My father made it clear to me that medical folks can't allow their emotions to get the best of them. We aren't of any use to people when we're falling apart like I did."

"But you didn't fall apart with the patient. You didn't begin to cry until you were out of the tent—with me."

Gwyn nodded. "Yes, but I should have managed my reaction better. I should have stayed to help you and Nasnana. I want you to know that I'm sorry. I hope you don't think less of me."

Jeremiah didn't quite know what to think. He didn't think less of her. If anything, he thought more highly of Gwyn Hillerman. She was a woman of feeling and compassion. She sorrowed over the loss of an infant. Nurse or not, she had every right to her feelings.

He wanted to say something more but could see that Gwyn had returned her gaze to the game, and Sadzi approached with her newly procured popcorn.

"I suppose I should get back to the clinic," Jeremiah murmured.

"Hello, Jeremiah," Sadzi called in greeting. "Are you enjoying the celebration?"

He looked from her to Gwyn, still watching the game, and then back to Sadzi. "It's been interesting but a bit confusing."

"Oh, you aren't familiar with baseball either?" Sadzi asked. "I thought I was the only one. I can tell you what I know, but it isn't much."

He smiled and shook his head. "No. I understand baseball just fine. It's the rest of the world that confuses me. Especially the female occupants of it."

A black cloud descended on the colony. It had been only eight days since the celebration of America's independence. But within forty-eight hours, four children died in camp eight. Jeremiah sat on a stump outside the clinic, his eyes stinging.

A few days ago, he'd been elated to deliver the first baby to be born in the colony. As he'd held little Laura Norena Van Wormer, his thoughts went to Gwyn. For the first time in a long time, Jeremiah longed for a family of his own. But was that even possible anymore? His future was all based on lies here in Alaska.

And then the deaths of the children. Without adequate sanitation and the remoteness of the camps, when one child got sick, it quickly spread. This time it had been measles and polio. Another baby was at the hospital in Anchorage—the measles had progressed into pneumonia.

Thirteen families left that day. And the reason hung thick in the summer air: They didn't want to watch their children die too.

The weight of the loss pushed Jeremiah into a dark place. Where was God in all this? Couldn't He have saved those children? Couldn't He help them get the correct supplies and provide them with a vehicle to be able to reach people faster?

The train whistle sounded in the distance. The colony was shrouded in sadness—the loss of children, the loss of friends.

"Jeremiah?" Dr. H. stood beside him.

Jeremiah wiped his eyes. "Sorry, do you need me?"

"No, no. I'm just concerned for you. This hasn't been easy."

Words wouldn't come. While Jeremiah had known the loss of patients, including baby Daniel, he hadn't lost children—children he'd laughed with, played games with. Maybe coming to this small community hadn't been a good idea. Maybe he needed to give up medicine altogether.

"I can see this tearing you up, and I'm sorry. But we've got to keep faith. God is still in control."

Jeremiah looked long at his mentor. Dr. Harold Hillerman had aged during the past few weeks. More lines creased his forehead and around his eyes than before. "I know you think that, Dr. H., but I'm not so sure anymore. The past few months have been horrible for me, and most of it, God could have fixed. But I'm guessing I'm not worthy enough for Him to intercede on my behalf." He stood, paced. "Maybe that's why those children are dead. God is punishing me. I shouldn't be here."

"What on earth are you saying, son?" Harold put a hand on his shoulder. "You're not making sense. God isn't punishing you. We did everything we could with the little time we had with those kids—"

At that moment one of the ARRC trucks raced up to the clinic. Mr. Carr and another man stepped out. "Dr. Hillerman, I'd like you to meet Dr. Earl Albrecht. He's been at the railroad hospital in Anchorage for a few weeks and has agreed to stay on here at the colony to help out. Dr. Romig and Colonel Ohlson made arrangements for him to use the speeder to get him here. They heard about the deaths and want to help us with medical care for the colony."

Dr. H. shook the other doctor's hand. "Thank you for coming, Doctor. We can use the help." Dr. H. sighed and Jeremiah sensed his relief—their workload had increased in recent days—but he found himself a little hesitant. Where was Dr. Albrecht from? What if he knew physicians in Chicago? Could he have heard about Jeremiah's license being revoked?

Eugene Carr continued, "We've also made arrangements for the colony's community building to be converted to a hospital. We will assist in moving everything from the clinic there immediately, if that's all right with you."

Harold nodded. "I've been saying for some time that we need to move closer to the town center."

"We've brought cots, mattresses, linens, and an abundance of medicine." Dr. Albrecht stepped forward. "They were also gracious to send three additional nurses. You'll meet them at the hospital."

"Thank you," Dr. H. said. "This will be huge for the community."

Jeremiah watched the interaction. He didn't recognize Dr. Albrecht. Hopefully he wasn't from anywhere near Chicago.

He shook his head. There were children dying, and he was worried about himself. What kind of selfish man was he? He headed inside to grab his medical bag. There were several chicken pox patients he wanted to keep a close eye on in camp six.

As Dr. H. and Dr. Albrecht instructed the workers to load up the truck, Eugene Carr stopped Jeremiah. "Son, I'm not sure we've had the chance to talk."

"I apologize, Mr. Carr, but I do need to check on some of our patients." He attempted to leave.

"I totally understand. I was just curious as to where you gained your medical training."

The question burned a hole in Jeremiah's back. His first instinct was to keep walking, but if he ignored the man sent by the president, that could give him away. "Chicago," he threw over his shoulder.

"Oh, so you probably know Randolph Brewster?"

The commissioner's words stopped him cold. And for a moment, Jeremiah couldn't breathe.

A worker ran toward them. "Mr. Carr? They need you at the office."

"Excuse me, Jeremiah."

The relief of the interruption was short-lived. It wouldn't take much for Eugene Carr to learn the truth.

14

The mosquitoes swarmed. Gwyn pulled her netting closer in around her neck. With all the clearing the construction crews were doing, the pests were worse than ever. Every time a stump was pulled up, thousands more of the almost-bird-sized bugs emerged.

But other than the Buhach powder they burned and the netting, there wasn't anything they could do until winter killed off the pesky bloodsuckers. Both people and animals suffered—no one was exempt. A couple of the men had even taken to making a paste out of the Buhach and putting it on their faces as they worked.

Gwyn reached into the dirt with a hoe. She was helping the women at camp four with their garden. Since the arrival of Dr. Albrecht and the other nurses and the moving of their clinic, she'd been able to spend more time in the camps. She missed working at her father's side, but with professionally trained nurses now able to assist, she was content to work in the fresh air. Besides, the more time she spent at the hospital, the more Dr. Vaughan distracted her. He occupied such a large portion of her thoughts that it couldn't be healthy for her to be around him too often. She didn't want to have her heart broken if he didn't return her growing feelings.

"Gwyn, what do you think of this?" Julia Lewis, one of the younger moms in the colony, approached her in the garden with a couple of signs. *Alaska Grown* and *Handmade in Alaska*. "Those wealthy tourists keep coming through to get a glimpse of 'the pioneers,' so we thought we'd come up with a little stand where we could sell things to them when they come through."

"I think it's a brilliant idea, and I love the signs. They look great." Rarely had any tourists come to the valley in the past, but now the colony had become a curiosity for the wealthy who could afford to cruise to Alaska. "How many of you are involved in it?"

Two more ladies entered the conversation. Arm in arm they were carrying some of the things they'd made. The taller one smiled at Gwyn. "Oh, a bunch of us at each camp. On the boat on the way up here, we actually talked about ideas for the valley and how we could make extra money, but we didn't realize we'd get tourists this soon."

A little twinge of jealousy hit Gwyn as she watched the ladies laugh and brainstorm together. The bonds of friendship that had been created on the voyage here had turned into long-term relationships. A couple of the ladies she'd met were sisters-in-law. Both newlyweds, they'd come here to start fresh.

The crowd of smiling faces made Gwyn smile too. This was how it was supposed to be. A community. A family.

One of the younger girls thrust a bunch of fireweed at her. "Pretty."

Gwyn patted the little girl's head. "Yes, very pretty." The

smell of the fireweed was one of her favorites. She couldn't wait until it was time to make fireweed jelly and fireweed honey. She'd promised several of the women she would teach them. They'd all fallen in love with the sourdough pancakes and bread.

For the women who still looked at the colony as an adventure, life was joyous and fun. But for the few who didn't seem happy—no matter what—it was the worst location on the planet. Gwyn and Sadzi and Nasnana had done their best to encourage and cheer everyone on, but there would always be a negative few in the bunch.

Laughter and voices drifted off as the group of ladies walked away. Gwyn surveyed her work and leaned the hoe back against the fence post. A walk sounded nice. A few moments to stretch and think.

Gwyn kicked a rock down the path as she hummed "Amazing Grace." God had been so good to her. She had no right to complain. But her heart yearned for a husband. Watching all the young couples in the colony had given her a glimpse of what she'd been missing. And the busyness of the summer increased her longings.

She hadn't seen Jeremiah in days. What she wouldn't give to run into him again. She'd never forget the comfort of his arms.

What was wrong with her? Goodness, she needed Nasnana and her good sense.

But the path from Nasnana's was quiet. There'd been no answer at the door. No sign of her outside in the garden. The wild flowers in full bloom and a strong breeze carrying the birds from tree to tree made Gwyn breathe deeply. Not finding Nasnana home made Gwyn's mind even more unsettled.

Should she tell her what she really thought about Jeremiah? Reveal her deepest longings and desires? The older woman cared for her more than any other woman in her life. Maybe she'd have some guidance or wise words to help Gwyn. But maybe since she wasn't home, God was telling her to keep it to herself. Maybe her feelings were in vain.

The crack of a stick behind her made her jump.

"Not to worry, Gwyn. It's just me." Clarence ambled toward her.

Ugh. There was plenty to worry about when that man was about. He was so annoying. God surely didn't want her to hate anyone. They were commanded in the Bible to love one another, but Gwyn had to admit that she couldn't stand the man now in front of her. "You startled me."

"I do apologize. It's a lovely day, isn't it?"

"Yes. What are you doing out here?" Her question came out harsher than she'd intended.

He tilted his head. "Why, coming to check on you. That's all."

"Why would you come all the way out here?"

"I know how close you are to the old woman and her beautiful granddaughter . . . uh . . . Sadzi? So when I couldn't find you anywhere else, I headed this way."

Just hearing him speak her friend's name made her cringe. What was it about him that irritated her so? And why did he keep seeking her out?

"They are kind people. I've enjoyed getting to know everyone here." He locked his hands behind him and walked beside her.

"That's nice. We have wonderful friends in this valley." Small talk wasn't her favorite, but this man seemed determined to stick to her side. *Lord, please help me be nice.*

"It's a lovely place, Gwyn. But I do look forward to the time when we can get away from here. I'd love to show you Paris and Rome and New York City."

"We?" She stopped, unable to take another step. Her boots seemed stuck to the ground. What on earth was he implying?

"I'm sorry. Maybe that was a bit presumptuous of me. I haven't even had the chance to escort you to dinner yet." He reached out and touched her elbow. "Would you do me the honor of accompanying me to Anchorage sometime soon?"

Her abhorrence for the man propelled her forward. Eyes down, she prayed for the right words. It struck her that they were alone in the woods, and her heartbeat quickened. "I appreciate your kindness to me, Clarence, but no thank you. There's far too much to be done around here."

"Don't you long for a life away from all the hard work? I'm offering you a night of luxury and my undivided attention."

She stopped again. "Clarence, you obviously don't know me. I don't like attention. I don't long for luxury. I enjoy hard work."

"Oh, my dear, but that's only because you haven't yet tasted the wondrous things the world has to offer." He tried to grab her hands, but she stepped back.

Maybe she just needed to be bold, no matter how hard that was—it wasn't her forte. "Clarence, how can you afford such luxuries anyhow? You are living with your brother and his family in a tent."

"But, Gwyn—"

"Miss Hillerman."

"Miss Hillerman, I am a wealthy man. I came here simply to spend some time with my family and see them off to a good start. I'd like to financially make it possible for them to succeed."

Succeed, in a pig's eye. She didn't believe that for a minute.

Sure, the man was always clean, dressed nice. She didn't care for the way he slicked back his hair, but at least he was groomed. In fact, he was always a bit *too* polished. That bothered her. That, and the fact that he always seemed to know where to find her, he never seemed to lift a finger to help anyone else, and his words dripped of condescension.

"You seem lost in thought."

"I just have a lot on my mind."

"Can I help you in any way?"

She wanted to tell him that he could leave her alone, but thought it might be too rude. "I'm off to see the Bouwens family."

"That's wonderful. Which camp are they at?"

"Camp two."

"That's quite a trek from here. Would you mind if I accompanied you?"

Every time he caught her, he asked the same question. And no matter how she responded, he walked with her anyway. Maybe if she ignored him, he would get the hint. But how could she accomplish that when it was just the two of them?

"Remind me about the Bouwens family."

"Oh, they're amazing. Mrs. Bouwens is teaching me how to tat. Mr. Bouwens was a butcher and a deputy sheriff before they came here."

He faltered for a minute. "I'm sorry. I must have tripped."

"They also are the largest family sent up to the colony."

"Is that so?" He looked off into the distance. "How many children do they have?"

"Eleven." Gwyn couldn't help but smile. "I just love those

kids. Mrs. Bouwens is incredible. Every one of them is hard-working and well mannered."

"Eleven children?"

"Yes."

"Eleven." Clarence's lips disappeared into a thin line as his eyebrows rose in obvious objection.

So this was her way out. Gwyn wanted to giggle at the thought. "I just love children, don't you? And big families. Big families are the best. One day when I do marry and settle down, I want to do it right here with a dozen or more children." Ducking her head, she hid a smile at the sound of his groan. "Is something wrong?" she asked in an innocent manner.

Clarence said nothing for a moment and then his words came in rapid fire. "I am so sorry. I totally forgot that I'm expected elsewhere. I apologize, Gwyn. I was actually on my way to find William when I thought of you. You see, William needs me back at the house site. I'm sorry to cut our conversation short." He turned on his heel and left. In the opposite direction of William Novak's house.

Gwyn shook her head and watched as Clarence disappeared. It was the fastest she'd ever seen him move. She laughed out loud and continued on her way. So Clarence didn't like children. That much was apparent. If she could just surround herself with a crowd of children everywhere she went, maybe he'd leave her alone.

But in less than thirty seconds, he was at her side again.

"Did you forget something?" She tried not to smile.

"Actually, I did." He cleared his throat. "And I also headed the wrong way. But before I go help William, I believe there is something of an urgent matter that you need to know."

"All right."

"I'm only telling you this out of the deepest concern I have for you in my heart . . . for your safety." He looked very serious. "I would never want to speak ill of anyone."

"Of course." If he would just get on with it.

"It's about Dr. Vaughan."

Now he had her attention. "What about Dr. Vaughan?"

"You need to be wary of the man, Gwyn. I know you have worked with him for quite some time, and your father is very close to him as well, but . . ." He grimaced and shook his head.

"But what?"

"He's hiding something horrendous that he doesn't want anyone to find out."

What? If anyone was hiding something, she'd think it was Clarence, not Jeremiah. "I'm afraid you must be mistaken, Mr. Novak. Dr. Vaughan is of the highest integrity. He's dedicated to healing people."

Clarence grabbed her arm.

She tried to pull it free, but his grip was firm. "Please, let go."

"Gwyn, I'm saying this because I want to protect you."

"Let go, Clarence." She yanked again.

He released her but stepped closer. "You wouldn't be too happy if you knew the truth about *Doctor* Jeremiah Vaughan's past."

Gwyn moved away. "This is really uncalled for, Mr. Novak. I won't allow you to slander a friend."

"Well, once you learn the truth, you won't call him a friend. Just remember when that happens, I was the one who warned you."

She narrowed her eyes. "I'll remember exactly what you've said . . . and done."

The hard bench beneath Jeremiah was a welcome relief. With the addition of Dr. Albrecht and the new nurses, sicknesses were under control. Jeremiah had even had time yesterday to work at one of the sawmills cutting lumber for the homes. As much as his feet usually ached from standing up all day, today his shoulders and arms felt ten times worse. The doctors and nurses had all agreed to a strict rotational schedule to enable them to get away from the clinic for several hours each week. But time on his hands wasn't what he wanted.

The church service began and Jeremiah straightened on the bench in this church without walls. During the prayer, he glanced around at the mountains, jutting thousands of feet above the beautiful valley they now occupied. While their beauty was magnificent, the rocky and rugged peaks evoked awe, reverence, and a heavy dose of fear. This was no land to be tamed or trifled with.

Even on the muddiest of days when souls were weary from work and the camps were a mess, all one had to do was look up and see the fingerprints of the Creator. Jeremiah shook his head. He might not be on good terms with Him right now, but there was no mistaking His handiwork when you gazed around this wondrous land.

No doubt about it, he loved Alaska. And he longed to stay. But that would mean he'd have to tell the truth. His secret couldn't stay hidden forever.

Especially with Eugene Carr knowing Mr. Brewster, the

man whose wife had died after Jeremiah's use of intravenous anesthesia.

When the people all stood to sing a hymn, Jeremiah jolted off his seat. He'd chosen the Presbyterian service because that was what he'd attended at home. But the colony was well stocked with clergymen. In fact, three had been chosen to be among the original colonists. Father Merrill Soltzman was a Catholic priest. He played the saxophone every Saturday night for the dance at camp one in the community hall, and was also chief of the volunteer fire department. Reverend Walter Georg was the Lutheran minister. He, along with Bert Bingle, the Presbyterian minister, tried to keep morale high and offered a lot of support and comfort to the people.

Voices rose in song around him, as beautiful and strong as if they were in one of the world's greatest cathedrals. Jeremiah longed for that same vibrant spirit. If only he had the same hope for the future that these people had. Here, on hard benches, their sanctuary the outdoors, they still sang and praised God, simply happy to be able to worship together.

Reverend Bingle read from his Bible, but Jeremiah allowed the words to float over him. The single reason he attended was to keep any rumors at bay. Just because he and God weren't on speaking terms right now didn't mean the whole community needed to think he was a heathen. Doctors needed respect.

He looked across the small gathering and spotted Gwyn. He hadn't seen her much over the past few days. But Dr. H. had kept him up-to-date on how she was doing. Since the Red Cross nurses arrived, she'd had the freedom to help the ladies in the colony and work at the huge co-op garden run by the university. He missed her presence.

As if sensing his gaze, Gwyn looked up. Their eyes met. A

small smile lifted her lips, and she gave him a tiny wave. The gesture made his heart leap. But what right did he have to look for Gwyn's affections? She was pure and sweet. Simple and strong.

And he . . . was nothing but a mess. The façade might still be intact, but his insides were crumbling under the weight of his lies. Even if he did come clean about the medical board taking his license, there was still the matter of his having been engaged to Gwyn's sister. That would probably cause her even more discomfort than his revoked license. After all, Gwyn knew that doctors were human and sometimes patients were lost even when the best medical skills were available. No, Gwyn would have a problem learning that he'd been engaged to Sophia and hadn't bothered to tell her or her father. But even with guilt eating up his gut, he couldn't resist looking at her. Staring. Longing.

Over the past few months, she'd taught him so much about Alaska. And even though she didn't know it, she'd taught him about people as well. That there were people in the world who actually cared for others rather than focusing on their social standing or their bank account.

For years, he'd spent every spare second he could with Randolph Brewster. The wealthy politician had it all. A beautiful wife, handsome sons, money, and position. He'd convinced Jeremiah that they could change the world with a new hospital and new medical technology.

Brewster had even convinced Jeremiah that a successful career in medicine was just the first step. Jeremiah could one day run for political office himself and could leave his mark for all mankind. Change the way hospitals were designed and perhaps even develop new medicines and life-saving techniques.

Brewster had encouraged—no, he had demanded—that Jeremiah reach for the stars. And if reaching those stars meant walking over a few people along the way, well, so be it. That was just the way it went.

Jeremiah hung his head. What had ever made him think that reaching for the highest achievements—climbing that ladder of prestige—would be beneficial for him? It would require that he go completely against his nature. All he'd ever really wanted to do was benefit his fellowman. Heal the sick. Find new ways to ease suffering. Walking on people, using them for whatever he could get out of them, was not his style. Even so, he'd given in to Brewster's pressure. Jeremiah had convinced himself that the means were justified by the end results.

The good reverend's voice rose and fell as his sermon continued. "Hypocrite!"

The one word—the only word he'd heard—struck Jeremiah to the core. *Hypocrite*. That summed up Randolph Brewster. The man was a liar. But it also summed up his own choices.

What would Gwyn think of *him* when she found out the truth? She'd call him a hypocrite too. And in all likelihood worse, much worse. Just as Sophia had.

Jeremiah shook his head. He had to stop comparing Gwyn to her sister.

Gwyn wasn't anything like Sophia.

Just one more reason why he could never have her. A woman of integrity deserved a man of integrity.

Jeremiah wasn't that man.

15

The colonists began singing "Onward Christian Soldiers" while a young mother accompanied on a small pump organ. The joy and happiness that floated through the crowd was unmistakable. If only he could grab on to it.

As everyone gathered their things, Jeremiah couldn't resist looking over to Gwyn. He watched her talking to her father. She became so animated sometimes—her hands helping to express her thoughts. He loved to watch her face. Even though she was quiet and reserved with most people, her openness with her father touched Jeremiah's soul. What an interesting lady—one he'd love to take a lifetime getting to know.

Hypocrite. The word ripped through his heart. He had to do something to get Gwyn off his mind. And the sooner the better.

Several families greeted him on the way back to their camps. Sunday mornings were often a rush, since people had to walk a good distance to get to the church services. The closest camp, camp one, still showed many tents with the dark tarps covering the tops. Many of the mothers had begged the ARRC to do something to help them darken the tents at night so they could convince their children it indeed was bedtime, even though the sun still shone. With the white tents and the long hours of daylight, the children's energy seemed endless. How did you convince small children they had to go to bed when it still appeared to be afternoon? Alaska was a grand adventure to the youngsters, and as long as the sun shone, it seemed only right they should be out and about. Parents were very nearly pulling out their hair.

Jeremiah laughed to himself. He'd even had a mother come to the clinic because she couldn't get her six-month-old to sleep because her three-year-old thought it was still playtime. And with families living in sixteen-by-twenty-foot tents, there weren't other rooms in which to put a baby to sleep. Someone had suggested partitions be built, but with the focus on building houses before winter, there simply wasn't time.

Thankfully, the hardworking people were also creative. When the ARRC discovered they could get black tarps, the people were all for it. That way they could cover the tents at night and pull the tarps off in the morning.

Walking toward the camp, Jeremiah spotted David Williams, the man in charge of platting out the new town of Palmer, standing in the center of the street. David had come for only a week or two, but Jeremiah liked the man and his creative influences for the town. "Hi, David. Is there anything I can help with?"

The man stood staring at the mountains around him. He turned and gazed at Pioneer Peak. "You know, Jeremiah, I think I need to move the location of everything."

"What do you mean?"

David continued to turn in each direction. "The town needs to be shifted from what I have in the plans."

"I'm still not following you, David. I'm sorry."

He unrolled a large sheet. "Look. Here's the original layout I had for the town of Palmer."

"All right." Jeremiah looked at the well-thought-out plan. "It looks great."

"Yes, but there's one major flaw."

"And that is?"

David shook his head and rerolled the design. "I need to turn the entire town ninety degrees. The folks can't take advantage of these God-given views if I don't."

From looking at the plan, Jeremiah hadn't even thought of that. "Very observant. It's a good thing you figured it out when you did. It's a beautiful place to live, for sure, and fifty years from now, the people who live in this town will thank you for thinking of them. I know how much I love to look at the mountains every day."

David shook his hand. "And people will thank you and Dr. Hillerman and Dr. Albrecht for what you are doing to provide medical care here. When there's a full-fledged hospital in this valley, you'll be able to rest in confidence, knowing that thousands of people will have the best medicine for their children and their grandchildren for years to come." With those words, David walked away.

The warm encouragement should have given Jeremiah a sense of pride. And would have if he were actually doing something as honorable as Dr. H. and Dr. Albrecht. Instead, the glowing commendation soured Jeremiah's stomach.

Maybe he needed a walk to clear his head. What he wouldn't give to be the honorable man everyone thought he was. Then he'd be able to hold his head up high in this community. He wouldn't have to avoid the press, or the questions, or even love. But God hadn't granted him that chance. He thought again about writing to his cousin in Chicago. Surely Howard had heard something by now. Then again, maybe the news was so grim he didn't want to share it with Jeremiah. Maybe Brewster had managed to get charges of negligent homicide filed against him. He had threatened it.

But Jeremiah had to know the truth either way. He determined then and there to go back to the office and write Howard a letter.

Eugene Carr strode up to him. "Were you just speaking with David Williams?"

"Yes, I was."

"Oh good, I've been looking for him all morning." He shoved a hand into his suit pocket. "But before I traipse after him again, I thought we could finish our conversation."

The jig was up. Jeremiah swallowed. "What conversation?"

"You. Training in Chicago. I asked if you knew Randolph Brewster."

"Oh, right. I remember that conversation." It wouldn't be right to lie. Then he'd be even more of a hypocrite than Brewster.

"Well?"

"Yes, sir. I know Mr. Brewster."

The older man clapped him on the shoulder. "Well then, how is he? I haven't seen him in ages."

Jeremiah breathed a sigh. Carr didn't know. "When I left Chicago, he was doing very well for himself."

"Good to hear! We were childhood friends, you know. Kept up for many years, but I'm ashamed to admit, we both grew too busy to stay in touch." Carr squeezed Jeremiah's shoulder. "Next time you speak with him, tell him his old friend Eugene says hello. Can you do that for me?"

"Certainly."

"Thank you. I'd better go track down Mr. Williams. We've got a lot to do." The man turned and hurried off.

Jeremiah watched Mr. Carr's retreating form. As long as Eugene didn't get the sudden urge to look up his old friend, Jeremiah would be fine.

The breeze picked up as he walked toward the small community building that was now the temporary hospital. A small tent in the back housed the Red Cross nurses. One day this place would be a true hospital. But would he be around to see it?

Dr. H. spent a lot of time with Dr. Albrecht. Jeremiah was sure at first that the two just needed to get to know each other, but he often spotted them having what looked like serious discussions. Could Dr. Albrecht have found out?

Jeremiah passed up the commissary and smiled at several of the children running around outside. Oh, the freedom of childhood. He hardly remembered those days anymore.

"Come play ball with us, Jeremiah!" one of the children called out. Several of the others added their approval to that request.

"You can help us practice catching fly balls," one of the boys declared.

"Not right now," Jeremiah replied. "But I promise to do just that later this afternoon. Right now I have something to attend to." There were moans of disappointment, but Jeremiah just gave them a wave and continued on his way. The guilt burned in his stomach. Fear at every turn that someone new would pop up and spill the whole sordid story. He had no business attaching himself to this beloved community.

"Well, well. Good day, Jeremiah." Clarence's smooth voice greeted him.

Ugh. The skulker was back. "Hello, Clarence." He started to walk past, but Clarence stepped into his path.

"Gwyn sure looked lovely at church this morning, didn't she?"

Jeremiah just stared at him. "I need to get back to the hospital."

"You do that . . . *Doctor.*" The look in Clarence's eyes gave Jeremiah the impression that they knew each other. But he was sure he'd never met Novak before.

Jeremiah gritted his teeth. He was in no mood for the man's games. Nor the snide way he said *doctor*. He shook his head and stepped past Clarence.

The one place that called him was the hospital. Inside, with patients, medicine, and his medical journals, Jeremiah felt alive. He loved to help people—and yet he'd learned to love solitude, because people were what hurt him the most.

The building was quiet when Jeremiah entered. He went to the small bookshelf in the corner of what had been deemed the doctors' office. Taking out pen and paper, he wrote a hurried letter to Howard. He stressed that no matter how bad the news might be, he needed to know the truth so that he could decide his future. When the letter was complete, Jeremiah tucked it into his pocket. He'd get it posted first thing in the morning. With that out of the way, he pulled out a new medical journal and began to thumb through the pages.

For many years, he'd wanted to be one of the physicians listed, to have articles written about him and his new discoveries. Why had he wasted so much time aiming for such pitiful heights? He disgusted himself the more he thought about it. His dreams had been based on politics and gaining people's favor. How easily influenced he'd been by Randolph Brewster.

He'd completely bought into the man's principles and goals, yet they had never been a part of Jeremiah's original plan.

Prestige and accolades. What were they worth?

Jeremiah leaned back. Nothing. Absolutely nothing.

Dr. H. walked in. "Oh, Jeremiah, I didn't know you were here. How are you feeling? You look exhausted."

"I'm fine, Dr. H., really—"

"Son, after all these years, you could just call me Harold. While I know Dr. H. is a habit, I'd much prefer the camaraderie. I think you've only called me by my name twice since you've been here. We are friends and fellow physicians. Please." The man's eyes crinkled as he smiled.

Jeremiah swallowed his guilt. "All right . . . Harold. I am tired, but I'm fine. It's just too easy to slip into the old habit. In my mind, you'll always be Dr. H. But I will try. As long as you continue to remind me." He took a deep breath. "I do have a question for you—if you have a minute."

Harold sat across from him. "All right. This sounds serious."

"Why did you become a doctor?"

"Because I wanted to help people get well. I wanted to be an instrument of the Great Physician."

Jeremiah thought about that for a moment. "You could have gone anywhere. I read everything they wrote about you before you left Chicago. You were known as one of the greatest doctors of our time."

"Oh, that's rubbish. What did those people know, Jeremiah? Part of that was driven by Edith's father. He wanted his son-in-law to be prominent in the community. Prestige and impressive news stories can always be bought for a price. The same is true for negative reports. It's amazing how the truth can be bent for a dollar."

"I don't think you give yourself enough credit, Harold."

"It's not about credit, son. It's about helping people. We should be doctors for *them*, not for ourselves."

"Is that why you came up here?" Jeremiah leaned forward, elbows on his knees.

Harold did the same and sighed. "In part I came up here to escape Edith's family. The constant push to be more, acquire more, be seen more just made me sick to my stomach. I wanted to simply be a doctor, a man who helped people. I don't even know how we did it. It's a bit of a blur. The fact that Edith followed me to this place is still beyond me. But as you have probably noticed, the wealthy are fascinated with Alaska. Her friends thought it a grand adventure, so she went along. Until she realized what she'd gotten into. I'm sure she believed we would build a luxurious vacation home up here after I did my little missionary journey, and we would live out the rest of our days back in Chicago among the elite of society."

Jeremiah nodded. He understood all too well. But Harold was different. Harold had defied Edith and her family to do what was right, while Jeremiah had played right into the greedy woman's hands. In a sense, she had paved the way for Jeremiah to fulfill the dreams she'd had for her own husband.

It took all of it blowing up in his face for him to change course. Why couldn't he be more like his mentor? Where had Jeremiah strayed?

"You look like you've got a lot on your mind."

"You've never sought the world's favor, have you?"

A sad laugh escaped Harold. "Oh, there was a short while when I thought money and esteem were everything. That's how I met Edith."

"But?"

"Those are days I'm not proud of. But I am glad to say that God got ahold of me." Harold cleared his throat. "I learned right away that the only favor I am to seek is that of my Lord. And when I put it all into perspective, my life completely changed. I knew without a doubt what I was supposed to do."

How could he know exactly what had been on Jeremiah's mind? "How did God get ahold of you?"

The older man sighed and stood. "I was offered a prominent position in a hospital—much like you—and delivered the child of our most wealthy benefactor." Harold looked at Jeremiah, the sadness in his eyes almost overpowering. "The child was weak, sickly. Another child was born at the exact same time. This one was robust and healthy but belonged to a very poor, underprivileged family."

Jeremiah held his breath.

Harold continued. "I overheard the physician above me and the father discussing switching babies. Oh, the reasons were lengthy. The poor family would never be able to raise the child. They'd have to send the child to work at a young age. Look how much the child could benefit from all the wealthy family had to offer."

He swiped a hand down his face. "I was in shock. Yes, I knew that these things happened, but I couldn't imagine our hospital being a part of it. And I thought my opinion held power. So I went to the doctor I'd overheard and discovered they'd already done the deed. That night, the sickly child died. The poor couple—those sweet people—they were devastated. They sobbed in front of me, not understanding. Their baby had been so healthy and strong. They were told they had to leave the hospital immediately. They were disturbing other patients. But I never said a word.

"The next day their bodies were found in the river. Apparently, they'd jumped into the river together, since all hope was lost." He turned toward the wall, his shoulders shaking. "I made a vow that day: I would never put man's bidding before God's. I would never put one person ahead of another because of class or rank or money. And I vowed to leave that horrid city behind, no matter the cost."

The depth of Harold's confession jolted Jeremiah to his very core. Dr. H.'s vow "no matter the cost" had indeed cost him a hefty price.

His marriage and one of his daughters.

"So you left everything behind—all the opportunities and prestige."

Harold nodded, tears glistening in his eyes. "I was proud. Thought I could do something about it but quickly found out that the hospital—and many like it across the country—did the practice on a regular basis. In my arrogance, I went to the police and said I wanted to give my testimony . . . to stop such things." His head lowered. "The detective laughed at me. Then he told me that if I wanted to save my reputation, I'd better run."

Jeremiah swallowed the lump in his throat. "So you came here. . . ."

His mentor turned back to face him and gripped his shoulders. "Son, the most important thing you can do for your patients and for yourself is to allow God to be in control. We are here to serve Him—no one else."

Jeremiah paced the floor, Harold's words ringing in his ears. Instead of turning away from God, the man had turned toward

Him and lived a fulfilling and happy life. Was there hope for Jeremiah to have the same? Even with all his lies and hypocrisy?

Shouts jolted Jeremiah from his reverie. They increased in volume. He ran outside to find out what was causing the ruckus and saw Gertrude dragging Nasnana by the arm. The old woman could barely keep up.

"What are you doing?" Jeremiah raced to rescue his friend from the clutches of the screaming Gertrude.

"This woman stole from me!"

A crowd had already formed. Gertrude's face was beet red. Jeremiah tried to pull Nasnana from her grasp.

"Oh, no you don't!" the angry woman hissed. "I'm not letting her go until I get some justice. Didn't you hear me? She stole from me!"

Don Irwin ran over, followed by Eugene Carr, David Williams, and half the ARRC staff.

Jeremiah needed a different tactic. "What did she steal?"

"My mother's pearl necklace. It's been in my family for years, and the only thing of value we had left when we had to sell everything."

"How do you know she stole it? Did you see her?" Jeremiah pressed.

"She was sneaking around the corner of my tent when I caught her—"

"I think Dr. Vaughan's question has merit," Don said, jumping into the fray. "Did you see Nasnana steal it?"

Gertrude narrowed her eyes. "No, I didn't see her steal it, but what thief takes something from the owner directly in front of them—"

"So why do you think she stole it?" Mr. Irwin pressed further.

She placed one hand on her hip and yanked at Nasnana's arm. "Like I said, I saw her sneaking around my tent."

"But what makes you think *she's* the one who stole the pearls?" Mr. Carr stared the woman down.

Gertrude stomped her foot. "Because when I discovered they were missing, I ran out of the tent and right into her. She dropped something, and when I bent to look, I saw my pearls on the ground."

Jeremiah had heard enough of the woman's accusations. "There is no proof that Nasnana took the pearls. You could have just as easily dropped them." He turned away from the hateful woman and looked to the two men who were in charge. "Gentlemen, I am loath to repeat it here, but you know Gertrude has shown great prejudice toward the native people and dislikes Nasnana."

"How dare you—"

"If I may continue," he said, sending a scathing look, "I know Nasnana quite well, and she's never stolen anything. In fact, she's always giving of her own possessions to help others."

The men nodded. Don moved forward. "Gertrude, unhand Nasnana. You have your pearls. I suggest you lock them up. We will discuss this in the morning with clear heads. I would like to see Dr. Vaughan, Nasnana, Gertrude, and Mr. Carr in my office at eight o'clock sharp."

Nasnana hadn't said a word. Jeremiah took her elbow and watched Gertrude storm off in a rage. He looked down at her. "Are you all right?"

"I'm fine. Thank you, Jeremiah."

"Want to tell me what happened?"

She took a deep breath. "I'm not really sure. I was just

walking through the camp. I'd just brought some food to the Brunswicks and to Rose when Gertrude flew at me in a rage. My heart aches for the woman. She's filled with bitterness and hatred."

"Did you see anyone else?"

Her dark eyes shimmered. "Unfortunately, yes."

"Who did you see?"

Another heavy breath. "Clarence."

16

Her heart had soared last night when she stepped out of the hospital and heard Jeremiah defending Nasnana. Even though she could probably never tell him how she felt, Gwyn gave a little more of her heart to the handsome doctor.

Linked arm in arm with Sadzi, Gwyn walked in the sunny morning air to Mr. Irwin's office. Mr. Irwin was well liked by everyone. He was fair and understanding. She couldn't see him locking up Nasnana for something she didn't do.

Her older friend had asked to walk alone that morning. She wanted to pray on her way in, so Sadzi and Gwyn walked with a slow cadence together.

"What do you think they'll do, Gwyn?"

"I'm sure it will be fine. Gertrude just got her feathers in a ruffle. That's all." She hoped those words were true.

"Grandmother's not worried about it. She told me last night that God was in control." Sadzi gripped Gwyn's arm tighter. "I know she's right. But I'm still worried."

"Worry is—"

"A sin." Sadzi laughed. "Yes, I know."

Gwyn gave her friend a sideways hug as they continued on. "It will be all right."

When they reached Mr. Irwin's office, he was walking out the door with Nasnana and smiling. "I'm sorry all this happened."

"God bless you, Mr. Irwin." Nasnana looked up and saw the girls.

Mr. Irwin smiled at Gwyn and went back inside.

"Is everything okay, Grandmother?"

"Yes, dear, everything is fine. Gertrude's husband came with her this morning. They were both angry and said some hateful things, but Mr. Irwin and Mr. Carr had already talked to many people in the camp. There were too many witnesses that stated I was just walking by, and they'd seen other people by Gertrude's tent." Nasnana looked heavenward. "Praise the Lord, there's not any other complaints, but I think I need to stay at home for a while. Let things settle down. This has caused some unsettled feelings within the camp, and I don't want to be the cause of any more strife." She looked at Gwyn and Sadzi. "I think Sadzi should stay home with me as well."

Gwyn wasn't sure what to say. Since all the medical personnel had arrived, Gwyn had been spending most of her time with one or both of the ladies in front of her. Many of the colony women relied heavily on Nasnana and Sadzi and their wisdom about growing things in the valley. And with her father still running the hospital, they were all she had. "All right. If you're sure that's the best plan."

"I think it is. And I'm going to warn my people to avoid the area for a time. There were comments about other natives stealing from the site. I think the colonists are skeptical of anyone who looks different, and when things disappear, it's easier to blame someone other than their own kind."

"But that's not right. The natives here have been good

213

to us. Father said they were helpful with the first group of homesteaders as well." Gwyn looked at Sadzi. "We're all Alaskans."

"Most white people do not feel that way," Sadzi reminded her.

"Well, I don't care. I feel that way. You are my friends, my family. I'll come visit every day at your house." She pasted on a smile that she hoped looked more casual than she felt. She wasn't naïve. She knew the matter was complicated and could erupt at any time into something bigger than all of them.

Prejudice and animosity toward those of a different culture and color really bothered Gwyn. Her father had often spoken of the way the blacks had been treated in the States. They were often seen as lazy and stupid. Now some of the comments she'd heard in the camps echoed those same attitudes toward the natives here. The arrogance behind those statements was most alarming. It seemed it took nothing more than a tiny spark to get a fire started. A fire that could well destroy them all.

The days blurred as they headed into August. So much to do and so very little time. Gwyn looked up from the huge garden at the experimental station. The sky was dark and the wind's intensity picked up. It didn't look good. She knew what those foreboding clouds meant. She picked up her tools and raced to find Lilly. She spotted her friend from the university across the potato field. "Lilly!"

Her friend didn't hear her and was on her hands and knees, unaware of the approaching storm behind her.

Gwyn ran faster. "Lilly!"

Finally her friend heard her.

Waving her arms, Gwyn continued to run. "Storm!"

Lilly jumped to her feet and looked behind her. Hail had already begun to pelt the far end of the fields. There wasn't any time to try to cover any of the crops. All they could do was run to shelter.

Inside the tool shack, Gwyn watched the storm. "Do you think we'll lose it all?"

A deep sigh left Lilly's mouth. "I don't know, Gwyn. But it doesn't look good."

For five long minutes, no words passed between them as they stared at the hailstorm. It pounded the ground with a ferocity Gwyn hadn't seen in many years. One thing was for certain, though. The weather in Alaska was always unpredictable.

A break in the storm moved Lilly to the door. "I'm going to go see the damage."

"I'm coming too." Gwyn pulled her gardening hat back onto her head. "But we'd better be careful. It might not be over yet."

In silence, they walked through the fields. Row after row was demolished. There were patches of vegetables that were sturdy enough to withstand the hail and others that had taken more of a beating. And to shock them the most, an entire patch of potatoes was destroyed by the largest of the hailstones. Their only consolation was that it was only one of the patches, but still, they needed this food. Continuing on their inspection for several minutes, Gwyn felt a deep sense of discouragement. They needed these crops to feed the people. Why couldn't God have kept them safe?

"Most of it survived," Lilly said, as if to convince herself. "It's not a total loss."

"No, but it's a loss just the same. We needed this food to can and store up for the long winter to come."

A chill now filled the air, as if to remind them both that winter would soon be upon the colony. Lilly moved farther down the rows of damaged vegetation, stopping here and there to give closer inspection.

Gwyn shivered and looked up to the sky. As the storm moved on and the clouds rolled away, the mountains now wore a new coat of snow. The colonists wouldn't be ready for that. Only a few of the families had moved into their homes. Dread washed over Gwyn. The people would be in an uproar. Gwyn ran toward Lilly for the second time that day.

Lilly stood with her hands on her hips surveying the damage. "It's not pretty, is it? Dr. Miller from the university is supposed to come out and inspect us next week. I imagine this will not go over well."

"Look, Lilly, I'm sorry to abandon you in this, but I'm worried about people in the colony. I want to go do what I can to keep them from panicking."

Lilly's brow furrowed. "I'm sure they're fine, Gwyn. Most of them probably took shelter from the storm."

"Look at the mountains." Gwyn pointed.

A slow nod as her friend surveyed the land around them. "Oh, I hadn't thought about the possibility of snow on the mountains. You're right to worry. They'll probably think a blizzard is right around the corner. You'd better go. Poor Mr. Irwin is probably getting run over by all the people who don't have homes yet."

"I knew you'd understand."

Gwyn walked toward the tent city and then picked up her pace. Panic among the colonists could be devastating—even dangerous. It was only the beginning of August. Snow covering the mountains now would make them think that winter was upon them. Gwyn had seen some of the people get into scrapes over issues far less important. She'd better hurry and help calm everyone down.

Out of breath, she reached the edge of the small town that had popped up over the summer. The ARRC construction office had a large crowd of people around it. But instead of panic and complaints, she heard only one voice. Her father's.

"There's nothing to worry about. While sometimes we get snow early—yes, even in August—the cold season is not upon us yet. We will continue to have long days of sun to keep things warm until the end of September."

Gwyn tried to breathe normally as she listened to the people's reactions. Most of them were content to listen to her father, a man who had lived in this valley for almost two decades. A few rumbles of questions, though, brought Mr. Irwin forward.

"I understand you are concerned. But we are still on schedule for the most part. We've put aside any other building until the homes are done. That's the priority. Seventy-five more workers arrived a week or so ago, and a hundred fifty new men arrived two days ago."

Gwyn watched as several of the families looked toward the tent city that made up the transient workers' housing. A bustle of activity was present everywhere.

Mr. Irwin continued. "With the portable sawmill up and in use and other sawmills running in the camps, we should have things under control."

A few more hands and caps were raised in the air. Don pointed to a gentleman.

"Mr. Irwin, we're concerned for our children. The school building hasn't been started, but we noticed that desks have arrived. Will there be any teachers? We didn't come up here to have our children uneducated."

"Yes, I know it's true about the school building, but like I just stated, we've decided to put the construction of other buildings on hold until the homes are completed." Mr. Irwin raised a hand as others tried to interrupt. "Please let me finish. As to the teachers, we've got fifteen high-quality teachers coming. They will be here before school is scheduled to begin, and at that point, we'll coordinate how the schooling of the children will take place this fall."

More hands shot up. Mr. Irwin began addressing another question in his calm manner.

Mr. Schaleben from the *Milwaukee Journal* circled the crowd, taking pictures and writing notes on his pad.

Gwyn spotted her father walking back to the clinic. She left the crowd and hurried to catch up with him. "You look exhausted," she teased.

"I am." His smile was genuine, but the bags under his eyes looked horrible.

"We haven't had a chance to talk in a long time, other than seeing each other in passing. You've been working so late into the night that I'm often asleep by the time you get back. Then when I wake up in the morning you're already gone. I think you're working too hard."

Her father gripped her shoulder. "I'm sorry we haven't had time together. We're doing well containing everything right now. We finally have enough hands. But in preparing the hospital for winter, we are a little behind schedule."

Gwyn nodded. Preparing a colony of thousands for a harsh

Alaskan winter would be difficult. Especially with how easily sickness spread among the children. Fortunately, most of these families had come from areas that were acquainted with temperatures below zero and lots of wind and ice. But they were much more isolated now. And she doubted all the homes would be up before the first real snow flew.

"When I saw the snow on the mountains, I worried about how the people would react. They know little of our weather up here. Because we're so far north, I'm sure they fear we'll be buried in snow by next week."

Her father nodded. "I thought the same. That's why I went out to offer my thoughts as soon as the storm passed."

"Why don't you come back to the cabin and I'll fix you something to eat," Gwyn suggested. "We can have a little time to ourselves."

He shook his head. "I wish I could, but there's just too much to do."

"Can I help you with anything?"

Again he shook his head. "No. You have your hands full getting our place ready for winter. I haven't had a chance to ask you about the garden or our wood supply. And we haven't made up a list of supplies to order. I'm afraid I'll have to leave it all to you."

Gwyn frowned but looked away quickly so her father wouldn't see. "I can manage."

They walked in silence for a moment. Would she ever have any leisure time with her father again? She would never accuse him of abandoning her, but she couldn't help feeling a nagging sense of loss. He loved her. She knew that and wouldn't want to hurt him. But that didn't take away her feelings of loneliness.

Overall, the only word she could find to define how she truly felt was *unsettled*. Everything was changing, including her relationships, which was something she hadn't bargained for. Nasnana and Sadzi felt the need to stay more with their own people, and now Father was far more concerned with the new hospital and colonists than anything else. All that had been a constant in her life was quickly being altered, and Gwyn didn't like it one bit.

She missed the quiet times she'd spent with her father all these years. And even though her fears about the new colony had been unfounded, for she loved the people and their new town of Palmer, she still couldn't help but wonder—what did her future hold?

Harold's heart ached. In the week since he'd walked with Gwyn, they hadn't had one conversation. How could that be? She was his daughter, and he hadn't taken the time to find her even once to see how she was doing.

Guilt flooded through him. Since the ARRC first contacted him about the Matanuska Project, he'd been elated. And it had given him excitement and hope for the future. There'd always been too much time alone at night to think of Edith before the president's announcement. Now he had barely enough time for his head to hit his pillow before exhaustion overtook him.

Dr. Albrecht was the greatest asset the valley had seen all summer. With his arrival and the arrival of more staff and equipment, Harold finally had hope for a successful hospital. Jeremiah was amazing as well. But Harold knew he still needed to speak with his young mentee.

He glanced to the mountains. Thankfully, the snow from the storm a week ago had melted, but he was hearing plenty of rumbling among the colonists. This was Alaska, after all, and many were afraid they wouldn't be in their homes before snow fell on the valley. The duskiness of midnight forced Harold to call it quits and go home. He was so close to finishing all the notes and files on each case. Things were quiet in the hospital. But as the lingering light dimmed, Harold decided he'd rather go home and sleep than turn on a lamp and try to finish. He'd be worthless tomorrow if he didn't catch a few hours of rest.

He straightened the table they all used as a desk and stored all the confidential notes away.

A noise outside the window startled him. He stopped for a moment and listened. Nothing. Must've just been a bird or something.

He had the urge to pray at that moment and sat back down. The Holy Spirit must have been prodding him because his brain didn't even have the words to lift up to the Father. But he took several moments to pray, lifting up Gwyn, Jeremiah, Earl, all the patients, Nasnana and Sadzi, and everyone in the colony he could remember off the top of his head.

Feeling refreshed, he smiled. Prayer was always a balm to his soul. Now he just needed some sleep and all would be right with the world again.

In the quiet of the hospital, Harold picked up his things and tiptoed out of the room so as not to wake Earl. The other doctor had fallen asleep around midnight, and Harold didn't have the nerve to wake him. At this point in time, they all needed their rest no matter when or where they got it.

Something out of the corner of his eye caught his attention.

The movement was silent, but there was no mistaking the fact that he'd seen it. Harold changed direction and went toward the medical supply room.

A slight rustling caught his attention and confirmed that he wasn't dreaming things. When he reached the door, he quickly flicked on the light.

"Clarence?" Harold wasn't sure what to make of the situation. "What are you doing in there?"

Clarence Novak stood to his full height. He slipped something into his pocket.

Harold reached into Clarence's jacket and pulled it out. "Morphine?" He pushed Clarence out of the way and headed to the cabinet where they locked all the medications. "How did you get in here?" Dr. Albrecht had recommended they put a lock on the cabinet. He said that all the larger hospitals were doing it now to keep anyone from stealing the medicines. At first, he'd thought it ludicrous. In this little area of the world, Harold had never encountered any problems with people stealing their supplies, but now he realized what a wise decision it had been. "Where's the lock? Did you break into this cabinet?"

A smile that appeared all too fake creased Clarence's lips. He held his hands out in front of him. "I didn't want to disturb anyone, but I was concerned about my niece. She fell down this morning and has been in a lot of pain."

"So you just assumed that you could come in here and take what you wanted?"

"No, no. Not at all. There just wasn't a doctor around. I didn't want her to suffer all night." The man was too prim. Too smooth. "I've been in here the whole time, Clarence. You didn't call out for anyone. You didn't even check to see if anyone was here." His temper was getting the best of him. Harold tried to remain calm.

"Please, come with me now, Doctor. You could help the poor child yourself and see that I'm not lying."

Why would Clarence invite him out if he wasn't telling the truth? But then why would he sneak into the hospital and steal morphine? Could he be addicted? Harold hadn't noticed the regular symptoms, but still, he didn't trust Clarence.

Too little sleep and distrust for the man in front of him clouded Harold's judgment. He'd better take Clarence at face value for now and see if there really was a child in need of help. "All right. Let me get my things and I'll head on over."

"Thank you, Dr. Hillerman. Thank you." Clarence smiled again. "I'll run back and let Suzanne know you are coming."

Harold allowed Clarence to leave and looked back to the bottle containing the morphine powder in his hand. What was that man up to?

He wrote Earl a note and headed to the construction office. Irwin had told him that during the night if they needed to use one of the vehicles, they could, so Harold found the keys the construction manager left for him and headed to the truck. Maybe if he arrived before Clarence, he could find out the truth.

Driving over the bumpy terrain at night at least kept him awake. When Harold reached the Novaks' tent, Clarence was nowhere to be seen. He knocked on the frame of the tent and whispered, "Suzanne? William?"

Suzanne Novak appeared in seconds. "Oh, Dr. Hillerman, how did you know?"

"Didn't you send Clarence?"

"Well, no. But I'm glad he went to get you." She looked

surprised and pulled him inside. "Heather has been moaning all night. She can't sleep because of the pain."

"What happened?"

"She fell out of a tree this morning. Said she landed on her feet, but her ankle twisted."

Harold reached under the covers to look at the young girl's foot. After a quick exam, he left Suzanne with some aspirin. "She'll be fine. It's just a sprain. I've written on that paper how much you can give her and how often."

Suzanne's shoulders slumped. She looked relieved.

"Keep it elevated and keep wrapping it in cool cloths. The swelling is what's causing her the pain right now."

"Thank you, Doctor." The mother's red-rimmed eyes spoke volumes. "I'm sorry you had to come in the middle of the night, but thank you again."

"You're most welcome. Just bring Heather in to see me in a day or two so that I can check up on her, all right?"

Suzanne nodded and closed the flap to their tent.

Harold climbed back into the ARRC truck and started the engine. Something didn't add up. Granted, it was a long hike to the camp where the Novaks lived, but Clarence should have returned if he'd truly run like he said he would.

And then there was the morphine. Why had he snuck around like a thief, broken into the medical cabinet, and put it in his pocket?

Harold's thoughts went every which way as he drove back to the hospital. Clarence had spent entirely too much time pursuing his Gwyn. She'd been nice enough to him, but Harold knew she was annoyed with the attentions of the man.

Maybe he needed to sit down with Gwyn tomorrow and talk to her.

Something about Clarence Novak put his senses on edge.

Now if only he could find a few minutes to talk to his daughter to warn her to keep her distance from him.

Harold shook his head. With their busy schedules, he wasn't sure when that would be.

Hopefully not months down the road.

17

The doctor had to go. Somehow, some way. Clarence paced in the woods. Ever since Dr. Hillerman caught him stealing the morphine, the man had been watching him like a hawk. The goody-two-shoes never said a word to him about it the past week, but Clarence needed to keep a step ahead of the game.

One hand shook with a brief tremor. The symptoms had come and gone more often the past week or two. Without liquor readily available, he'd turned to morphine. He'd gotten the idea when he'd seen one of the injured workers given the drug. Unfortunately, stealing it was getting harder and harder. He didn't need much. Just enough to get him through until he could finalize his plans and get back to the States or, better yet, abroad.

Shoving his hand into his pocket, Clarence thought about his options. As his fingers met the cool metal of the diamond ring, he longed to look at the finery again. That's what his life should be full of—fine things. Gold. Diamonds. Money. Anything his heart desired. He pulled the ring out.

"Whatcha got, Uncle Clarence?" The tiniest brat of his brother's brood looked at the ring with eyes as big as saucers.

Clarence shoved it back in his pocket. "Oh, nothing. Just a

prize I found in a Cracker Jack box." He wasn't sure the kid bought it. "Don't you need to be heading to bed?"

The boy didn't respond. Just frowned at him and walked away.

The longer he stayed, the more he wanted to leave this place and his horrible family in the tiny tent. The kids wanted his attention all the time, William wanted Clarence to be his slave, and Suzanne was content to wipe snotty noses all day.

Clarence was ready for the real world again. He wanted to leave. But it would be with the lovely Gwyn on his arm. There wasn't any reason he shouldn't have her.

He had enough money.

They could run away to Europe and never return. He knew he could convince her; after all, what woman couldn't be persuaded with a little sweet talk and promises? She would see him as a hero when the truth came out about her precious Jeremiah. She wouldn't continue to defend him once she knew how he'd lied. The trouble was, Clarence was hard-pressed to get her alone.

There were three rather large obstacles in his way. Nasnana. Dr. Hillerman. And Jeremiah Vaughan.

"I just need to bide my time," he reminded himself. "Just as I have been. I need to be patient and let everything fall into place." He smiled. Three obstacles—three hurdles to overcome—three very irritating, interfering complications.

In a few more weeks, none of them would stand in his way.

Gwyn looked down at her hands. They were wrinkled and rough from the canning process, but she and the other women had made a lot of progress. The end of August was upon them, and winter would appear sooner than they'd like.

Mrs. Lydia Fohn-Hansen had traveled to the colony from the University of Alaska to teach the colonists how to can salmon. And with the last of the coho salmon run in the past week, they'd all had their hands full. More than twenty-five hundred cans of salmon had been prepared by the women as a group, and many of the colonists were catching more and preserving the fish on their own.

As Gwyn stood at the large makeshift sink washing all the canning tools, she allowed her thoughts to wander. Most of the other women were carrying on conversations outside the tent while the cans were distributed and hauled to their tents and homes. Gwyn enjoyed the silence and the menial task of scrubbing.

The summer had flown by. She missed her father, and Jeremiah. But even more so Nasnana and Sadzi. She'd tried to get out to their cabin every day, but it hadn't happened. Gwyn spent her days racing from camp to camp, helping with anything and everything she could. She often performed simple nursing duties, patching a boo-boo here, removing a large splinter or two there, and other things the mothers didn't want to drag their children all the way to the hospital to see tended. The women also had lots of questions about projects for the winter and their gardens. The men stayed hard at work building the cabins and frame houses.

The construction of homes had really picked up. Originally the ARRC had intended to use timber from the valley, but the monumental task of cutting and trimming all those trees wasn't possible. They simply didn't have the time. So they'd spent more money and brought in lumber. Now there were frame houses going up all over the valley as well.

The women worked hard in their gardens, and the group

canning the fish had shown a true pioneer spirit. It was obvious they wanted this endeavor to work. Gwyn marveled at these women. They'd given up so much for the opportunity to give their children a brighter future. At times, she even found herself jealous—of the families, the relationships, the excitement.

She had to admit, it felt good to be a part of something like this. Not only the project, but the community itself. Gwyn loved this place. Loved this land. If she had allowed her initial fear and worry to rule, she would never have experienced this wonderful time.

But . . . would she be able to stay here? Did she still belong? Was this where God wanted her to minister?

Her heart yearned for a family of her own. Especially since she hardly had the chance to see her father anymore. Loneliness often overwhelmed her, even though she was surrounded by people. That thought sent her mind wandering.

The colonists had all been chosen because they were families. The only single men were transient workers, and the ARRC planned to have them all shipped out by mid-October. None of those men had caught her attention anyway. Many of them were married. Some had girls back home. And a lot of them didn't share her faith.

She sighed. Only one man caught her eye.

Jeremiah Vaughan.

As much as she tried to banish thoughts of him, they still intruded. She prayed every morning for him, and also prayed that if it be the Lord's will, He take away all the yearnings she had.

But for now, they remained. Without any seeming return of affection. She huffed and blew the curls off her forehead. Men. What a conundrum.

Sadzi peeked around the corner and caught her attention. "Gwyn!"

Gwyn raced over and threw her soap-covered arms around her friend. "What are you doing here?"

"Oh, you know Grandmother. She wanted us to stay quiet for a while and let everything settle down. But after a couple weeks, I was about to go crazy." Sadzi plopped onto a bench. "So she sent me fishing and hunting and berry picking and anything else she could think of. When we had enough meat and fish for ten people for the winter and enough berries, jams, jellies, and honeys all canned, I finally urged her to allow me to come help you."

"Wouldn't she come with you? It's been a month already since she was accused of stealing the pearls." Gwyn didn't understand the older woman in this situation.

"No, I'm afraid I couldn't convince her. She's content to stay at home and read her Bible. She keeps saying that she's tired; the years are catching up to her. She'd had such hope for the community. I think she wants to make sure that she isn't a stumbling block to anyone else. And she says over and over that 'Everything takes time. We must be patient.'"

Stumbling block. *Humph*. The only stumbling blocks were the naysayers like Gertrude and the annoying Clarence. "I hear what you're saying, but I don't have to like it. Nasnana is the sweetest person I've ever known."

Several of the colony wives entered with smiles, laughter, and more to wash.

"So, what can I help with?" Sadzi rolled up her sleeves.

Her heart panged. Hopefully none of these women had been tainted by Gertrude's hatred of the Alaskan natives. "Well, we're almost done here, but you can help me finish cleaning up."

Gwyn thrust her hands back into the soapy water. "After that, I promised to go visit Rose. She said she hasn't been feeling well."

"I'm surprised she's still here. I figured after losing both her husband and son, she would clear out. Especially since they stopped working on building her a house."

"I don't think she's been in any shape to travel, and because of that no one has been pushing her to do anything. The women have been good to her, seeing that she has food and such. As for a house, I think most folks figured it was better to get families settled before one woman. One colonist even mentioned the possibility of Rose being taken in by another family if she stays."

"Well, I'll come with you," Sadzi declared. "Between the two of us we can help with anything she needs. Grandmother sent me with a letter for her, hoping you could deliver it. I'll just deliver it myself, and we can pray with her too."

"Maybe. She was so angry at God for her losses that I'm not sure she believes He hears our prayers."

Sadzi elbowed her slightly. "Well, we know He does, and that's enough."

The two made quick work of finishing the cleanup, and Sadzi sang some beautiful hymns while a few other women hummed along and stacked the cans. Several ladies buried all the fish bones so they wouldn't attract bears to the site, and a few poured lye soap, mixed with water, out onto the dirt floor to finish the cleanup.

Gwyn lifted a hand to her nose after she waved good-bye to the other ladies, thankful that they'd all been open and welcoming to Sadzi. "I think my hands will smell of salmon for another week."

Sadzi grabbed her hand and sniffed. "*Eww*. I think you're

right. Better keep them in your pocket so the bears don't get wind of it."

They laughed together as they walked to Rose Benson's tent. The young widow had endured so much. But Nasnana had reached her in a short time like no one else had. Maybe the letter would do Rose a world of good. God hadn't given up on Rose, if only Gwyn and Sadzi could help convince her of that.

"When I saw Rose yesterday, she was so pale and told me she hadn't been feeling very well," Gwyn said. "I asked her if she wanted to walk with me to see our friend, but she said she was too tired and weak."

"I know Grandmother has missed seeing her most of all. That was her biggest regret in staying away. Even so, she prays for her daily."

They approached Rose's tent, and Gwyn called, "Rose, it's Gwyn and Sadzi. May we come in?"

An awful retching sound reached her ears. Gwyn headed to the back of the tent and found Rose huddled over a bucket. "Rose! Are you all right?"

The young woman barely lifted her head and nodded. "I think so. I'm just so weak."

Gwyn looked to Sadzi. "Help me carry her back to her bed."

They struggled but managed to get Rose to the edge of the bed. As soon as she was seated, Gwyn looked into the young woman's eyes. "Rose, we need to get you to the hospital. How long have you been sick?"

Her head wobbled. "Oh, off and on for a couple months now. After Daniel's death I was too tired to care, and I wasn't eating. Then when I lost baby Daniel . . ." Her eyes filled with tears and her lips trembled. "I wasn't hungry for a long time. But lately, I've had a strong appetite. I'm hungry and I feel

like I could eat a horse, but my stomach just doesn't want
to . . ." She passed out and fell back on the mattress.

"Sadzi, run and see if you can find some construction workers and a truck anywhere close by. Tell them we need to get
someone to the hospital right away."

Sadzi ran out the door and Gwyn reached for a towel. She
wet it down in the fresh water bucket and started to wipe
Rose's face. Gwyn assessed the young widow as she lay still.
Her pulse was strong and steady, but she was all too thin.
And very pale. Had she been eating something bad? Or could
her water be contaminated?

Gwyn checked for signs of a fever, but there weren't any.

The rumbling of a truck sounded in the distance. *Thank
you, Lord!*

Two workers helped load Rose into the back of the truck,
and Gwyn asked one if he would drive them to the hospital.

The bumpy road wasn't more than a grooved path from
construction trucks and tractors moving back and forth over the
dirt. Gwyn had a rough time keeping Rose's head from banging
around, so she lifted the young woman's shoulders and head to
rest in her lap while Sadzi held on to the young widow's legs.

As they reached the hospital, Jeremiah and her father both
exited the building.

Her father was first to reach the truck. "What've you got?"

"It's Rose." Gwyn stroked her friend's head. "I don't think
she's been able to keep much down for a while now. She's pale
and thin but has a steady pulse and no fever."

Jeremiah lifted the young widow out of the back of the
truck. "Is she unconscious? Did she hit her head?"

"No. We were with her when she passed out. She didn't
hit anything."

Both doctors nodded.

Her father directed Jeremiah to lay Rose on a nearby cot, and both men reached for their medical bags. "Gwyn, we need clean linens and a bucket." He already had his stethoscope around his neck. "And pull that curtain closed so we have some privacy."

It took several minutes to collect the things her father wanted. By the time Gwyn finally found everything, her mind had worked into a frenzy of worry. Poor Rose. She had suffered so much. How could it be that yet another trouble was allowed to wound her?

Gwyn caught sight of Sadzi kneeling on the floor. She seemed completely oblivious to her location. Sadzi's head rose for only a moment. "I figured we could help best on our knees."

"I'm sure you're right." Gwyn sank down beside her. "I do believe the best thing for Rose right now is prayer." The girls fell silent and focused on their petitions to God. Gwyn wanted so much for the young woman to be all right. *Please, God. Please heal her.*

"Gwyn."

Her father's hand was on her shoulder. Gwyn wasn't sure how long they'd actually been praying. She looked to her father and saw his smile. "I'm sorry to interrupt you two, but I wanted to give you an update."

Gwyn wiped the tears from her eyes. She'd been pouring her heart out to the Lord and had drenched her hankie in the process. "Is Rose all right?"

18

"Mr. Novak!"

Clarence cringed. He recognized that nasal voice but kept walking.

"Mr. Novak! Clarence!" Gertrude was relentless. If only he could get that pushy woman off his back.

With practiced ease, he pasted a small smile on and turned around. "Gertrude. How good to see you today, but I must admit, I'm off on a very important errand."

The heavy woman caught up and gasped for breath. "Errand? In the woods?" She huffed. "That's a lot of nonsense, and you know it." She pointed a finger in his face. "We had an agreement, and I'm getting tired of waiting." The haughty woman lifted her chin and narrowed her eyes.

Like she could do anything at all to intimidate *him*. Please. The woman was nothing but a nuisance. Useful for a time, but that had worn off like the plating on cheap jewelry. "I truly am on an urgent errand."

"But you've missed our last two appointments. I hate to be a nag"—she leaned in close and dropped her voice to a whisper—"but you have yet to fulfill your end of the bargain. I've done my part, now you best follow through or—"

"Or you'll do *what*, exactly?" He allowed his gentleman façade to drop. His anger emerged in his hissed words, "Do not attempt to threaten *me*, Gertrude. Or I will gladly tell the ARRC board and managers exactly what you've been up to."

"You wouldn't dare!"

He stepped very close. "Oh, wouldn't I? You forget your place. And I'm the one holding all the cards. The colony would hate to find out that one of their own was behind all the thefts. *Tsk, tsk.* And trying to blame the Indians." He narrowed his eyes. "You'll be reimbursed, woman. Now shut up and go home."

Gwyn steadied herself for the truth. To her surprise, however, Father laughed.

"Rose is pregnant. She'll be fine."

"Pregnant? But . . ." Gwyn fell silent and shook her head.

Her father helped her up off her knees. "Indeed, but I'm afraid her sickness is worse than most. When she woke for a few minutes, she admitted that she's been throwing up quite a bit since the boat trip up here. She thought it was seasickness at first and then thought it was from all the loss she's endured."

"No wonder she's gotten so thin." Gwyn looked to Sadzi. "And we never once guessed she could be pregnant. What with the baby and her nursing. Well, it didn't seem possible."

Gwyn's father shrugged. "It happens. We'll need someone to stay with her."

"Let me stay with her, Dr. Hillerman," Sadzi piped up.

"It's the least I can do, and I have the time to spare. I can stay with her around the clock and pray with her. Maybe this is how the Lord will help heal her heart."

"Perhaps. At least now she'll have something more positive to think on."

"But what if things go wrong with this baby too?" Gwyn's question hung on the air for a moment. She didn't want to seem negative, but the concern was heavy on her mind.

"We won't borrow trouble," her father replied. "For now, we'll rejoice that a new life is given—a gift from the Lord."

"Yes." A smile lifted Sadzi's lips. "A gift of His love for Rose."

CHICAGO

So Tony Griffin wasn't really Tony Griffin.

Frank Rhoads studied the paper work in front of him. How had they missed this? The real Tony had been dead for over ten years.

The police hadn't been a lot of help; they had so many cases on their hands right now. The Depression just made people more desperate. And petty crimes were up.

But Frank needed a break in this case and fast. He knew they were close. He just needed to fit a few more pieces to the puzzle. It was a game he had often played—one he actually took great pleasure in—but there was always a deep sense of frustration when nothing seemed to go right.

He snapped his fingers. Maybe he'd missed something at the bank. Especially now that he knew Tony wasn't *Tony*.

It only took a few minutes to drive over to First National. When he entered, the new manager greeted him.

"I just need to see Mr. Griffin's office again." Frank didn't slow his pace.

"Yes, sir."

"Have you touched or moved anything?"

"Not a thing, sir." The manager straightened his shoulders. "We want this solved as much as you do." When they reached Griffin's office, the manager unlocked the door. "I don't even let the cleaning service in here, so please excuse the dust."

"Not a problem. Thank you."

The manager walked out and closed the door.

Now if Frank could just focus on what he was looking for. But he hadn't a clue. Something was here, his gut told him, but it would have to jump out at him.

Tony, whoever he was, had been immaculate. Everything was in its place. Like he never meant to leave—just disappeared. But that was what it was *supposed* to look like. Now that Frank knew the truth, he knew it was all an elaborate setup.

"Come on, come on . . ." What was he missing?

Frank opened each drawer of the desk. Files, pencils, paper clips, change, mail, papers. All posed to look like Tony had just been there. Another drawer produced a photo of several well-dressed bank officials. He gave it a cursory glance and placed the framed photograph back in the drawer.

Then it hit him. One of the men in the picture seemed familiar. He picked up the frame again and looked at the less than perfect image. It was a bit fuzzy but clear enough. He studied the man third from the right. It was Tony—the imposter. The man looked rather distracted—almost indignant. Perhaps he resented having his picture taken. Then again, maybe he always looked that way.

Always looked that way?

Frank knew in that moment that he'd seen a similar image somewhere else . . . recently. But where?

In a newspaper. But what newspaper? Where?

Frank searched his memory. Where had he seen that face? It had been in another group shot. Not a business photograph like this one, but rather with a family. He shut his eyes and let the picture take root.

"Of course!" He slammed the desk drawer closed and raced out of the office.

He ran into the manager. "Please lock it up. I'll be back."

Traffic was picking up, but Frank still managed to make it back to his office in record time. He pulled his chair up to the desk and began to sift through a stack of newspapers.

"I know it's in here." The memory was quite clear now. He could almost detail the placement of the people in the picture. There had been a man and woman—several children.

He rifled through the stack and began to despair. Where was it? His fingers flipped through the pages of newsprint, but the picture wasn't there.

Worried that he'd somehow imagined it all, Frank threw one paper aside and picked up another from his visit to New York, and bingo. There it was. Front and center.

One William and Suzanne Novak were staring at the camera with a brood of children. The man wasn't Tony, but he was a dead ringer for him. Could this be a relative? A brother, perhaps, or a nephew?

Frank smiled to himself as he read the article about the Matanuska Colony in the Alaska Territory. It would take some time, but with a few queries, telegrams, and letters, he could have this wrapped up in a couple of months. The end was in sight, and he couldn't wait to catch this one!

The more he read, the more the same thought came to him over and over.

"What a perfect place to hide."

Gwyn sat on the floor of Nasnana's cabin with Sadzi as they untangled a mass of yarn.

"What did you do to this, Grandmother? It's a mess."

The older woman laughed. "Well, I was trying to get some fresh air. I've been cooped up lately, so I took my knitting outside. I went back inside to get my tea, and next thing I know there's a bear cub just a-squealing away 'cause he's all tangled up in the yarn."

"Oh my." Gwyn wrapped an untangled portion around her hands. "What did you do?"

"Well, I couldn't let that little cub tear up my yarn and all my hard work, so I went out there to untangle the little guy. He just squealed some more. And then his mama came looking for him."

"Grandmother! How did you get all the yarn off? You know better than to mess with a mama bear and her cubs."

"Oh, the mama bear was still a ways off. Thankfully, the ornery little cub had run a good distance before finding my yarn. But I did lose a couple yards because I had to cut him out." Nasnana shook her head. "Little guy didn't even say thank you. He just snorted at me and ran off."

Her description of the situation made Gwyn laugh. "Oh, Nasnana, I would have loved to see you scold that little bear. But I'm sure his mama did it for you."

Sadzi looked at Gwyn. "I'm going to leave with Gwyn this afternoon, Grandmother. Dr. Hillerman is going to send Rose home, and I'm going to stay with her until she gets back on her feet."

"I have some Scriptures and notes for you to take with you. Please read them to Rose when you feel she's ready."

"Yes, Grandmother. I will."

Gwyn treaded lightly. "It would be wonderful for Rose if you would go as well, Nasnana. There are so many who would love to see you."

"No. No. It's not time yet."

Maybe if she pushed a little harder. "But, Nasnana, Gertrude is the only one who still holds a grudge. Everyone else loves you and would enjoy seeing you again."

"No, Gwyn. It's not time." Nasnana continued her knitting and rocked in her chair.

She didn't want to contradict the woman who'd been so influential in her life all these years, but Gwyn didn't understand. It wasn't like her to push for her own way. Maybe it really was best to leave it alone. Nasnana would come around in time. Hopefully before the winter.

They worked in silence for several minutes. Gwyn kept picturing the baby bear tangled up in the yarn she now held. How funny that would have been to watch the scene. But Gwyn knew how dangerous wild animals could be. This was their land too, and people had to respect that. One of the young girls in the colony had defied them all when her father had shot one of the large mama bears, and she took one of the babies to be her pet. It was all fun and games to walk her baby bear around on a rope for now, but once that bear grew, Gwyn feared the young girl wouldn't be able to control it.

The sound of running footsteps came through the open window.

"Are you expecting someone, Nasnana?"

"No." She rose from her rocking chair.

Jeremiah burst through the door. "I'm sorry for barging in like this, but we've got an emergency."

Gwyn saw the fear on his face. "What is it?"

"They found Gertrude facedown in her garden. I'm sorry, Nasnana, but she's dead. And a couple of the colonists are accusing you."

19

"Dead? Gertrude's dead?" Gwyn couldn't believe it. The woman was a complainer and had been a thorn in Nasnana's side since she arrived, but who would kill her?

Nasnana sat down in her rocking chair. Tears spilled down her cheeks. "Oh, God, please help that family."

Sadzi knelt before her grandmother and shot an angry look at Jeremiah. "So what exactly are you saying? That you believe those people? That my *grandmother* killed her?"

Jeremiah held his hands up in front of him. "No, not at all. But I wanted to warn you. They are bringing in officials from Anchorage to deal with it. And they wanted you to come in."

"So they can accuse her in an angry mob and throw her in jail far away from home?" Sadzi jumped to her feet. "I won't let them do it. I won't!"

Gwyn looked to Jeremiah for help and wrapped an arm around her friend. "There's no way they can throw her in jail unless they arrest her, and they can't arrest her without evidence, right? And we all know that Nasnana hasn't left this house since the last altercation with Gertrude. There are plenty of witnesses."

Jeremiah nodded. "I think if Nasnana goes in willingly and

we talk with the people, we can avoid an angry mob. People are frightened. And fear often breeds violence, so we need to calm everyone down as quickly as possible."

"Let's all go. We can clear this up together." Gwyn was still gripping Sadzi's shoulder and tried to move her toward the door.

The rocking chair creaked as Nasnana stood.

Every eye was on her. "I know you are concerned for me, but there's a greater problem here. A family is suffering with the loss of Gertrude, and we have a murderer in our valley."

The crowd outside the government offices was huge. Gwyn looked at all the people and cringed. What would they say and do to Nasnana?

Don Irwin and Eugene Carr stood outside the offices. Don was the first to notice them as they approached. He walked over to Gwyn. "Miss Hillerman, Dr. Vaughan," he said with a nod, "thank you for bringing Nasnana."

A hush began in the crowd closest to them.

Mr. Irwin held up his hands. "Please, everyone calm down."

A male voice shouted through the crowd, "Someone's been killed. I don't want to be calm. Who's going to protect us at night? We ain't got doors or locks on those tents!"

This time a woman's voice penetrated the murmurs. "Gertrude was right. Are the Indians going to kill us all in our sleep?"

"Calm down, everyone!" Mr. Carr's voice boomed. Gwyn jumped at the authority in his voice. "We need quiet, right now!"

The crowd hushed.

"Nasnana is here and I want to set one thing straight right now. There are no charges against this woman. There is no evidence that she did anything. We have been investigating this awful crime since Gertrude's body was found."

"But she didn't like Gertrude!"

"Yeah, and Gertrude accused her of stealing!"

Another male voice sounded off. "But how many of *us* didn't like Gertrude? Gertrude wasn't a likable person."

Another woman piped up. "Do not speak ill of the dead!"

"Even though it's the truth? What are you here for? A witch-hunt or the truth?"

Gwyn watched in horror as angry words flew back and forth in the crowd. She tightened her grip on Nasnana's arm. The older woman stood strong, her shoulders straight.

Don Irwin stepped forward and joined Eugene. "We have several witnesses who can attest to the fact that Nasnana hasn't left her home since Gertrude accused her of stealing. Before that, she'd been gracious to everyone—helping out, bringing meals, and even praying with many of you since you arrived."

Murmurs rose like ocean waves.

Don held his hands out again. "Let me remind you that this has been her home for a long time. Drs. Hillerman and Albrecht are trying to determine the cause of Gertrude's death, but I'm asking all of you *not* to jump to conclusions."

Several glances were shot their way. Gwyn watched closely. Suspicion seemed present in most people's eyes. How could they conquer prejudice and hate when fear made them so quick to judge?

Lord, we need your help. What do we do?

Jeremiah stepped forward. "Ladies and gentlemen, we need

to remember our American rights. Let's not forget that we are all innocent until proven guilty, and as such, we should treat Nasnana with respect. She has sacrificed so much to stay out of everything, to give you all time to learn to trust and love the native people."

A few people nodded. Then someone else tossed out more suspicions. "Yeah, and you defended her last time too. Maybe we should suspect you too, *Doctor*."

Gwyn was shocked. How could they suspect one of their own doctors? That was more ludicrous than thinking Nasnana was a killer.

Stu Campbell came forward and stood among the crowd. "All right, you all are acting like children. We've had a murder. It's awful. But standing around speculating and accusing is only dividing you. Go back to your work. Let the officials who are trained to deal with these situations do their jobs. And stop all the gossip. It's ridiculous." The FERA administrator strode up to the platform where the other government men stood.

Gwyn watched the crowd disperse. Mr. Campbell's no-nonsense ways always amused her. But would the accusations against Jeremiah and Nasnana stick? Would people always be doubtful and condemning?

Mr. Irwin called Nasnana and Sadzi over.

Jeremiah touched her elbow.

She turned and looked into his eyes. He looked vulnerable and weary.

"Gwyn, we need to talk." His voice was hushed.

"All right." She snuck a glance at her friends. Mr. Irwin smiled at them.

"I'm really concerned. I think I know who is behind all this."

"Who?" She leaned in closer.

Jeremiah glanced around him and grabbed Gwyn's hand. "I'm almost positive it's Clarence, but I don't have any proof."

Truth was, Gwyn thought Jeremiah was on the right track. And she enjoyed the warmth of his hand covering hers. "Do we have to have proof? He's done plenty to make me suspicious of him. What have you observed?"

"I saw him with Gertrude several times. Like they were conspiring together. And your father caught him in the hospital stealing morphine."

"What?" She covered her mouth at her exclamation. Then whispered, "Why didn't he say anything to me about it?"

"He told me he hasn't had time, but he let Dr. Albrecht and me know about it so that we could keep an eye out."

Gwyn glanced down at their hands. "So what do you think it means? Do you really think Clarence is capable of murder? He's not exactly my favorite person, and he annoys me, but . . . murder?"

Jeremiah squeezed her hand and then let go. "I've noticed all the attention he gives you, and I'm ashamed to say that I'm glad he annoys you, because you need to be very careful. Don't be alone with him if you can help it." His face turned very serious again. "As to murder? I honestly don't know, Gwyn. But I don't trust him. I think he's capable of saying or doing almost anything to get his own way."

He rather liked doing his own dirty work. In Chicago, he'd always kept his hands clean. But Clarence felt a new little thrill with each of his accomplishments in this backward little colony.

And who would ever blame him? He'd had no dispute with Gertrude. Not that anyone else knew about. If he played his hand well, the colonists would not only be suspicious of that native woman but also of the popular young doctor.

Clarence smiled. He would, of course, come to the rescue of Gwyn's precious friend and help tighten the noose around Jeremiah Vaughan's neck. Miss Hillerman would be so relieved—so pleased to see the old Athabascan woman saved by Clarence's intercession that she might very well fall into his arms in gratitude. And if he couldn't get her that way, perhaps threatening Dr. Vaughan with exposure and arrest would convince her. There was always a way to get what one wanted. The thought pleased him.

Maybe he should stay a little longer. It wasn't that bad of a place. He could arrange for regular whiskey shipments and with the right connections get just about anything else he wanted. He'd already made a few friends among some of the workers, and while he'd kept his wealth hidden, it just might be time to reveal his prosperity. The colony needed a strong, business-minded man like himself. Maybe he could even become a politician and help run things. He could still travel, and he could bring in enough supplies to build a fine home for himself and Gwyn.

The thought of her wanting a dozen children came to mind, and Clarence shook his head. There would be no children if he had his way. Children were just an unneeded complication. No, he would woo Gwyn and keep her so dazzled and amazed by trinkets and baubles that the idea of having a brood of brats would no longer appeal.

The idea took root and gave him a boost of confidence. He could even open a bank. Invest in the community, or at least appear to. He could make a small fortune by charging interest and assessing fees, all while appearing to be helping the town. He could start with small low-interest loans and put clauses in the small print that would allow the rates to increase when the loans weren't paid back in a certain amount of time. There were all sorts of possibilities. He could make it all appear very innocent, very positive for the colony, and by the time everyone realized how powerful he'd become . . . well . . . it would be too late.

No one would dare accuse him of underhanded dealings. He would be too important to their survival. He chuckled at the thought. "And Miss Hillerman, beloved as she is, will be right in the middle of it all." He'd finally have absolute power over her and the community. He rubbed his hands together in anticipation. The tremors started up again. If he could just get enough powder to keep him calm and his head clear, he'd be able to tackle the rest of his plan.

He just needed to get rid of a few more hindrances and things would be perfect.

On his way to the hospital, Jeremiah saw Arville Schaleben taking a picture outside the mess hall. September was upon them, and the bounty from the gardens overflowed wheelbarrows and buckets.

Jeremiah moved in closer and spied the largest cabbage he'd ever seen. He chuckled. Only in Alaska.

Arville noticed him. "Hey, Dr. Vaughan, could you come do me a favor real quick?"

"I'll try."

"Would you put your hand in the picture for me, you know, for perspective?"

Jeremiah froze. A photograph? He looked at the man. "I'm

hardly prepared to be in a picture. As you can see I've been working all day and—"

"I don't need to take a full picture of you, Dr. Vaughan. Just put your hand in so that we can show it against the cabbage."

"All . . . right." Jeremiah hesitated a moment and then smiled. The young lad holding the cabbage looked as if his arms were about to fall off. "Better make it quick. We wouldn't want him to drop it."

The skinny boy looked a bit relieved and moved his knee up under the giant vegetable.

"A little to the left."

Jeremiah moved his hand and made sure his face was aimed the opposite direction.

"Perfect." The reporter got the shot.

The boy let all the air out of his mouth and set the cabbage down on a crate.

"How much does it weigh?" Jeremiah asked, patting the boy's shoulder.

"Over twenty pounds, sir. And he's had me holding it for almost thirty minutes." The boy flexed his little arms.

"That's pretty amazing."

"Yes, sir. But I better get this into the kitchen." He picked up the cabbage and walked into the mess hall.

Arville walked toward him. "The cook's gonna see how many people it will feed. He'll announce it at lunch, and we'll put it in the paper."

Though giant cabbage was interesting, Jeremiah found himself chuckling at the antics of the press. He guessed that anything new and different would be fun for people to read back in the States.

He'd all but forgotten the cabbage and photograph until

the mess hall bell rang sometime later. He'd managed to clean up a bit and change clothes as well as check his mail. There was still no word from his cousin Howard. Making his way to the mess, he wasn't surprised when Dr. H. joined him.

"I see you managed to wash up," Dr. H. said with a smile.

"I did," Jeremiah admitted, "but you don't look to have had that same luxury."

The older man shook his head. "Afraid not. Had another injury to deal with. Speed is causing some of the workers to take unneeded chances. One of the men nearly cut his finger off. He came in just after you left."

"Could you save the finger?"

Harold shook his head. "No. I finished clipping it off and then sewed the end closed. Hopefully it won't get infected."

There was quite a crowd gathering at the dining hall. Jeremiah leaned closer to his mentor. "They had a twenty-pound cabbage to prepare. Should be interesting to see just how far they could stretch it."

A man turned to Jeremiah. "Twenty-four men, two servings each, with a little to spare."

Harold laughed. "Not too bad . . . if you like cabbage."

"If you don't, they're growing lots of other things big up here," someone else threw in. "I ain't ever seen the likes down in Minnesota."

"It's the long days," Harold explained. "They're good for something other than keeping you awake." The people around them laughed.

Jeremiah adjusted his tie and wiped his sweaty palms on a towel. Earl had insisted that Jeremiah and Harold take the evening to go to the social affair at the newly completed community center. The only reason they'd both agreed was because Dr. Albrecht's fiancée was scheduled to arrive in a few days, and he would need time off for his honeymoon. But Jeremiah couldn't help the strange butterflies in his stomach. He'd known Gwyn all these months but only recently had allowed himself to admit that his feelings toward her weren't going to fade. All this time, he'd been squashing down any attraction that bubbled up, and he'd even tried to convince himself that women were trouble.

But the more he observed her, the more he realized Gwyn Hillerman was a woman he wanted to know. She fascinated him. Her beauty, her intelligence, her giving spirit, her compassionate nature—all these things added up to a woman unlike any he'd ever known.

Why was he so nervous tonight? He saw her almost every day. Didn't always have the chance to speak with her, but he did *see* her every day. No matter how much he tried to calm his nervous energy, the jitters remained. Maybe it wasn't Gwyn he was nervous about. Maybe it was the large crowd and the possibility of photographers. Yeah, that was it.

But even with all his attempts to convince himself otherwise, he knew the truth.

He couldn't wait to see Gwyn.

Pacing the floor, he pulled his pocket watch out for the fifth time. He didn't want to seem too eager and get there early, only to stand around making small talk. Neither did he want to arrive too late and miss the social time at the beginning. If he didn't time it right, he'd walk in during the recital and everyone would notice.

He shook his head. Thirty-four years old and yet behaving like a schoolboy. Is this what real love did to grown men?

He took a deep breath. Might as well just head on over.

The walk in the cool air settled Jeremiah's mind a little. Alaska was a beautiful land. He would never tire of the magnificent views or the moose, bear, and eagles. Of course, he'd only seen a small portion of the territory. He couldn't wait to explore more of the country around him. He'd heard several of the colonists talking about someone who had written about their journey up the Yukon River from Nome. It was during the gold rush at the end of the last century, and the story sounded quite interesting. With a smile he wondered if Gwyn would ever want to take on such an endeavor.

Noise from the community center—a giant warehouse—reached his ears. Laughter, music, talking. He hoped it wouldn't be hard for him to find Gwyn.

When he reached the open doorway, Jeremiah gasped. Hundreds of people milled about. He hadn't expected so many would be able to attend. Workers were still furiously building homes, and many of the families were beginning to harvest their gardens. But the turnout was tremendous.

The band played a few short blasts a little louder, and Stu Campbell mounted the stage. It took several moments for everyone to find a seat, but eventually the crowd quieted.

"Welcome to tonight's historic occasion. It's our first social affair in the new community center."

Applause rippled through the room.

"Thank you, thank you." Stu nodded to the crowd and waited for it to quiet. "We'd like to thank Miss Harriet Malstrom of Seattle for coming all this way to grace us with her talent tonight." Stu held out a hand toward her. "Miss Malstrom."

The pianist started the introduction. The band joined in

and soon Miss Malstrom's voice soared over the hall. Jeremiah appreciated the music, but that wasn't why he'd come. Standing at the back of the room, he searched through the large crowd.

His stomach leaped when he spotted her. There she was, seated in the back corner with her father. Her eyes were closed. He wasn't sure if she was appreciating the music or just exhausted and taking the opportunity to rest for a moment, but no matter what, he loved that he had the chance to watch her. She wore a lovely blouse that came high on her neck and was trimmed with lace. Accompanying this was a dark blue skirt that fell almost to her ankles. Her long curly hair was tied at the nape of her neck with a ribbon. Simple and modest was always Gwyn's style.

And it was lovely.

At the close of the song, the room erupted in thunderous applause, and Gwyn's eyes opened. For a moment, Jeremiah thought she might look his way, but instead, she dabbed at her eyes with a hankie.

His heart swelled. What he wouldn't give at that moment to hold her in his arms. He wasn't sure where the strong emotions came from, but he realized for the first time in a long time, he really felt alive. Gwyn, her father, and these amazing people had awakened him. For once, he was doing the right thing. Giving of himself to help others. That's what life was all about.

As he watched Gwyn, his thoughts turned to God. The anger he'd felt all these months faded. The truth of the matter was simple—he'd been headed down the wrong road. In God's infinite mercy, He'd spared him a lifetime of misery. Jeremiah wasn't sure he appreciated the circumstances that led to his downfall, but for the first time in months, he thanked God for intervening. Now, if only he could tell the truth.

As Gwyn turned her face, a light from above shone down on her golden hair. Had God sent him an angel? To help him heal?

As the vocalist started a new song, Jeremiah couldn't keep his eyes off Gwyn. He made a decision. He had to talk to her. Tonight.

Every time a song ended and people shifted and applauded, Jeremiah moved a little closer to her. Maybe by the time the concert ended, he'd be right there, ready to escort her and ask if she'd like to take a walk.

Miss Malstrom announced her last song and stated the band would play so that everyone could dance and socialize for a bit. Then she would return for the finale. This was his chance.

The song was peppy and happy. Gwyn smiled and swayed a little to the music. Jeremiah watched. A throat cleared.

Jeremiah looked away and caught Dr. H. watching him. The half smile on the man's face told him he'd seen the way Jeremiah looked at his daughter. He winked at Jeremiah.

It took forever for the song to end. But as everyone stood and clapped, Jeremiah stepped closer to Gwyn.

Mrs. Hawthorne, one of the women from camp three, stopped him. "Thank you, Dr. Vaughan, for taking care of my Billy. We're so thankful to have you here."

"You're welcome. Is he doing better?"

"Oh yes. We'll be in this week for you to check his arm."

Jeremiah nodded and the woman walked away. He turned.

But instead of finding Gwyn in front of him, he found Clarence taking Gwyn's elbow and steering her away.

Enough was enough! He was going to punch the man in the nose! Tell him to stay away from Gwyn. But as he stepped forward, Harold was there rescuing his daughter. The trio spoke for several moments, and Dr. H. walked Gwyn to the front of the room.

Away from Clarence.

And Jeremiah.

Doubt crept back in and his joy faded. Maybe that was his sign. It didn't matter how he felt. He still hadn't told anyone the truth. What right did he have to happiness?

20

Gwyn piled more produce onto the wagon. Four months after their arrival, the "Publicized Pioneers," as the settlers were sometimes called, were deep into harvest. She looked up to see a photographer taking yet another photo of one of the colonists with a wheelbarrow full of giant vegetables. She shook her head. The newsmen and photographers still journeyed to their valley nearly every day to record the latest stories and happenings. Mr. Irwin assured her at the concert that it would slow down once all the transient workers left for the winter, and she couldn't wait for that day.

Every time they tried to take a picture of her, she asked them to focus on the colonists. The attention wasn't anything she wanted.

As she helped with the harvest at the experimental station, Gwyn thanked God for the bounty. Even though a lot had been lost in the hailstorm, they still had plenty. Huge vegetables, lots of grain, wheat, potatoes, and cabbage. The time she'd spent helping with the gardens this summer had been wonderful. It hadn't given her much time with her father or Jeremiah, but there was something about digging in the dirt and making things grow that made her happy. All this food, added to the native berries, fish, and wild game, would feed people in the valley over the long winter months. And that thought made her smile.

Faces of children and colony families rolled through her mind. And to think she'd been worried about all the change and all the new people. God had known what she needed, and He'd seen her through the adjustment. Her worry had been unfounded and borne out of the unknown. It gave her cause to think about her future and other things that were yet unknown. Instead of worrying about them, perhaps she could use this example to remind herself to simply take one day at a time and trust God to know what was best for her. Before the colony was established, she couldn't have imagined her quiet existence disturbed by thousands of strangers. Now she couldn't think of her life without all her new friends.

She hefted another crate of vegetables to the truck then paused to stretch. Her back and shoulders ached from the hard labor she'd put in the last few days, but again she thanked God. The winter would soon be upon them, and she'd be cooped up indoors a good bit of the time. Several of the Red Cross nurses would be leaving with the transient workers, and the hospital would need her on a daily basis again.

"Hello, Gwyn." Clarence's overly smooth voice ruined her afternoon.

She closed her eyes. Why did that man have to show up everywhere she went? He found her every single day now and took it upon himself to escort her around the valley. She tried to avoid him, but he always found her. She picked up a shovel and stabbed it into the ground. She almost wished she could stab it into his foot.

"Hello, Clarence." *Lord, forgive me.* But the prayer didn't help her produce a smile for the man.

"I've got a picnic lunch all prepared in a basket, just waiting for your approval. When would you like to take lunch?" His smile showed off his shiny teeth.

Gwyn looked down and counted to ten. One of these days, her temper would get the best of her and she'd say something she regretted. No one would expect the flames her tongue was capable of shooting. She needed an excuse and fast. Her coveralls were covered in soil. "I'm not exactly dressed for a picnic, Clarence. And as you can see, we're really busy with harvest."

"I won't take no for an answer, Gwyn. I've been a gentleman all summer, but you work entirely too hard—"

"I'm afraid you'll *have* to take no for an answer. Because that is the only answer you'll be receiving." *Lord, give me patience and help me not to accidentally run over him with my wheelbarrow.*

"Gwyn—"

"Gwyn, there you are!" Her father's rich voice rolled across the field.

Thank you, Lord. She waved at her father. "Excuse me, Clarence."

"Of course." She heard the irritation in his tone and ignored it. Perhaps now he would see that she had no desire to be with him.

She ran to her father and couldn't help the smile. "You came just in time."

"I know." His eyes crinkled. "Sadzi told me that Clarence has been quite a pest lately. I don't know what that man is up to, but I don't trust him. I think it's time for you to come back to the clinic. That way Jeremiah and I can keep you occupied and away from your admirer."

"But that means I won't be able to help with the rest of the harvest." She pulled off the heavy leather gloves.

"I know you enjoy helping, Gwyn. I'm sure everyone appreciates it, but it is nearly complete, and the colonists can manage without you. It's more important that I keep you safe."

Gwyn linked her arm around his. "I feel completely safe when I'm with you. I've missed you terribly."

He smiled and gave her hand a pat. "I've missed the peace and quiet we used to have and our long talks, but even so, I'm glad to see new life come to this territory. Just imagine it, Gwyn, years from now maybe all of this area will be settled. Perhaps Alaska will even become a state."

"I can't imagine they would want it. It's so far removed from the rest of the country. I heard one of the colonists saying that some legislators think it should be sold off to Canada, since it only connects to that country."

"I've heard the same thing, but I doubt it will ever happen. Men who know this territory know she has a lot to offer. They won't let Alaska slip away easily."

"I pray not. I know I won't." She smiled up into his face. "This is my home, and I love it more every day."

"I think perhaps there is someone else you love more every day as well."

Gwyn felt her cheeks grow hot. Could he really know her heart that well? "I can say with honesty that I've come to love a great many people—especially the children. Children make the world a better place."

"And children of your own will bless you more than you can imagine," her father replied. "A husband and children are exactly what you need."

"Is that what the doctor is ordering?" she asked with a giggle.

Her father laughed. "Perhaps I am. With the right man . . . say . . . someone like Jeremiah . . ." He let the words trail off and waited for Gwyn to respond.

She looked to the ground. "Someone like Jeremiah would meet with your approval? Is that it?"

"I think he's a fine man, and I believe he would make a wonderful son-in-law. And it doesn't hurt that he looks at you with the same heart of love."

"What?" Gwyn asked, stopping in midstep. "How can you say that? He's said nothing to me."

Her father chuckled. "Of course he hasn't. Sometimes a fellow can't see the forest for the trees. But give him time. He'll figure it out."

Hours later, Gwyn was still thinking on her father's words. The time with him had been all too short. But work took priority and the needs of the three-year-old lying on the cot in front of her were far more pressing. Nurses filled the hospital tonight, as several more cases had been brought in. Measles spread all too fast in the camps, and quarantines were almost impossible. Not that they didn't try, but the children seemed to travel between the camps at will, and with them went the various strains of disease. This, coupled with the visitors and transient workers, made it impossible to keep the sick isolated. One man had shown up to work on one of the trains and broke out in measles spots later that evening, exposing all he'd been around on the trip and in the campsites.

Gwyn wiped the brow of the listless cherub in her care. The fever wouldn't break, and her father was concerned. When the child first arrived, she had been alert and babbling, but with the steady rise of her temperature, the girl grew quiet. The child's mother was busy helping to care for her two other sick children in the next room, so Gwyn's father had asked her to stay and help. At this rate, it would be a long night.

Gwyn's thoughts drifted back to the conversation with her father. He'd guessed correctly about her feelings for Jeremiah. It was encouraging that she held her father's approval, but was Jeremiah even interested?

Her father said yes, but Gwyn wasn't so sure. How did a girl know that a man was really interested anyway? And not interested the way Clarence was interested. Gwyn could happily go her whole life without having another man like *that* follow her around.

The curtain slid over and Dr. Jeremiah Vaughan stood in his white coat, his brown hair covering one eye. With one hand, he pushed it back. "Hi." He looked tired but nevertheless offered her a smile.

"Hi." How could this one man take her breath away? Was that even good?

He slid a chair close to the cot and pulled the curtain closed again. "How is she doing?" His voice barely audible.

"Fever's still up. Not much change. She's so little—so precious. I wish the children didn't have to suffer so." The whispered words choked her up. How she hated to watch children suffer. She pulled out her hankie and wiped her eyes. "Sorry. I'm not going to fall apart again."

"Don't apologize." Jeremiah reached a hand out and covered hers. "Your heart is what makes you a great nurse, Gwyn. Your father was right that we medical folk have to guard our hearts, but that doesn't mean we turn them to stone. I don't believe we can be any use to anyone when we do that. I think you're an amazing woman, and your heart is one of the best things about you."

The compliment made more tears spring to her eyes. Who was this man? At moments like this, he was the most wonderful man she'd ever met. Then at others, he seemed to carry a heavy weight and keep her at a distance. Her heart longed to know the real Jeremiah Vaughan. But to do that, she'd have to open up to him. Was she prepared to do that? Even if he rejected her just like her mother had?

"Did you always want to go into nursing?"

The question jolted her back. She focused on the man in front of her. "Um, yes. I guess so. Just watching Father with his patients made me want to be like him. I loved his caring spirit. Loved watching people get well and the smiles he put on their faces."

He scooted the chair closer and leaned over. "That's what did it for me as well. When I was a kid, I would bring anything injured I could find for your dad to 'fix.' He would talk me through whatever he was doing and tell me how it applied to treating people. He's the only adult in my life who took the time to care."

The pain in his voice squeezed her heart. And opened a door she desperately wanted to walk through. "What about your parents?"

"Oh, they were around. It's not that they didn't care about me. They were too busy with everything else. Society and all. They had a business to run and appearances to keep up the family name." He cleared his throat. "They loved the idea of my becoming a doctor."

His small smile did little to soothe Gwyn's heart. So much

pain in those few words. How could she help him? What should she say? "My mother left my father because of society."

His brow furrowed as he looked at her.

Unsure whether or not to go on, she took a deep breath. Would he open up to her if she bared her soul? "Well, she used the excuse of my grandfather having had a heart attack, but she's stayed away all these years because she didn't want to be here. She called it a 'Godforsaken land' and asked how anyone could live in such primitive conditions. She was raised with money and a mansion full of servants. It didn't matter how beautiful this land was, or that she had the undying love of my father. All she wanted was to return to the life of comfort that she'd known."

The memory hurt, but Gwyn's heart felt lighter after sharing with him. "You know, she groomed my little sister to be just like her. The only things they care about are precisely that: things. They don't care about people. They care only about what people *think of them*. It's all about money and prestige and parties and social events and who you know." She huffed and looked down. She'd twisted the handkerchief in her hands into a knot. A nervous habit her mother would've scolded her for. "I'm sorry. That was horrible of me to say."

"No it wasn't." He covered her hands again with his own. "I've known . . . how people like that can be."

The gesture meant more to Gwyn than anything else she'd ever experienced. Did he understand? As much as she enjoyed the warmth and exhilaration from his touch, she hated what she had to say. "But it was wrong of me to malign them, and I'm sorry. Not many know about my mother and Sophia. And I should watch my tongue. It's not honoring to God to speak ill of them. Definitely not honoring my mother as the Bible says I should. I came to the awful realization the other day that I've been selfish in how I've prayed for them. I should be praying for their hearts, that they would know God, not for what *I* want." She tried to pull her hands away.

Jeremiah moved closer and took both of her hands in his. "And what is it that you wanted?"

"To be loved. Accepted." Tears stung her eyes. She blinked. "To rid myself of these feelings that I'd been abandoned because I wasn't good enough. Because I wasn't like them."

"Gwyn, you are so much more than that." He reached up and touched a curl at her temple. "What do you want now?"

She thought of her father's comment that Jeremiah looked at her with a heart of love. She studied his face for a moment. Was it love she saw there?

"Mommy . . ." The raspy voice from the bed startled Gwyn. Jumping up, she knocked her chair backward. The little girl in her care started to flail about, and Gwyn tried to hold her still.

Jeremiah moved to the child's other side and touched her forehead. "She's burning up—convulsing. Get that tub over there." He gripped the child's shoulders and pulled a tongue depressor from his pocket at the same time. With one fluid motion, he put the stick between her teeth.

Pouring two buckets of lukewarm water they kept by the stove into the tub, Gwyn prayed. *Father, please bring this child's fever down. She's so precious and has just begun to live. The colony doesn't need to bury another child. Please, God.* More tears streamed down her face.

Jeremiah placed the toddler in the water, keeping the tongue depressor in place so that she wouldn't bite her tongue. Gwyn bathed the child's face and head as the seizing lessened. It seemed an eternity passed, and still the little girl's body shook.

Gwyn reminded herself to keep breathing. The child was in God's hands. "Come on, little one, be strong."

Jeremiah stood up. "Keep bathing her with the water and try to keep the depressor in place. I'm going to get more aspirin. When was her last dose?"

"About three hours ago."

He returned in less than a minute. "We've got to get her calm enough to swallow. It won't do any good if we can't get her fever down."

Gwyn continued to drench the child with water and pray. If they could just get the medicine into the precious baby, maybe they could keep her temperature down for good.

All of a sudden, the little girl went limp. Her jaw relaxed and dropped open. The convulsions stopped.

Gwyn held her breath while Jeremiah listened to the child's heart with his stethoscope. Then he checked her temperature. The waiting seemed unbearable.

He took the thermometer out. "The water is helping. Her temperature is coming down."

She closed her eyes. "Thank you, God."

The clink of a glass against metal drew her eyes open. Jeremiah was crushing an aspirin and mixing it with sugar water. He looked at Gwyn. "I don't want her to spit it out."

She nodded. They needed to get a full dose into the little girl. "Let me help. I'll sit her up and coax her to swallow."

Minutes later, they had accomplished their goal and had their patient dressed in a dry gown and tucked back into her hospital bed.

Gwyn laid a hand on the little girl's forehead. For the first time in hours, her skin felt cooler to the touch. A deep breath left the tiny child's pink lips, followed by a shudder. Relief and gratitude poured through Gwyn. It seemed like even the child's body was relaxing after battling the sickness.

"It's always amazed me that children are both so resilient and fragile." Jeremiah washed his hands in the basin next to the bed.

"A beautiful mix, isn't it?"

He nodded. "I've got to check on the other patients. Keep cooling her down with a cloth and see if you can get her to drink some water." At the curtain, he turned back. "I wish we had more time to talk." And then he was gone.

"Me too." Her whispered words couldn't reach him, but her heart hoped that he knew.

Thick sawdust covered his feet, his hair, and everything in between. Even after working twenty-four hours at the hospital, Jeremiah couldn't rest. Dr. Albrecht had relieved him a few hours ago, and he still couldn't shut his mind down. The conversation with Gwyn ran through his mind over and over. But guilt always replaced the happiness those few minutes had given him.

He grabbed log after log off the mill and laid them out in a pattern on the ground. Then he'd mark each one. The menial task didn't take a lot of thought, but it made his muscles burn. Maybe that would help ease the ache in his heart.

"This wall is complete!" the foreman yelled.

Several men came and grabbed the logs and loaded them into the truck. They'd be back as soon as they delivered the load. Jeremiah needed to have the next wall's pieces cut and numbered before they returned.

Everyone in the valley felt a sense of urgency to get all the colonists out of their tents by winter. A number of families had left, either because of sickness or difficulty in adjusting, but Stu Campbell was recruiting more families, and they'd be arriving soon. Jeremiah found it fulfilling to know he was helping these men construct the two hundred homes needed for the colony. But not as fulfilling as healing the sick.

And definitely not as fulfilling as seeing Gwyn.

His pulse drummed in his ears. Thoughts of her invaded all too often. He had to tell her the truth. But he couldn't. Jeremiah's mind volleyed back and forth. For the longest time he'd tried to convince himself that Gwyn couldn't be different. She had to be just like her mother and her sister.

But that argument didn't hold water for long. Every time he judged her and kept her as far as he could from his mind, reality settled in.

The facts all pointed to one thing—something he'd tried to deny for months—he cared for Gwyn Hillerman. In a way he'd never cared for anyone else. Could this be *real* love? Not the superficial physical-appearance love that he thought he'd had for Sophia. But the real thing?

He longed to tell Gwyn how he felt. But what would she say, since she didn't know the truth?

All those lies. He'd lived them. Now there wouldn't be any chance of his gaining Gwyn's affection. When she found out what had happened in Chicago and that he'd been engaged to her sister, she'd never forgive him.

Dr. Hillerman wouldn't forgive him.

The colonists wouldn't forgive him.

And he'd never be able to practice medicine again.

21

The pen fell from between his teeth onto the desk. Jackpot.

Frank sat down hard and studied the papers in his hand. William Novak had a brother.

Clarence Novak. And according to his contact in Anchorage, Clarence was still in Alaska.

AKA Tony Griffin. Former bank manager at First National Bank of Chicago.

William and his wife, Suzanne, had been chosen as one of two hundred and three families for President Roosevelt's now famous New Deal project—the Matanuska Colony Project. Right now, Clarence resided in a tent with his brother's family. The perfect hiding place. Where no one would find him.

Except Frank Rhoads. Everyone else had given up on the case. But he hadn't. He was a Pinkerton. And he didn't fail.

He typed a memo to his boss, using all the notes from the case. Hunting and pecking with his index fingers didn't go as fast as he wanted. Maybe one of these days he would learn how to type the real way. He jammed the pen back in between his teeth as he pulled the sheet of paper out of the barrel and checked for mistakes. As soon as his boss approved it, he'd head to Alaska. And one Clarence Novak—mastermind behind the First National Bank robbery—would be his.

───────

It didn't take much for Frank to pack. Most of the time, he kept a bag ready with everything he needed since he was on the road constantly. There was always some criminal waiting to be apprehended or a crime scene that needed review. One day Frank hoped to settle down. Have a family. But he couldn't put anyone through the life that he lived now. Besides, when would he meet a woman to marry? On his next arrest? The thought made him chuckle.

He carried the bag back into his office. His boss wanted to see him one more time and discuss the plan before he left.

He picked up the phone's earpiece and then stuck his pen in the zero slot on the rotary and slid it around.

"Operator—"

"Frank!" a man called from the door. "I'm so glad I caught you!" The familiar voice caused Frank to hang up on the poor operator.

"Howard, what are you doing down here?" He stuck out his hand.

"I need your help." His old friend shook it.

"Anything." Howard Vaughan had saved Frank's life ten years ago on Lake Michigan. "You know it."

"It's my cousin."

"The doctor? Sorry about that, Howie. When I read that in the papers, my heart broke for your family."

Howard sat down and removed his hat. "That's the thing. I've been appealing his case, and I had a hard time tracking him down. That's where you come in."

"Whatcha got?"

"I spoke with your boss this morning on the phone, and he told me you were about to go to Alaska—to the FDR colony in Matanuska. I finally had a letter catch up with me from Jeremiah. He's there." Howard handed over a picture. "The letter was posted months ago and must have gotten lost on its way. I need to get in touch with him, and I don't want to send a letter and have it go astray. Since you're heading there, I thought maybe you'd be willing to help me."

"Well, I've got another case that's first priority, but I'll be glad to find Jeremiah as soon as it's concluded." Frank looked his friend in the eye. "You look plum worn out. Is it pretty serious?"

"Yes." Howard nodded. "It's urgent."

MATANUSKA VALLEY

Very little sleep the past week was not helping her mood. Gwyn's brain was muddled. Like a big bowl of mush. There'd been no time to talk to Jeremiah in more days than she'd counted. Everyone had to pitch in with harvest, canning, and building colonists' homes. Only half of the families had moved in to a home with a solid roof over their heads, and way too many of the other homes weren't even framed all the way. Cooler temperatures had arrived, and Gwyn was certain the snow would fly soon. Oh, they'd have plenty of time before the brutal cold arrived and stayed, but these first few signs were glaring reminders of all that was left to do.

The only consolation she'd had was a long chat with her father last night. They'd stayed up late eating sugar cookies Gwyn had made for the students celebrating their first full week of school. With all the new teachers finally in Alaska, they'd started their rounds to the camps and homes, giving homework and grading papers. The plan—at least until schools were built—was for the teachers to make it to each family once a week, assign work for the children, and then head back the next week for more lessons and to pick up the papers completed by the children. It was far from perfect, but it would have to do. A small cabin next to the community hall had been temporarily assigned to the teachers. Only one room, it would have to do until all the colonists' homes were done.

Her father had mentioned Jeremiah last night and commented on what a wonderful doctor he had turned out to be. He spoke of the great love Jeremiah showed for the children, that he'd supplied them with new baseballs and bats for their games.

Gwyn had wanted to tell her father about her feelings, but she'd been hesitant to share too much. In her heart, she'd wanted to share everything. All her fears and innermost thoughts she shared only with the Lord. Something held her back from opening her heart to her father.

But Father knew. He didn't push. He encouraged her to talk to Nasnana about it.

If she talked to Nasnana, would the woman who knew her almost as well as she knew herself look into her eyes and see the turmoil and confusion? The fear? The longing?

The . . . love?

There was no denying it any longer. Her strong feelings for Dr. Jeremiah Vaughan couldn't be hidden or ignored.

But Gwyn didn't know or understand what she was supposed to do or how she was supposed to do it. She didn't have a textbook. She didn't have an older sister. She didn't even have a mother she could turn to for guidance.

While there were other native people nearby, Nasnana, Sadzi, and Father had been her only close companions for a great many years. There'd never been any secrets. Never anything she couldn't share.

But this was different.

And Gwyn had no idea why.

Thoughts tormented her like buzzing flies. Now she wished her father hadn't demanded she stay home from the hospital today. There was plenty to get done, but she'd gotten so used to staying busy around people that she feared her own thoughts and emotions.

Was love always so complicated, so painful? *Lord, what do I do?*

"Knock, knock!" Sadzi's voice came through the window.

Gwyn ran to the door. "Come in!" She glanced down. "What are you up to?"

Sadzi held the handles of two large buckets in each hand. "I noticed you hadn't had time to do any blueberry picking. I saw your father at the hospital, and he informed me you were home today. So . . . change your clothes. Let's go before the bears eat them all."

A giggle bubbled up to the surface. Just what she needed. "All right, give me two minutes."

"I'll give you one."

"Ah!" Gwyn laughed all the way to her room, knowing her friend meant it. She flung off the dress she'd worn that morning, grabbed an old shirt of her father's she used for gardening, and slipped it on. She could hear Sadzi counting outside.

". . . twenty-one . . . twenty-two . . . twenty-three . . ."

Gwyn stepped into her overalls, snatched her leather gloves, and ran to the door.

". . . forty-eight . . . forty-nine . . . fifty . . ." Sadzi looked down at Gwyn's feet. "Uh, you might want shoes . . . fifty-one . . . fifty-two . . ."

Only Sadzi knew how to make her laugh this way. *Thank you, Lord, for this friend*. Gwyn grabbed two pairs of thick wool socks, yanked them on, and stuffed her feet into her rubber boots.

"Sixty!" Sadzi grimaced and laughed. "Well, you made it, but you look a fright. Look on the bright side—maybe you will scare the wildlife away."

Gwyn looked down. One pant leg was stuffed into a boot; the other was half in and half out. The buttons on her shirt were buttoned crooked, and one shoulder of her overalls wasn't hooked. "Easy now. I made it, didn't I?" She held out her arms and twirled.

Their laughter filled the air outside as Gwyn shut the door and tried to adjust herself and keep up with Sadzi at the same time.

Trekking up the hill to their favorite blueberry gullies, they caught up on all the happenings around the valley.

Sadzi moved closer and bumped a bucket on Gwyn's leg. "Grandmother wants you to know that she misses you."

"I miss her too." A long sigh escaped. "I know it hurt that she was accused of Gertrude's murder, and I know she wants to give people space, but I wish she'd come out more often."

"She's getting old, Gwyn. Her heart longs to help more, but I think her body is slowing down."

"If only Gertrude hadn't stirred up all that mess to begin with. If only they could find out who killed her. If only . . ."

"All the *if only*s in the world won't change it." Sadzi's sad smile said it all.

Since sin entered God's beautiful creation, there'd been prejudice and gossip. Gwyn couldn't stop it. Neither could Sadzi. But Gwyn loved her friend's spirit. Having given the colony several weeks after the initial confrontation, Sadzi dove right back in to help with anything and everything she could. If someone was uncomfortable around her, she slipped away to help elsewhere and didn't force the issue.

"You're right. Me and my worry. One of these days I'll conquer it . . . with God's help."

Sadzi laughed. "I've known you since before I can even remember. You've always been a worrier. Always. Not that God can't change that, but how many handkerchiefs alone have you destroyed?"

"Oh, don't get me started. My father now gives me a new package of hankies every Christmas and every birthday."

The path narrowed and Sadzi led the way. When they reached the top, she sidestepped her way down the steep gully. Gwyn knew the routine well. Every year growing up, they'd spend days in the late summer and fall picking berries. The best times were when they'd had plenty of rain. They'd climb to the top and work their way down the gully as they picked.

A comfortable silence settled over them as the first berries plunked into their buckets. Years of practice came back, and they picked up speed. It wouldn't take them too long to fill the four ten-gallon buckets.

"So . . ." Sadzi picked with both hands and popped a blueberry into her mouth. "Are you going to tell me about how you're madly in love with Jeremiah Vaughan, or do I need to make up my own story?"

The barking cough of his two-year-old patient woke Harold from his nap in the chair. The warmth of their makeshift steam tent must've put him to sleep. Swiping a hand down his face, he stood and went to the boy. Harold sat the child up and checked his lungs.

Croup was such a nasty illness for the little ones. Mothers hated to hear their children struggling to breathe, and Harold had never gotten used to it either. Thankfully, this was the first case in the colony, but they were approaching the season. How many nights would he spend in a chair like this over the next winter?

He smiled at the boy who looked up at him. The little guy patted his hand and went limp. Asleep in an instant after the awful coughing spasm.

Harold wouldn't change a thing about his life. Other than the fact that he hadn't spent enough time with Gwyn lately. How many days had it been since their chat over sugar cookies? He glanced up at the calendar on the wall. October was only two days away.

His mind drifted back to other years. Would he change anything? Even with Edith gone, he still knew that God was in charge, and this was where he was supposed to be.

Stretching his back and neck, he decided another little nap wouldn't hurt. He'd check on the other patients in the hospital and take up residence by little Tim again.

Six other colonists and one carpenter took up the cots in the hospital that night. Thankfully, the numbers were down. Harold scribbled a few notes as he checked each one and found his chair back in the steamy curtained-off area.

The clunking of booted feet alerted him to someone else entering the hospital. Oh, he hoped it wasn't another patient.

He wanted the people to stay well. About to stand, Harold stopped with his hands on the arms of the chair when Jeremiah's head poked through the curtain.

"Dr. H., mind if I join you?"

He leaned back. "Not at all, Jeremiah. Come on in. Pull up a chair." Sleep could wait. The young doctor's face was serious.

"Something bothering you, son?"

Jeremiah sat down, his hat smashed in his hands.

Harold chuckled. "You know. You're as bad as Gwyn. When she's got something on her mind or she's worried about something, she'll twist and fray her hankie to shreds."

His words elicited a small smile but nothing more. Jeremiah stared down at the floor.

Harold had been around the block a few times. He knew what was on the young man's mind. "Well, since I don't want to use a scalpel to pry it out of you, I should probably tell you that I know the truth."

22

Jeremiah's head shot up, his eyes as round as saucers. "You do?"

"I do. I know how much you care about my daughter. I see it on your face. Love bit me once too, you know."

"It's not just about your daughter, Harold. It's the fact that I don't deserve your daughter. I . . . I . . ."

Lord, help this young man. He's carrying so much anger and hurt.

Jeremiah sighed. His head hung low, shoulders slumped.

"I know, Jeremiah."

"No, Dr. H., you don't. As much as I care for Gwyn . . . I . . . I . . . just can't."

Harold slid his chair closer and leaned with his elbows on his knees. "I do, Jeremiah. Son, look at me."

The anguish in Jeremiah's eyes was almost more than Harold could take. This man was broken.

"I know about Chicago." Harold took a deep breath and prayed for the right words. "I know about Mrs. Brewster. I know about the proceedings against you, and I know that your license was revoked."

Jeremiah slumped even further into the chair and leaned his head back. "How long have you known?"

"Only a week. It took over six weeks for the letter to reach me. It had gone out to one of the islands first and then had to come back up here."

"What letter?"

"I wrote to an old colleague of mine this summer. I was so excited about the colony and the work we were doing. Ecstatic that you were here."

"And you let me continue practicing medicine? Why?"

Harold looked away. "I'm not real sure. Other than the fact that I know you are a phenomenal physician. I've been debating all week whether I should discuss it with Dr. Albrecht before I brought it up with you, but we haven't had the time."

"Dr. Albrecht will be furious."

"No, I don't think he will, son." Harold crossed his arms over his chest. "He's a good man. And he believes in you. He's told me on several occasions how much you've taught him and how much he respects you. I also know that your cousin has been appealing your case. My friend back in Chicago thinks you have a chance, even if the bigwigs aren't on your side."

"What do I do now?"

"Well, first, we send a telegram to your parents and find out how the appeal is going."

Jeremiah shook his head. "I'm sorry. I never should have put you—"

Harold held up a hand. "I can't say that I wouldn't have done exactly the same thing. No one can know what they might do in another's situation, so no more apologies. You are forgiven. Now we move forward."

"But how?"

"You need to tell the truth. The sooner you do, the sooner everything can be resolved."

"But there's more—"

"Sophia?"

Jeremiah's eyebrows shot up. "How'd you know? Mrs. Hillerman made it very clear that she didn't communicate with you."

"My friend. He shared that not only had you lost your career, but you'd lost your engagement to my daughter all in the same day." Harold stood and checked the little boy's temperature. "I can't say it surprises me. Sophia and her mother only care about the appearance of things and where they stand in society. I'm sure hearing that you had lost face was enough to cause Edith to force an end to the betrothal."

"I don't think it was just Sophia's mother who wanted to put an end to the engagement."

"I'm certain that Sophia has turned into a beautiful young woman. I just wish her heart were as beautiful as her exterior. I'm afraid she's too much like her mother."

"So you know." Jeremiah cleared his throat. "You know that she's . . . well . . ."

"A snob? Vain? Money hungry?" He let those thoughts hang for a few minutes. "Yes. It makes me so sad. Edith turned Sophia into a replica of herself years ago." He paused. "Unfortunately, I could have stopped it. I wish I would have."

"How can I ever tell Gwyn? I mean, you've already guessed correctly about how I feel for her. But I've been lying to her all these months, and when she finds out I was engaged to her sister, I don't think it will go over very well." The young man's voice rose. The line of his jaw tightened.

"You need to tell her the truth. But there's something else you have to do first."

Jeremiah sat straighter. Every muscled looked rigid. "What?"

"You've got to get your heart right with the Lord." Harold sat down, hoping that he could reach this young man that he loved like a son.

Jeremiah leaped to his feet, his face red. "God took everything away from me!"

"No He didn't. We live in a sin-filled world with sin-filled people. You can't blame your circumstances on God."

"But why didn't He save Mrs. Brewster? Why couldn't He have kept the board from ruling against me? Why didn't He open my eyes to Sophia's façade and true character before I fell in love with her?"

"Would you be here?"

"Well, no. Maybe. I don't know. But that's not the point."

"What is the point? You want someone to blame?"

"Well . . . yes. My life was ruined—"

"Your life wasn't ruined. If you had died without reconciling to God through Christ, then your life would have been ruined. Is that what happened?"

Jeremiah looked away.

"Son, you told me that as a young boy you accepted Jesus as your Savior. Weren't you about nine years old? Ten maybe?"

Jeremiah sat down heavily in the chair. He nodded. "I just don't understand. I had my life all in order. I was going to be the hospital head, Dr. H., did you know that? During one of the worst economic times in our country, I was going to be making a decent salary. I was going to get married and have a family and be successful."

"In other words, you were storing up earthly treasures."

"What?" Jeremiah looked confused.

"Give me a second. I'll be right back." Harold went to his little desk in the corner of the hospital building and grabbed his Bible, praying all the way back to Jeremiah. "Look at this, son. Matthew 6:19–21 says this: 'Lay not up for yourselves treasures upon earth, where moth and rust doth corrupt, and where thieves break through and steal: But lay up for yourselves treasures in heaven, where neither moth nor rust doth corrupt, and where thieves do not break through nor steal: For where your treasure is, there will your heart be also.'

"You see, Jeremiah, moth and rust corrupted all those things you listed earlier, because you weren't laying up your treasures in the right place. That means your heart wasn't in the right place either. God wants to be first and foremost in your life. No matter what you do, who you are, where you work, how much money you have, or who you're married to."

The younger man leaned forward. "May I see that?"

"You can even borrow it. I've got another at home."

Jeremiah sat silent for several moments as he gazed at Harold's Bible.

Lord, please reach his heart. Heal him, Father. He's hurting.

"You know. You're right." Head bowed. "When I packed to come here, I didn't even bring my Bible. I brought all my medical books instead. What kind of a man am I?"

Harold gripped his shoulder. "A man that I love as much as if he were my own son. And a man that God loves even more. He wants to use you, Jeremiah, for His glory. He's given you amazing gifts. You are an incredible physician. And you love my daughter. I couldn't ask for a better son-in-law." He squeezed hard, and the young man's hazel eyes met his. "But you've got to get your heart straight with the Lord first. You've got to tell the truth. And I'll help you appeal that case until we've exhausted every resource."

Clarence knelt beneath the open window of the hospital. So Dr. Hillerman knew. And wanted to help Jeremiah.

And wanted to take Gwyn away from him.

He couldn't let that happen. Not ever.

Footsteps echoed off the wood floors. Someone was coming. Clarence ran behind a tree and watched as Jeremiah stood in the doorway talking to Dr. Hillerman.

"I'll be back in a few hours. Thank you. For everything."

The older doctor hugged the young man. It made Clarence sick to his stomach. This was not part of his plan.

He watched Jeremiah walk away and the door close.

What could he do? He needed to think—to clear his mind. He pulled the small envelope out of his pocket. There wasn't much morphine left, and the man who'd promised to bring him some from Anchorage never returned.

A new plan formed in his mind. He could take care of things and get what he wanted all at the same time. He turned and searched the ground.

Grabbing a heavy log about the length of his arm, he headed for the hospital. At the tree, he took off his shoes and then crept in the same door Jeremiah Vaughan had just exited.

He slid one foot in front of the other, listening for any sound that would give away his presence. A slit in the curtain to the right gave him a perfect view. The good doctor was sitting down, head bowed, eyes closed.

Clarence counted to ten and then slid through the opening.

Crack!

Dr. Hillerman fell face first onto the floor. Clarence ran to the other room, smashed the glass in the case where they locked up the medicine, and grabbed what he wanted.

He yanked a pillowcase off the linen shelf and shoved everything inside. Then he went back to the door and looked around. How would he do it? Wrapping his jacket snugly around the good doctor's face, Clarence chuckled to himself. He amazed himself with his own brilliance. With a glance back to the clinic, Clarence dragged the old doctor's limp body to the river.

23

Gwyn twisted yet another handkerchief in her hands. She hadn't seen her father in two days. The group gathered outside of the hospital was discussing where they would search next. Ten different search parties had looked for her father. But they hadn't found him. Her worst fears played out in her mind. What if they did find him . . . and he was dead? What would she do?

No. She couldn't allow her thoughts to take her to that dark place. She needed to place it all in the Lord's hands and leave it there.

She walked closer to the group.

"You must admit that Dr. Vaughan is acting very strange." Clarence bounced on his toes as he spoke with Don Irwin.

Mr. Irwin frowned at Clarence. "Wouldn't you act different if you'd lost someone close to you?"

"Humph. He was the last one to see Dr. Hillerman alive. He even admits that, like it somehow frees him from suspicion." The accusation was unspoken in the undertones of sarcasm.

"I think our time is best served looking for Dr. Hillerman, not speculating."

Clarence looked at Gwyn. His expression changed. Apparently he realized she'd heard the whole thing. Now his voice sounded sympathetic. "Yes, of course, Mr. Irwin." He held her gaze. "Of course."

"Group six!" Stewart Campbell yelled over everyone. "You'll need to search the next half mile of banks along the river. Group eight posted a flag where they left off."

The last two groups left, Clarence among them. Gwyn wasn't sure she was relieved or angry. The man had no right to talk about Jeremiah that way. She saw the hateful looks Clarence sent toward the man she loved. And even though Jeremiah had been the last one to see her father, she knew in her heart that he had nothing to do with her father's disappearance.

But Jeremiah had barely spoken to her. He seemed to carry the weight of the world on his shoulders.

Then Clarence's words sank into her mind. *"He was the last one to see Dr. Hillerman alive."*

Could it be true? Did everyone assume that her father was dead?

The rustle of footsteps on the fallen leaves broke her thoughts. Nasnana handed her a cup of tea. "Here, let's go back inside, dear."

"Thank you." Gwyn followed the older woman into the building. Around her were cots and curtains and medical paraphernalia. This hospital had been her father's dream for years. And here it was, serving the people.

He should be here.

She walked from bed to bed. Little reminders of her father were everywhere. *Oh, Lord, I don't know what to do. I'm afraid the worst has happened. Please show me how to rely on you, Father. And please keep my father safe. Thy will be done.*

Yelling reached her ears through the window. And then more voices added to the cacophony. Nasnana was at her side and grabbed her hand.

Gwyn pulled her friend out the door with her. Her hand shot to her mouth.

Mr. Bouwens was carrying her father's limp form.

As the group approached, the crowd grew. The fire bell rang.

More people came running.

They came closer.

"No!" The scream left her lips, and she sank to the ground.

Jeremiah ran to her side. "I'm so sorry, Gwyn. I'm so—"

"I demand that you remove this man and take him into custody." Clarence had a wild look in his eyes. He'd dragged Mr. Carr and Mr. Irwin with him. "He admitted that he was with Dr. Hillerman in the middle of the night—the night he disappeared. And we have the testimony of the Gray boy who was in the hospital that night. He heard them arguing."

"We weren't arguing." Jeremiah's voice broke. "We were discussing some important matters."

"Matters that enraged you and caused you to take the situation into your own hands! When are we going to learn the *truth*, Dr. Vaughan?"

"That's enough!" Mr. Carr pushed Clarence back. "The authorities are on their way." He held up his hands. "I need everyone to move back, please." He turned to Gwyn. "I'm so sorry about your father. He was one of the best men I've ever met."

Gwyn nodded. The shock of seeing her father's lifeless form in front of her caused her stomach to ache and her head to spin. This wasn't real. It couldn't be.

Dr. Albrecht appeared. "I'd like your permission to examine the body."

She nodded again. Mr. Irwin was saying something to the other doctor.

"We need to get her inside—"

Was that Jeremiah's voice? Black spots danced in front of her eyes. All the sound around her turned into a deafening roar. And then nothing.

Someone pinched her arm. Hard. Her eyes flew open. Nasnana was bent over her. "There you are." The lines around her eyes crinkled.

"My father—" She didn't want to say the words. "Is he? Is he dead?"

The dark eyes deepened and pooled with tears. "Yes, my child. I'm sorry. Your father's gone on to be with the Lord."

"How can this be? Oh, Nasnana, what will I do without him?" Gwyn's sobs filled the air. She needed more time with him. They were going to have more time once the houses were built and the people were settled. "I can't bear this alone."

"Child, no one is asking you to." Nasnana stroked her hair.

They would bury Harold Hillerman tomorrow. Nasnana couldn't believe the man she'd known all these years was really gone.

Rose Benson sat next to Gwyn on the couch in the Hillerman home. It was Rose's turn to be the comforter. Even after months of heartbreak and pain, the rosy cheeks of the new child of God attested to His goodness, even in the midst of all their sorrow. Rose had one hand on her growing belly and one hand in Gwyn's.

Rose started humming. The sound swelled through the room, and then her voice lifted in song:

> "'Tis so sweet to trust in Jesus,
> Just to take Him at His Word . . ."

Sadzi and Nasnana joined in.

> "Just to rest upon His promise,
> Just to know, 'Thus saith the Lord!'
> Jesus, Jesus, how I trust Him!
> How I've proved Him o'er and o'er!
> Jesus, Jesus, precious Jesus!
> O for grace to trust Him more!"

Tears ran down Gwyn's cheeks. Nasnana moved forward and knelt in front of this precious girl and wiped them away with her hands. "We will rest in His promise, won't we, child?"

Gwyn nodded again and again. "I somehow have to let Mother and Sophia know."

"I know, child. I wrote them a letter already."

"Thank you." Her blond head dipped again.

"We will trust Him, child. And even in the midst of all this hardship, with the worry for what your mother or sister will do, and when your world feels upside down, we will trust Him."

Gwyn closed her eyes and bit her lip. She continued to nod. Rose started another verse, her voice soothing, sad:

> "I'm so glad I learned to trust Thee,
> Precious Jesus, Savior, Friend;
> And I know that Thou art with me,
> Wilt be with me to the end."

Gwyn opened her eyes. "I love that hymn. And so did my father." Her bottom lip trembled, but she kept going. "Thank you for sharing that, Rose."

"I sang it because your father was the first one to tell me about it. He told me that the woman who wrote the words had just lost her husband too. Even after that, she was without a husband, had a little daughter, and they became destitute. But she still trusted Jesus."

Rose looked at Nasnana. "He visited every day and brought me letters from Nasnana. They wouldn't leave me alone. Wouldn't let me lie in bed and die along with those I'd lost. Told me that God had a purpose for me. So I got out of bed one day and went to see Reverend Bingle. I asked him if he had a copy of that hymn, and he gave me a songbook. I took it home and memorized it. Whenever I get low, I sing it."

More tears streamed down Gwyn's face. She hugged Rose. "Thank you. I know my father would want me not to mourn. He'd want me to celebrate that he's with Jesus. But it's hard to think of life without him. I don't even know how to work at the hospital without him. He's the one who trained me. Guided me. Taught me everything I know. And not just about medicine." She sniffed.

"I always thought my father would be here when I got married and had children. . . ." A sob overtook her. Then she straightened and sucked in a breath. "But I know that God's will is not our will. His ways are not our ways. I want to find joy in this. I do. But it's really hard." Gwyn turned her head and sobbed into Rose's shoulder.

Nasnana motioned for Sadzi to help her up. "These old bones don't like the floor anymore. This past summer seems to have aged me ten years."

When Nasnana was back in a chair, she closed her eyes. Gwyn needed a few minutes. "Sadzi, would you bring me my Bible?" Nasnana said. "It's in my basket by the door."

"Here it is, Grandmother."

"This morning—" she flipped through the onionskin pages that had been well read and were well worn—"I was reading in Job." She settled on the right spot.

"The story of Job fascinates me. Here's a man of God, upright and wealthy. When Satan goes to God and basically says that the only reason Job is upright is because God has placed a hedge about him and blessed him, then God allows Satan to strip all of Job's family and wealth away.

"And you know what Job says? He says, 'Naked came I out of my mother's womb, and naked shall I return thither: the Lord gave, and the Lord hath taken away; blessed be the name of the Lord.'

"But that just riles old Satan up some more. So he goes back to God and tells Him the only reason Job is still upright is because he's still got his health. So God once again allows Satan to hurt Job, but He won't allow Satan to kill him.

"So now we have poor Job, who's lost all his children and his wealth, covered with boils from the top of his head to the bottom of his feet. His wife tells him to curse God and die. But what does Job say? He says, 'Shall we receive good at the hand of God, and shall we not receive evil?' In Job chapter two we read, 'In all this did not Job sin with his lips.'"

Rose leaned as far forward as her belly would allow. "What happened after that?"

"Then to compound things, Job has three *wonderful* friends come to visit him. They even sit in silence with him for seven whole days."

"Wow. Now, that's a friend." Rose nodded. "Seven days is a long time to sit in silence."

Nasnana laughed. She looked at Gwyn. Her teary eyes crinkled up and she smiled.

Nasnana winked at her and continued, "Well, it would seem that way. But after those seven days, they began to make speeches to Job. And for the next thirty-some odd chapters, we have these three friends accusing Job of sinning. Because that's why he's suffering, right? There must be some hidden sin in his life? As Job debates with these men, he attests to the fact that he doesn't understand why God is allowing all this suffering in his life, but he rests in God's sovereignty and the fact that he knows the Lord. In chapter nineteen, Job says, 'For I know that my redeemer liveth, and that he shall stand at the latter day upon the earth.' You see, Job had an intimate relationship with God. And even though he'd been beaten up and battered by life, he still trusted."

Gwyn shifted in her seat. "I want to be like that. I want to praise God now, even though it hurts, and I want to be able to come out on the other side of all this and still be praising God. ''Tis so sweet to trust in Jesus. . . .'" She closed her eyes again.

Rose wrapped an arm around Gwyn's shoulder. "Nasnana, how does the story of Job end?"

"Well, after all the debates with his three friends. God answers them all in a whirlwind and tells Job's friends that they must repent and sacrifice, because they didn't speak of Him correctly, like Job did. And then He blessed Job abundantly with more than he'd had before."

"Oh my goodness. That's an amazing story." Rose's eyes locked with hers.

Nasnana knew the Lord was doing a mighty work in this young woman. He was doing a mighty work in them all.

Gwyn stood up. "My heart may be broken in loss, but I know where my strength is found." A tear slid down her cheek. "'The Lord gave, and the Lord hath taken away; blessed be the name of the Lord.'"

Nasnana, Rose, and Sadzi all stood. Nasnana reached out. "Let's join hands and sing that hymn again. Rose, would you lead us?"

Their voices rose in praise and adoration. Nasnana watched each girl the Lord had blessed her with. Her beautiful granddaughter, Sadzi, her adopted granddaughter, Gwyn, and this precious new young woman, Rose. The beauty of them choked her up. *Father, thank you. Thank you.*

A knock sounded on the doorframe, and they stopped singing.

Nasnana opened the door. "Mr. Irwin, won't you come in?"

"If you all don't mind, we need you at the hospital, Gwyn. Nasnana, we were hoping you could accompany her."

"Of course. Now?"

"Yes, as soon as possible." He nodded and left the house.

"Well, I guess we better head on over." Nasnana grabbed her shawl. "Rose, would you mind staying and cleaning up a little?"

"Of course. I'll have some lunch ready when you return."

Sadzi and Nasnana walked the long path on each side of Gwyn, there to comfort and support. At the hospital, Nasnana took an offered chair while Gwyn sat on the floor at her feet, as she had when a child. And now, as they waited, she stroked Gwyn's head. The young woman had been so quiet since Mr. Irwin came to the house, her peaceful demeanor now replaced with fear. Where would they go from here? The mourning journey would take time, but bad news could make it seem even longer.

Dr. Albrecht entered with Mr. Carr, Mr. Irwin, Mr. Campbell, and the officers from Anchorage. They all nodded their heads in greeting.

"Ma'am, Miss, Miss Hillerman," the officer in the front began, his southern heritage apparent in the drawl of his words, "we asked you to be here today because we have some news. First we'd like to give you this." He held out a pocket watch. "The young Bouwens boy found it next to your father."

Gwyn took it. "This is Jeremiah's. My father must have borrowed it."

The officers exchanged a glance, then the one who handed Gwyn the watch continued. "Dr. Albrecht did an examination of the body after they found him and noticed something unusual. Doctor, would you mind explaining what you told us?"

Dr. Albrecht moved forward. "Your father had petechial hemorrhages present around and in his eyes. That's when I realized he didn't die of natural causes. He didn't fall in the river and drown, because there was no water in his lungs."

Nasnana looked at Gwyn. Her face was pale, eyes wide.

"I'm sorry, Gwyn. Your father was suffocated. Someone killed him."

24

This shouldn't be happening. Not to her. Not to her father.

Gwyn sobbed, burying her face in Nasnana's lap. Why? Why would someone *kill* her father?

"Miss Hillerman, I'm sorry. But we wanted you to be the first to know. We are greatly concerned about your safety and about the safety of the other people in the colony. Anchorage just sent the results from Gertrude Albany's autopsy. At first they thought she had died of cardiac arrest, but they found a large amount of snakeberries—baneberry fruit—in her stomach, which is poisonous and can cause cardiac arrest. Her husband says that she hated any kind of berry and wouldn't touch it with a ten-foot pole. There weren't any berries in the house, so we fear she was poisoned. We've got a murderer on our hands. We need your help."

The officer questioning her blurred in front of her. Couldn't they just leave her alone? She wanted to mourn. She wanted to curl up in her bed and cry herself to sleep and stay there forever.

She lifted her head, the tears still flowing. "My help? I just lost my father." She shook her head and started to give them all a good upbraiding.

But then Rose's hymn played through her mind. She couldn't give in to the anger and depression. She couldn't let the enemy win. The thought completely sobered her. "What do you need?" She sat up, straightened her dress, and blew her nose.

"Do you believe there's any validity to Mr. Novak's claims about Dr. Vaughan? Could he have had any motive to kill your father?"

"No. That's absurd. My father mentored Jeremiah when he was a boy and asked him to come here. Jeremiah adores my father."

"What about Dr. Vaughan's intentions toward you? Mr. Novak stated that Dr. Vaughan had a secret, and that he'd sworn no one would have you but himself. Could this be true?" the man pushed.

Gwyn was shocked. "I have no idea what Mr. Novak is talking about, but I know none of it can possibly be true."

"Was there anyone else who could have wanted to harm your father?"

"No. No one."

"Would you mind going through your father's things? See if there are any threatening letters or notes?"

She wasn't ready to go through her father's personal belongings. She wanted to leave them just like they were. Forever. Nasnana's hand reached over and grabbed hers. The older woman had to know what she was feeling.

"All right. I . . . I can do that."

"Thank you. Please let us know if you find anything."

Gwyn nodded. What had just happened? She wasn't sure she could handle the blur of events. Her pulse pounded in her ears.

"Miss Hillerman. We'd also like you to have someone with you at all times. Please don't go off alone. It's for your protection. Until we find out who's committed these heinous crimes."

Again she felt her head nod, but it didn't seem to be from her own strength. She was drained. Completely.

The walk home passed by in what seemed like seconds. She couldn't even remember walking. It was almost like she'd drifted.

Sadzi gave her a gentle push onto the bed, removed Gwyn's shoes, laid her down, and covered her with a quilt. Gwyn heard her friend say something, but the words didn't register.

Maybe it was all a bad dream. She closed her eyes and prayed it was.

Gwyn woke up in a fog. Someone was tapping her shoulder, calling her name.

"What?"

"Gwyn, wake up. You need to see something." Nasnana kept tapping. "If you don't wake up, I'll have to pinch you."

She opened eyes that felt full of sand. "I'm awake. Don't pinch." She sat up.

Nasnana sat beside her. Sadzi stood in front of her.

"What?"

"Here, drink some water first. It will clear your mind." Sadzi handed her a glass.

The water slid down her throat. She hadn't realized how parched she'd become. She drained the whole glass. "Okay, what is it?"

Sadzi handed her an envelope. "Rose found this. In your father's trunk."

Gwyn took the yellowed envelope. In her father's beautiful script was her name. "Gwyneth."

Fresh tears sprung to her eyes. She'd always loved it when her father used her full name. It sounded regal rolling off his tongue.

Gwyn ran her hand over the outside of the envelope. It hadn't been a bad dream. Her father was gone.

Nasnana hugged her and kissed her temple. "Do you want us to leave so you can read what's in it?"

She shook her head, unable to speak.

"We'll be here. Take your time."

Gwyn sucked in a breath. She couldn't do it. Not yet. "Did you go through all of my father's things?"

"Yes." Nasnana patted her knee. "It was my decision. I saw your face when they suggested it at the hospital and thought while you rested, it would be best if we just looked. Then when you are ready, you can take your time going through them."

"Thank you." A sigh of relief escaped her lips. "I didn't want to do that yet."

Sadzi sat on the floor and leaned against the wall.

Gwyn looked back at the envelope. She wanted to savor her father's words, wait until a day down the road when it didn't hurt quite so much. But it had to be done. What if there was some clue in there about his death?

With a prayer for strength, she ripped open the envelope and pulled out two sheets of paper folded in thirds. They smelled like his aftershave. She closed her eyes and inhaled deeply.

Hugging the letter to her chest, she said aloud, "'The Lord gave, and the Lord hath taken away; blessed be the name of the Lord.'"

Several moments passed in the quiet room. But she couldn't wait any longer. Her father had penned words to her. Words that might be the last she would ever read from him. She unfolded the paper. It was dated December 14, 1934.

My dearest Gwyneth,

She read the greeting three times. Funny how the words written by her father elicited a reaction in stark contrast to the words scrawled by her mother.

> *I've known for some time that I couldn't live forever, but the thought of writing a letter to you that you would then have to read after my death made me feel old. So I've put it off until now.*

More tears flowed, but she had to laugh. She could imagine her father saying that aloud to her with a twinkle in his eye. He'd been so full of life. *God, why? Why have you taken him home?*

> *As I sit here contemplating that I'll be with my Savior, it still saddens me to think of you alone. I know how I would feel if something happened to you. We've been two peas in a pod for so very long. Ever since you could walk, you've followed me around. I've loved it. Not only the time spent with you, but the fact that you share the same passion for helping people that I do. The good Lord was so gracious in giving me you as a daughter. I have always been proud to be your father.*
> *The awkwardness of writing this letter probably pales in comparison to the grief you must be feeling. I'm sorry,*

Gwyn. Sorry that I've left you, but not sorry for the life I've lived. I will never be sorry for eternity either.

More than anything, I want you to live your life to the fullest. Keep God as your focus and the utmost priority in your life. Study His Word. Live every day with His joy in your heart. Can you do that for me?

Yes, Father, I can. And I will. Two tears dropped onto the page, and she dabbed at them with her hankie. She couldn't bear for the last words of her father to be smeared.

I have another request as well. It concerns your mother. Please forgive her. No matter how she's hurt you, forgiveness is the only way you can be set free. I've seen the pain in your eyes and the bondage you seem to be in to the thought of abandonment. But you still need to forgive her. I've loved your mother all these years. I know you couldn't possibly remember, but there was a time when we were very happy.

Gwyn set the letter down in her lap. Her father knew her so well. But forgiving her mother would take an act of God. Maybe that was what he was expecting. She picked up the letter.

Unfortunately, those days are long gone. I'm ashamed to admit that I've kept the truth from you for many years. Among my things you will no doubt find a packet from your grandfather's lawyer. Sealed in that packet are divorce papers. Your mother tried to divorce me after she first left, but I let it drag on. A couple years ago now, I finally realized that I couldn't hold on to her any longer.

The law firm had been pressuring me for some time, even though I hid all those telegrams from you. I never wanted you to worry about me. Or about your mother. I didn't want you to give up hope that one day she would return. You clung to that dream, and I hated to shatter it.

Please forgive me for my dishonesty all this time. I imagine your mother won't even care that I am gone, but I have remained faithful to her all these years, despite the papers that declare our marriage abolished. Please forgive her as well and allow her to go on with her life.

On that note, my dearest Gwyn, I want to encourage **you** *to move on with your life. There's no reason you should stay here in the valley. I don't want you to be alone the rest of your life. Please, go find love. Even as much as you've seen the dark side of it, I still encourage you to find a young man worthy of you and to fall in love. Get married. Have children.*

Make this old man proud.

In closing, I want to tell you how very much I love you. You have been the light of my life. No man could have ever asked for a better daughter. Be brave and strong in the coming days. In my trunk, you will find boxes and boxes of handkerchiefs for you to fidget with, but I pray that one of these days you will no longer need them.

I leave all of my earthly possessions to you, dear Gwyn. In an unmarked envelope in the trunk, you will find a key and information about my bank accounts in Seattle. There's plenty there, Gwyn. Go . . . live your life.

With eternal love from your adoring father,

Harold H. Hillerman

The tears rushed down her face as she folded the letter. What would she do without her precious father?

Nasnana wrapped her arms around her, and Sadzi came and sat on the other side of her. Wrapped in their arms of love and comfort, Gwyn sobbed.

25

A tapping on her shoulder woke her again. Gwyn's eyelids felt like heavy rocks, swollen from the tears she'd spent. She didn't even want to try to open them.

"Gwyn. Wake up, child." Nasnana's singsong voice. "Don't make me pinch you. Jeremiah is here to see you."

Even in her foggy state, her heart did a little flip. She slowly sat up and worked to straighten her hair.

"Don't worry about it. You look fine. Besides, he won't care." Nasnana practically dragged her off the bed. Even in her decline, the woman could still muscle Gwyn around.

In the living room, Jeremiah stood by the couch. "Gwyn"— his bloodshot eyes gave away his lack of sleep—"I'm so sorry."

She shook her head. "You don't need to keep apologizing. At least I know where my father is now, and that gives me comfort. Though I will miss him every day for the rest of my life." She lowered herself to the cushions of the couch. She could still see her father sitting there, reading a book in the summer, or listening to the radio in the winter.

"I'm going to make us some tea." Nasnana shuffled away. "Jeremiah, sit down with Gwyn." The words flew over her shoulder.

Jeremiah sat next to Gwyn. He leaned over. "Is she always this bossy?"

She chuckled. "Yes. But only because she loves us."

He reached into his jacket and pulled out a small leather book. "I wanted to bring you this as soon as I found it. It was locked in your father's cabinet at the hospital. The officers opened everything, looking for clues."

The smooth leather was as soft as butter. Gwyn rubbed her hand back and forth. The book had been a journal of sorts for her father. She'd seen him write in it over the years. "Thank you for bringing it by." She opened it and flipped through the pages. The brief lines of her father's script made her heart catch. Page after page filled with dates and her father's thoughts. On life, on patients, on God.

When she reached the back, there were only five blank pages left. He had used the same volume for almost ten years. She turned the pages back and found his last entries.

September 26, 1935

So blessed to have Gwyn as a daughter. Wish we'd had more time together the past few months, but winter is coming.

September 27, 1935

The Zimmerman child is finally better. Will go home tomorrow. Need to find a better way to comfort the children here in the small hospital.

September 28, 1935

First croup case of the season came in tonight. Not looking forward to winter for this very reason. But they are finishing homes at a rapid pace.

September 29, 1935

Jeremiah Vaughan is a good man and a great physi-
cian. He's carrying a burden he thinks I know nothing
about, but I know it in full, and it doesn't matter. He's
much too hard on himself. When the truth comes out . . .
I know God will help him to see it. And when he is
finally free of this burden, I hope one day to see him
and Gwyn married. I look forward to being a doting
grandfather.

Tears stung her eyes. "Did you read it?"

"I'll admit I wanted to, and I hope one day you'll let me. I
bet he has a lot of insight in there. But no, I didn't read it."
He bowed his head and twirled the hat in his hands.

Gwyn scooted closer to him. "Here, read this last one."
She sniffed and wiped her nose.

Their hands touched as they both held on to the little
leather book. Jeremiah released a long sigh. "Your father
was such a good man, Gwyn."

"He thought pretty highly of you as well."

Jeremiah closed the volume and laid it on her lap, leaving
his hand on top. "Gwyn, your father and I talked for a long
time the night he disappeared. And there's a lot I need to
tell you."

"About your burden?" she asked.

He looked so grim. "Yes."

"All right." The tight tone of his voice worried her. Did
he not care for her after all? Had her father written that last
entry before he talked to Jeremiah?

"Gwyn, I don't know how to say this . . ." He moved his
hand from her lap. "I haven't had my heart right with the

Lord for a long time. And I'm just now getting back on track. Your father helped me with that."

She sighed. Okay, that wasn't so bad. She gave him a tentative smile.

"But there's more. I've been carrying around heavy guilt . . . and it's time I told you the truth."

Closing her eyes, Gwyn prayed. Jeremiah was a good man; she knew that. And if this was the man God had for her, she needed to be strong. No matter what it was. She opened her eyes. "Go on."

"I left Chicago because a woman died in my care, and the board stripped me of my medical license. I was also engaged. And my fiancée, well, she showed me the door, wanted nothing to do with me."

Her heart felt like it hit her shoes. "So you've been in love before?"

"I thought I was. But now that I know what love really is, I know better." His hazel eyes seemed to search hers.

"So you're not a doctor anymore? At least, not legally? What happened?"

"My cousin is appealing the case, but the woman who died was the wife of a very wealthy, very influential man." He took a deep breath. "Mrs. Brewster fell down a flight of stairs, and since I was Mr. Brewster's choice to head up his new hospital and the neurological department, he asked me to perform the surgery. He'd been my biggest supporter, my greatest ally. I had no idea he would turn on me. The fact is, I shouldn't have even tried. I knew her neck and head wounds were fatal. It was just a matter of time. But in my arrogance, I thought if I could save her, I could be the renowned physician I'd always wanted to be. We used a new technique—intravenous anesthesia—and she didn't respond well. It went downhill from there, and even though I relieved a little of the pressure off her brain, she died on the operating table."

"I'm so sorry, Jeremiah." This was too much to take in all at once. "And my father knew?"

"Yes, he did."

"Are you in trouble?"

"No. Well, I don't know. There was some talk of charging me with negligent homicide. But, Gwyn—" he got down on the floor and knelt before her, grabbing her hands—"there's something else you have to know. I have to tell you the whole truth. But I don't want to hurt you. Please know how much I care about you."

She bit her lip and held her breath. Could she take any more? Her mind couldn't make sense of any of this.

"The girl I was engaged to . . . was Sophia. Your sister."

Gwyn's legs pumped beneath her as she ran as fast as she could. Jeremiah called to her, but she ran harder.

Her thoughts spiraled out of control. He'd been engaged to Sophia? Her beautiful, delicate, sophisticated sister? How could she measure up to that? Even if Sophia was as horrible to him as he said, Gwyn knew she paled in comparison to her baby sister's beauty.

How could her father leave her at a time like this? How could he have known the truth and not told her?

Was everything in her life based on a lie? She loved Jeremiah. Of that she was certain. But how could he possibly love *her*?

She stopped at the edge of the river, where they'd found her father. Gasping for air, she bent over at the waist. *Lord, help me to understand the truth. Please, Lord. I love Jeremiah—I know that. He's a good man. But I'm so confused.* She fell to the ground on her hands and knees. *It hurts so bad that my father is gone. Please . . . Lord . . .*

She cried until there weren't any more tears to shed. Her nose and cheeks dripped. A crackle alerted her to someone else's presence. Jeremiah must have followed her. And she found she wanted him to.

She stood up and turned, wiping her face with her sleeves. "Jer—"

But it wasn't Jeremiah's eyes she looked into.

Clarence ran toward her and gripped her arms with his hands. "Gwyn, I've been worried sick." His eyes were wild.

"Clarence, please . . . you're hurting me."

"We've got to get away from here. Don't you see? Jeremiah killed your father!"

"No. No. Jeremiah loved my father. He—"

"Yes, he did!" Clarence shook her until her teeth rattled.

"Clarence! Let go of me! I don't want anything to do with you!" Tiny tendrils of fear crept up her back like fingers. The hair on her neck prickled. What could she do? The man was insane . . . crazy . . .

"I can give you everything and anything you've ever wanted! I am one of the wealthiest men in America." His glassy eyes grew wide and he smiled. "I've got more money than you could even imagine."

"I don't care about your money, Clarence."

"Shut up!" He shook her again. "Everyone cares about money. Everyone always thought they were smarter or better than me. Well, guess who's laughing now? I went after what

I wanted, and I got it. And now I intend to have *you*, and nothing is going to stand in my way."

Gwyn closed her eyes. Clarence wasn't acting normal. She bit her lip. What could she do? *Lord, help!*

"Let's go. You're coming with me."

Peace flooded her. All the worry and fear disappeared. For the first time in her life, Gwyn wasn't twisting a handkerchief to pieces. "No, Clarence. I won't." No matter what happened, she knew the truth.

And the truth was that all she needed was the Lord. Because *He is* truth.

His grip tightened.

She straightened.

"Oh, yes you are. I didn't come all this way and endure this horrible little place all summer long for you to tell me no." He shook her harder.

Gwyn tried to wiggle free, but Clarence held on tightly.

She clawed at his jacket. "Why did you come?"

A little envelope fell out of his pocket, its contents spilling in the dirt.

"No!" Clarence squeezed her arms until she thought her bones would break under the pressure. "Look at what you did!"

She watched him stare at the last remnants of powder floating to the ground. When his grip loosened, she bolted.

But she only made it two steps before he had one hand around her neck. He shook her like a rag doll, screaming in her face. Her ears thundered, black spots sprinkled her vision. "Please . . . stop!" She needed air.

"I said you're coming with me," he hissed in her face.

"No!" She struck his face with her hand. If she didn't get air soon, she'd join her father.

"No one tells me no!" He wrapped both hands around her neck and squeezed, his pupils dilated and his eyes bloodshot. "Not you. Not your stupid, nosy father. I showed him, and now I'll show you."

Gwyn's mind filled with panic. She couldn't breathe. He would kill her. She watched her arms flail about helpless to stop Clarence's attack.

And then his expression softened. He let go.

But it was too late. The world faded to black.

26

He'd killed her.

That wasn't part of the plan.

The powder on the ground next to Gwyn caught his attention. Clarence got down on all fours. Maybe some of it could be saved.

But what about Gwyn? He'd killed her!

No. He didn't. Someone else did.

He looked around. No one saw anything. Only the trees were witnesses.

His heart raced. Head pounded. He needed more medicine. But it was all hidden back at William's.

It was time to leave Alaska.

"Gwyn!"

"Gwyn!"

"Gwyn, where are you? Whistle if you hear me."

Voices! Too many of them. Who were they?

"Gwyn!"

The old Indian woman. He'd recognize that voice anywhere. He could blame *her*.

His brain buzzed and his focus darted around. He couldn't stand still, but he knew he'd better clean up his appearance.

He rinsed off his face and hands in the river and straightened his suit. Picking up a stick, he hid behind a tree. Hopefully the old woman would be the first one to find him.

"Gwyn!" Her voice drifted. But it was closer.

Clarence gripped the stick tighter in his hands, his palms slippery with sweat.

"Oh no! Gwyn!"

It was the Indian. She was here. Clarence watched her kneel beside Gwyn. Then he rushed her and grabbed her arms.

"Help, someone! Over here!"

"Wha—"

He slapped a hand over her mouth and yelled as loud as he could, "She killed Gwyn. Someone help! Quick!"

The woman kicked him in the shin.

"'Ahh! You witch!" He tried to suffocate her with his hand as the sound of voices grew.

He smiled as she fought. Then he yelled, "Call for the authorities. I have her. I have the one who killed the Hillermans."

Gwyn was dead? No! It couldn't be.

Jeremiah ran toward the shouts. Wait. That was Clarence's voice. What was he yelling?

He heard rustling ahead. Sadzi sprinted from the other direction.

Together they ran until they found Clarence and Nasnana, Clarence screaming that he'd caught the murderer. His eyes weren't right. They were darting around. And the man's hands shook as they gripped the tiny woman.

Dr. H. had suspected Clarence had an addiction, but they'd

never had proof. Now Jeremiah found plenty to be afraid of. An addicted man coming down off of a high.

"Whoa, Clarence. Calm down." He approached with slow steps, hands extended. "Why don't you let Nasnana go?"

"No! I won't! Look what she did to Gwyn."

Jeremiah followed his gaze to a still form on the ground— *No!*

He ran to Gwyn's side. She lay limp . . . lifeless. Her head rested on a large rock. He lifted her head with gentle trembling hands and his fingers examined her scalp. There was substantial swelling on the back of her head. Keeping his hand behind her head, he put his ear to her chest. *Oh, God, let her still be alive!*

"She's breathing!" Even shallow as it was, it gave him hope. His Gwyn wasn't dead. Relief rippled through him. *Thank you, God!* In that brief moment, he remembered to breathe. Noticed his heart still beat. So this was love. He didn't want to live without her.

His thoughts cleared. But there wasn't much time. "What happened?"

"I told you—Nasnana killed her. I saw it!"

"She's not dead, you idiot." Jeremiah lost his temper. But he couldn't—no, wouldn't—lose the woman he loved. "Sadzi, run and tell Dr. Albrecht that I'm carrying Gwyn in. He's going to have to get everything ready. I'm afraid she's going to need surgery."

The young native woman took off at a run.

"Clarence, let go of Nasnana. We've got to get Gwyn to the hospital."

"I will not let go! She's the murderer, I tell you!"

Jeremiah bolted to his feet hard and fast. Clarence stumbled back and let go of Nasnana, his eyes glazed and wide. Jeremiah's heart pounded. Without another thought, he jerked his right fist back and slugged Clarence.

When the man fell to the ground, Jeremiah lifted Gwyn as gently as he could in his arms and looked over his shoulder at Nasnana. "Are you all right?"

"Don't worry about me, son. Go. I'll keep up."

He started the trek to the hospital, trying to keep his steps soft. But the cursing and yelling behind reminded him that Clarence wasn't done. Jeremiah picked up his pace.

More ranting reached his ears. "I caught the murderer! She did it! You won't be safe! Someone catch the Indian woman!"

Jeremiah hoped someone else would hear the man's rants and come help them. But his priority was getting Gwyn to the hospital. And fast.

His heart pounded from the exertion, but Jeremiah forged ahead. What would Dr. H. do?

Pray.

Lord, I'm sorry for walking away from you. But please, Lord, heal Gwyn. I want to serve you for the rest of my days, and I want her by my side. Please, Lord. Forgive me. Help me to always follow your will for my life from today until the day you take me home.

He was almost there. People started coming toward them. Thank God for Clarence and his crazy ranting. Don, Stu, and Eugene exited the ARRC building, and Dr. Albrecht spotted him with Gwyn and ran toward them.

"What happened?" The doctor walked with him and lifted her head.

"I don't know. But she's got a large hematoma, and her

breathing is shallow. She must have hit her head. She was on the ground when I got to her."

Dr. Albrecht frowned as he examined the wound. "We'd better move fast. The swelling is putting pressure on the brain, and that could kill her."

27

Jeremiah heard the commotion outside, but he couldn't let that distract him. Dr. Albrecht had two nurses assisting and Jeremiah went to wash up.

"Jeremiah, come look at this."

He lifted his hands from the water and brought the towel with him. "What've you found, Earl?"

"Look. There's bruising around her neck and here on her arms. Look at the span. There's no way a tiny woman like Nasnana could have caused this damage."

Clarence. Jeremiah looked out the window. "Nurse Abigail, could you ask Mr. Irwin to join us in here? Be calm. Just make sure he comes. Immediately."

"Yes, Doctor." She rushed out the door.

"Earl, what do you think?"

"I think we need to operate. And I think you are the perfect man for the job."

Jeremiah sank to a chair. Could he really operate on the woman he loved? What if he messed up?

Gwyn started to moan on the table.

"I don't think we have much time, Jeremiah. That pressure has to be relieved off her brain before it does damage to the brain tissue. Harold said you had a great deal of experience in this area."

"Yes." He had studied under the top brain surgeons in the country. This was his field of expertise. "But, Earl, there's something you need to know—"

"We don't have time right now, Jeremiah. Her heart rate is erratic. Tell me later."

"But what about Clarence and Mr. Irwin?"

"I'll go tell Irwin. You prep for surgery. Now!"

Ten minutes later, Jeremiah was operating on Gwyn. He hated to shave part of her beautiful curls off, but they'd grow back. He didn't care how much hair she had. He just wanted her alive.

The procedure didn't take long, and as soon as all the fluid was drained, Gwyn started to stabilize.

Thank you, Lord.

Dr. Albrecht smiled at him. "I think you've done it. Good job, Dr. Vaughan."

Jeremiah breathed a small sigh. But he couldn't rest until he knew for sure that Gwyn would wake up.

The nurses cleaned up around him, and he washed up. Then he brought a chair to her side and waited.

He laid his head on the cot beside her and prayed. He understood now, more than ever, that God truly was in control. And Jeremiah realized he was thankful that it was out of his control. Let the Great Physician handle it.

Something moved above his head. And then fingers touched his hair. He slowly lifted his head. Gwyn's hand was in his hair, her eyes mere slits.

"Hi."

"Hi." Her voice cracked.

"Let me get you some water. But just a sip at a time, all right?"

She blinked.

He braced her neck and back and lifted her so she could take a sip.

She held a hand up. "That's enough."

Dr. Albrecht walked over. "She's awake."

"Yes, she is." Jeremiah squeezed her hand. "You're going to be all right, Gwyn."

"Clarence—"

"What about Clarence?"

"He attacked me. He's crazy."

Jeremiah looked to Earl. His friend nodded and raced out of the room. Her statement would be all the authorities needed.

"Gwyn, hang on, sweetie. They'll take care of Clarence."

"I don't want him to hurt anyone else—"

"Shh, it's okay. Don't try to talk. I love you, Gwyn." He squeezed her hand as her eyes closed. "Do you hear me? I love you, Gwyn. And I'll never let him hurt you again."

The train pulled into Palmer, and Frank stepped off before it came to a stop. He would find Clarence today. He hadn't followed the man's trail for months on end and traveled thousands of miles to quit now.

He spied the government office and made a beeline toward it. A group of men were in a lively discussion outside.

"Gentlemen, could one of you direct me to a Mr. Eugene Carr?"

Everyone stilled. A man stepped forward. "That's me. What can I help you with?"

"I'm Frank Rhoads with the Pinkertons. I'm looking for a Clarence Novak."

All eyes were now riveted on him.

"Let's step into my office." Mr. Carr ushered him into the small building and closed the door. "Mr. Rhoads, we're in the process of looking for Clarence right now."

"What's happened?"

"He attacked a woman and accused another woman of it, but the victim confirmed it was Clarence. She also stated that he was crazy. We also have a murder from a few days ago." He slid a paper to Frank. "Dr. Hillerman, who was suffocated. And then a woman died suspiciously of berry poisoning several weeks prior to that. We've also just confirmed that Dr. Hillerman had suspected Clarence of an addiction to morphine—apparently caught him trying to steal some from the hospital in the middle of the night."

"It wouldn't surprise me if Clarence was responsible for all of these." Frank laid the papers back down. "His past is strewn with dead bodies."

"Well, I know the colony would sleep a lot better if you could help us catch this guy. We've been watching the trains. There's no other way out, other than on foot."

"Where's the woman he attacked?"

"In the hospital. She had to have brain surgery earlier."

"Is she awake?"

"I don't know." Mr. Carr sat on the edge of his desk. "But I know that we will help you in any way we can, Mr. Rhoads. Why don't we go see Gwyn?"

Frank carried his one bag with him as they trekked to the hospital. Fortunately, it wasn't far. He was ready to end this. Justice would be served and Clarence Novak would pay.

Something cool was laid on her forehead. Gwyn opened her eyes. Confusion flooded her thoughts, making it impossible to understand her surroundings.

Jeremiah smiled at her. "Hi."

"Hi." Her voice seemed to croak.

"How are you feeling?"

"Tired." She could barely speak above a whisper. "My head . . . my throat . . . hurt."

"That's to be expected. You're going to have to take it easy for quite a while. Don't try to talk. You've got some swelling from the strangulation, but it will pass."

She nodded. Her eyelids were heavy.

"Dr. Vaughan." An unfamiliar male voice spoke outside the curtain.

She felt a kiss on her nose. "I'll be right back."

Whispers drifted over to her, but her brain was too tired to listen.

"Gwyn?" She heard Jeremiah whisper in her ear.

"Yes?" Only one eye obeyed. Then it shut again.

"Gwyn, this is Mr. Rhoads. He's a Pinkerton agent. He needs to ask you some questions about Clarence. I don't want you to strain your voice, so nod or shake your head when you can. If you can't answer that way then speak very softly—not above a whisper."

Using every bit of willpower within her, she forced her eyes to open.

"Miss Hillerman, I just have a few questions."

She nodded.

"I understand Clarence Novak attacked you."

She nodded in affirmation.

320

"And you're positive it was him?"

Another nod.

"Can you tell me why?"

"He wanted me to go away with him, and I said no."

Rhoads nodded. "And did he say where he wanted to take you?"

She struggled to remember and shook her head.

Leaning closer, Rhoads narrowed his eyes. "It's really important that you remember everything he said."

Gwyn frowned. "I'm trying to." She swallowed against the soreness in her throat. "He was mad that I'd said no. He said that no one told him no." She paused and closed her eyes for a moment. The feel of Clarence's hands around her throat caused her to shudder. "He said my father was stupid—nosy." Her eyes shot open. "He said he would show *me* . . . just like he'd shown my father."

In her dreams Gwyn saw her father, Jeremiah, and her sister standing in wedding attire. Sophia looked much as she had when she'd left six years ago—still a little girl, her chin high in the air.

"I'm going to marry Jeremiah," she said in a haughty voice. "You cannot have him because he's going to marry me."

Gwyn looked at Jeremiah. He was smiling, but he seemed sad. She turned to her father. "Why is he marrying Sophia? He said he loves me."

Her father shrugged. "The heart always knows."

She looked again to Jeremiah. "You said you loved me. You know that I love you."

Jeremiah shook his head. "No. You can't love me. I lied to you. You can't forgive me."

Her father nodded. "You can't forgive."

Gwyn felt tears form in her eyes. "But I can. I can forgive. I do forgive. I love you, Jeremiah." The images began to fade. "Come back. I love you. I forgive you." But they were gone.

When she awoke, it was dark outside. Her head still felt like someone was banging on it—using it as a drum. But her thoughts were a little clearer, and her throat hurt a little less. She tried to remember what had happened last, but thoughts of her dream came back to haunt her.

With a turn of her head, she found Jeremiah asleep in a chair, his hand holding hers. Her heart melted at the sight of him. Could she really have found love? It didn't seem possible.

Gwyn filled her lungs with a deep breath. "I forgive you."

Jeremiah opened his eyes and leaned forward. "Hey there. Sorry I fell asleep. Did you say something? How do you feel?"

"A little better. But not great." Her whisper made him smile.

He touched her forehead and pulled out his stethoscope. "May I?"

She nodded and he listened to her heart.

"Sounds strong. Much better. I think we're past the worst, but it's going to take some time for you to heal. Why don't you get some more rest? I won't leave. I'll be right here." He scooted the chair closer and picked up her hand again.

"But I need to tell you something."

He looked at her oddly. "Something you remember about Clarence?"

She shook her head. "About forgiveness." She smiled. "I forgive you, and I hope you'll forgive me."

"I'm most grateful for your mercy. God knows I don't

deserve it. But, Gwyn, I can't forgive you, because you've done nothing wrong."

She was too tired and her throat hurt too much to argue with him. "Were you telling the truth when you said you loved me?"

His smile lit his face. She could get lost in the depths of his eyes. "Yes. I was. I've loved you almost from the start, even though my stubbornness and pride got in the way. I thought for sure my past would ruin any chance of a future with you. I honestly never loved Sophia the way I love you. I never loved anyone the way I love you."

She smiled. "I feel the same way about you. But I do have one request."

"What is it?"

"That you never lie to me again."

"I never wanted to lie to you in the first place. I was foolish and selfish. I thought only of guarding myself—keeping others from knowing the truth so that I wouldn't have to bear the shame. I'm so sorry."

"Sorry isn't enough." He looked at her in confusion, and Gwyn couldn't help but giggle. "Promise me," she insisted.

Her laughter immediately changed his mood. "And what exactly do I get in return for agreeing to this request, miss?" His cocky grin only made his eyes twinkle more.

She smiled. "My whole heart."

"Your request is granted. I promise I will never lie to you again." He leaned forward, his smile growing. "Will you promise me something?"

"What?"

"Promise you will love me for the rest of my life and marry me."

She sighed. "Of course. I thought you'd never ask."

Harsh clapping sounded from behind the curtain. The curtain ripped open—

Clarence entered the room. "Very touching scene, worthy of the stage itself."

Even as Gwyn held back a scream, she felt Jeremiah tense beside her, knew he was about to stand, so she grabbed both of his hands in hers. He looked at her, and then followed her gaze back to Clarence's hand.

And the gun he held.

28

Jeremiah moved closer to Gwyn.

"Get away from her, *Doctor*. Or I'll be forced to kill her."

He wanted to tackle Clarence, to get him on the ground and strangle him. But even in his anger, he knew he couldn't get to Clarence before he pulled the trigger. And Jeremiah couldn't risk Gwyn being shot.

He'd better think. And fast. He gave the pretense of adhering to Clarence's command by holding up his hands and shifting his shoulders.

Clarence paced at the end of Gwyn's bed. "Now, this is how it's going to go. Gwyn will be my hostage as we leave the colony. No one will try to come after me, because they know I'll kill her if they do."

"But she can't be transported right now. Look at how weak she is." Maybe he could reason with the man. Or at least stall him until he could think of a better plan.

"No! You need to do whatever is necessary to make sure that she can come with me. I'll drag a nurse along as well if I have to. Hey, two hostages are better than one, right?"

Jeremiah straightened and got to his feet. "Won't that be

cumbersome? Why don't you take me instead? Then you'll still have your hostage, but I won't slow you down."

"No!" Gwyn cried from the bed.

Clarence pointed the gun at her again.

Jeremiah moved to the end of the bed—and the gun trained on him.

"Don't be stupid, Dr. Vaughan. You know I'd just kill you."

"I know that."

A young nurse entered the room. "Take me instead."

Clarence wrapped an arm around her neck and put the gun to her head. "So you sent a spy, did you? You thought you could sneak up on me?"

The young nurse started to cry. "No, I just thought you wanted a hostage, and Miss Gwyn will die if you take her."

Clarence blinked rapidly. His eyelid twitched. He released the nurse and shoved her toward the bed. "I'll just take you both. Nurse, you do whatever it takes to get Gwyn ready to leave." The arm holding the gun shook. "Now!"

She looked to Jeremiah and he nodded. "Better do what he says, Abigail." The woman moved to help Gwyn sit up.

"Hurry up!" Clarence demanded.

Abigail looked at him like he was crazy. "She can't move fast. She has a head injury that needs to be redressed. If she moves too quickly, she'll lose consciousness." Clarence studied the woman as if trying to perceive the truth of the matter.

It was now or never—

"Hands up, Novak!" Frank Rhoads's voice penetrated the room.

Clarence jerked at Frank's yell, and Jeremiah dove for the gun.

A thunderous report went off.

As Jeremiah and Clarence fell to the floor, Gwyn prayed for strength. Her legs wouldn't support her, and Abigail sat her back down on the bed. *Oh, Lord, please help. Please don't let Jeremiah be hurt!*

She heard a struggle and then another gunshot. Spots danced in front of her eyes again. The room spun.

"Miss Gwyn!" Abigail reached out and laid her down on the pillow.

Her eyelids were so heavy. But she had to know what was happening.

Another crash. Grunts. And then what sounded like a window breaking. Footsteps running away. Followed by more footsteps . . . yelling . . . another gunshot.

The silence that followed begged her attention. She wanted to stay awake, find out what happened. But exhaustion tugged at every fiber of her being.

"It's all over, Miss Gwyn." Abigail's voice penetrated the fog.

As much as she tried, Gwyn couldn't open her eyes. "What . . . happened?"

"Shhh. It's over. Don't worry."

And she surrendered to the blackness.

They'd laid her father in the ground today. A full week after when they'd planned the original burial, but Gwyn had been too weak after the attack and her surgery, and she had insisted that she be able to attend. Could it really be the tenth of October? This year of 1935 had been a year of excitement and anticipation for her father, and now he was gone. The bandage around her head itched and reminded her of all they'd gone through. Nasnana had knit her a hat for the occasion, but Gwyn didn't want to try to put it on—the entire back of her head still felt like one big bruise. In the months to come, the hat would come in handy as her hair grew back in, but she didn't care about her appearance right now. Her father was gone.

Gwyn knew that funerals were a source of closure for many people, but it was more the start of a different chapter for her. Her mother had telegrammed that she wouldn't be coming back. Ever. But the door was open for Gwyn to join the family in Chicago. Jeremiah had graciously responded to Edith Hillerman and said they were praying for Edith and Sophia to turn to the Lord in their grief.

Did Father's death have any effect at all on Mother? Would Mother ever be able to see past her vain and selfish ways and see the need in her soul for the Savior? Gwyn could only pray for the woman she'd longed to please for so many years. Maybe one day that ache in her heart would diminish.

For thirty minutes after the reverend walked away, Gwyn remained, silent, her right hand ensconced in Jeremiah's, her left hand in Sadzi's.

Every colony family had attended the funeral. And every man poured a shovelful of dirt over the roughhewn coffin. The children threw remnants of once lush lupine and fireweed, covering her father's grave in a carpet of his favorite Alaskan wild flowers.

Encouraging words were given: Praise for her father. Gratitude for all he'd done. Assurance that she wasn't alone in her journey.

But none of it made the anguish go away. Her father was truly gone.

She knew he now resided in heaven. She knew he'd want her to rejoice in that fact. But putting it into action proved harder than she'd expected.

Gwyn turned to see Nasnana. A beautiful light in the woman's eyes made her whole face glow.

"My child, it's not easy to say good-bye to someone you love." The older woman placed her hands on each side of Gwyn's face. "But the Lord will give you strength and peace."

Gwyn nodded. She knew that. She did. But why did she feel so lost? As though she were wandering around in a haze?

Nasnana removed her hands and made a little circle around Gwyn by joining hands with Jeremiah and Sadzi. "Things are unclear right now, Gwyn. Out of focus. I see the struggle in your eyes. Grief will do that. But Psalm 105 reminds us to 'Seek the Lord, and his strength: seek his face evermore.' We will be here for you. We are your family and we love you. But how exciting it will be to join your father in heaven one day.

"Jeremiah"—two tears slipped down her weathered face— "would you please pray for us?"

"I'd be honored."

His voice was a welcome balm. Gwyn closed her eyes. The smooth tenor of Jeremiah's voice washed over her, healing raw places in her heart. The words blurred, but the peace behind them overflowed her heart with joy. *Thank you, Lord!*

Tears streamed down her face.

And then Jeremiah concluded, "In Jesus' name we pray, amen."

Somewhere outside their little circle, a throat cleared.

"Excuse me. I'm sorry to intrude." Frank Rhoads stood with his hands folded in front of him. "How are you feeling, Miss Hillerman?"

"Weak and a little unsteady at times, but healing. I think my grief weighs me down more than my injuries. Thank you for asking."

"That's understandable. I've learned so much about your father in my investigation here. He was an amazing man and will be missed. I'm so sorry for your loss."

Gwyn looked at Jeremiah. "Yes, thank you, but I know where my father is, and that gives me great comfort."

Frank stepped closer. "Again, I'm sorry to intrude, but I need to speak with Jeremiah before I leave. I've got an urgent case back in Chicago."

"Of course." Jeremiah turned toward Frank but took Gwyn's hand in his own.

This time, she felt the warmth and the haze begin to lift. Another memory surfaced. She never wanted to forget opening her eyes to see Jeremiah praying over her after Clarence threatened to take her hostage. The man Jeremiah had become thrilled her heart. She'd slept for days after it was all over, but when she awoke clearheaded, he was still by her side.

Gwyn glanced at her wonderful fiancé. Again by her side. Through thick and thin.

"I'd like to thank you both for all you did to help us catch Clarence Novak. I was sorry to have to kill him. It's never something I take satisfaction in." He looked to the ground and then back to Gwyn. "I value every man's life—even one like Clarence's."

"How's his family?" Gwyn worried about the colonists.

"They are all right. A little shocked, but William said Clarence had never chosen to be close to any of his relatives. He'd stayed away and aloof for many years." Frank reached into his jacket and pulled out an envelope. Then he sat down on a stump and looked to Jeremiah. "What I really needed to speak to you about is this: Your cousin, Howard, asked me to find you."

Jeremiah stiffened. He looked at her. "It must be about the appeal."

Frank handed Jeremiah the letter.

Gwyn squeezed his hand. "Open it. God's in control, remember? No matter what it says, our trust is in Him."

He nodded. The rip of the envelope rent the air. Jeremiah inhaled long and deep.

Gwyn gave him a couple moments as he read, but the anxious thoughts swirling in her brain showed none of that patience. His eyes widened and he looked at her in disbelief. Gwyn couldn't stand it. "Well? What does it say?"

Jeremiah handed her the letter. She read it aloud.

"Jeremiah,

"After a full investigation, the medical board has cleared you of any wrongdoing and has reinstated your medical license, effective immediately. There will be no formal charges of negligence. Also, Randolph Brewster has been removed from the board of directors.

"Please contact me as soon as you receive this.

"Sincerely,
Howard"

Gwyn lowered the letter and met Jeremiah's smiling face. "You've been cleared! God has interceded for you!" She wrapped her arms around him and hugged him close. "Oh, this is the best possible news. I only wish Father could have lived to see it."

"He knows," Jeremiah said confidently. "He always knew. He told me as much." He glanced back toward the grave site. "Even when I didn't believe in myself, your father believed in me."

Gwyn nodded. "I know he did. He loved you very much. And so do I."

Epilogue

Everyone from the colony crammed into the community building. All the children were seated together on the floor at the front of the room.

Gwyn glanced around at all the smiling faces. They'd made it. Their first Christmas. As fall came in with a swift wind, the temperatures dropped and the snows came, but the people had kept their chins up and worked themselves to the bone, even though the nights in the tent homes grew chilly. Everyone came together and helped one another, chopping excessive amounts of wood for the stoves so that the families still living in tents would be able to keep the fires going.

But finally the last home had been finished, just a few days prior, and now everyone had at least four walls around them instead of the chilly tents. Most of the homes were still simple skeletons, but the colonists could spend their winter months finishing up the insides. They were happy simply to have a roof over their heads.

The harvest had been plentiful. And the men had hunted and fished, so no one was afraid of not having enough food to feed their families. All in all, the colonists were a family. They'd been through deaths, heartache, disappointment, and times of worry. But through it all, they knew they would stand by one another. Spirits were high in the little colony as they approached the festive season of celebrating Christ's birth.

Jeremiah walked up to Gwyn and put his arm around her waist. "Hi there, beautiful."

"Hi." She smiled up at him. Why the Lord had chosen to bless her with such a wonderful man was beyond her. But she would always be thankful.

Giggles and cheers brought her attention back to the children. The train that morning had brought an abundance of gifts for the colony children. The Alaska Railroad, steamship companies, and organizations all over the States had sent presents for the first Christmas up in the Matanuska Colony. Christmas would be spent with friends and neighbors rather than with extended family, but from the smiles around the room, Gwyn didn't think anyone minded.

She shook her head. They'd all come so far in seven short months.

The laughter filling the room reminded her of God's abundance and love. Even in one of the hardest times the country had ever seen, people came together and worked hard. They loved. They laughed. They had built a community.

Jeremiah squeezed her waist, and she leaned into him. It was almost time. The paper-strewn floor attested to the fact that the children were almost done.

Gwyn glanced out the window. The snow blew sideways and the wind howled. Her father used to tell her to hold on tight on days like these. And then he'd tell her about a time when she was little: One day the wind picked her up off her feet and she flew—but she was saved because she'd been holding on to her father's hand.

His words echoed through her mind, *"It's just like that in our spiritual walk too, Gwyn. The enemy is going to blow that wind as hard as he can, but you've got to hold on tight to your Father's hand."*

Gwyn smiled. But the tears still threatened to spill. She missed her earthly father today, but she knew her heavenly Father was watching every moment.

Rose walked up, her beautiful new little baby in her arms.

"Oh, she's so precious. What did you name her?" Gwyn reached out for the tiny one.

"Her name is Hope. For the future we have in Jesus and for our new start here in Alaska."

The beauty of the moment forced Gwyn to close her eyes, and a single tear escaped. "That's perfect, Rose." Opening her eyes, she hugged her friend and handed the baby back. "Thank you for standing up with me."

"You're welcome."

Women bustled around the room, cleaning up and scooting the children to the back corner. Men brought chairs forward, and Reverend Bingle strode to the front with his Bible.

Jeremiah grabbed her hand and took her to the window. "It's a beautiful day for a wedding, don't you think?"

She gazed at the blowing snow. "Yes, I believe it is."

Sadzi rushed in the side door and winked at Jeremiah.

Gwyn placed her hands on her hips. "Now, what exactly are you two up to?"

Her best friend swung off her coat and threw her black

braid over one shoulder. "Oh, nothing. Just helping Jeremiah with a small errand." Sadzi didn't look Gwyn in the eye, but her grin was unmistakable as she scooted around Gwyn and fluffed the skirt of her wedding gown.

Nasnana had ordered a beautiful, lush red velvet fabric in an overabundance of yardage so she could give Gwyn the gift of a beautiful gown. Trimmed in white satin and a wide white satin sash at the waist, Gwyn felt like a princess. The older woman had done so much for her through the years, and Gwyn appreciated this special gift. She'd be able to wear it today and also every Christmas and be reminded not only of God's love in sending His Son as a sacrifice for all mankind but also of the love of a very special man here on earth.

———

Tears pricked her eyes as the ceremony began a short time later and Sadzi passed her a bouquet of handmade paper flowers. Red and white ribbons flowed to the floor from their stems. A hush settled over the crowd as the pastor prayed over the couple.

Was her earthly father watching from heaven? Would her mother be proud of her? A dozen different thoughts flitted through her mind until Jeremiah took her hand in his and squeezed. All other thoughts left her brain as she trained her focus on the man in front of her. The man she would spend the rest of her life loving. Jeremiah's eyes twinkled as a smile lifted his lips, radiating through his whole face.

In a matter of minutes, their vows were spoken and the good reverend blessed their union with a reading of Scripture. "'But from the beginning of the creation God made them male and female. For this cause shall a man leave his father and mother, and cleave to his wife; And they twain shall be one flesh: so then they are no more twain, but one flesh. What therefore God hath joined together, let not man put asunder.'

"I now pronounce you man and wife! Ladies and gentlemen, let me introduce to you Dr. and Mrs. Jeremiah Vaughan."

Cheers erupted as two men pushed the huge outer doors of the community center open.

Nasnana threw a red velvet cape over Gwyn's shoulders, and Jeremiah grabbed his overcoat from Earl Albrecht as they ran out the doors.

In the middle of the snow-covered street, Jeremiah stopped and drew her close. "I love you, Gwyneth Vaughan."

The wind howled.

"I love you too." She reached up and kissed him. Long and deep. "Where are we going?"

"That, my dear, is part of the surprise." The train whistle blew in the distance. "But if we don't hurry, we'll miss our train."

"But I'm not packed! We didn't plan to go anywhere."

Sadzi appeared at her side and handed her a small velvet bag that matched her dress and cape. "Not to worry. We've taken care of everything."

Gwyn laughed as her new husband leaned in and kissed her again. "Our bags are already there," he said, his voice husky and deep as he pulled away. "Sadzi and Nasnana took care of everything for you." Grabbing her hand, he started running for the train.

Snowballs hit them from every angle—a good old Alaskan sendoff. The train whistle sounded again, and Jeremiah scooped her into his arms, snowballs pelting the ground around them.

Gwyn snuggled her face against his neck and giggled. The cold and snow didn't bother her one bit. She was with Jeremiah, and nothing else mattered.

All things hidden had been revealed—most important of all, the love they would share for a lifetime.

Dear Reader

We want to thank you for joining us on this journey.

The decision was made in January of 1935 for the Matanuska Project. In less than five months, the government had to plan and ship everything for the colony and choose all the families. (And the ARRC wasn't actually established until April!) In such a brief amount of time, there were sure to be mistakes—and there were many—but the brave colonists who stayed will go down in history as pioneers of the Alaska territory.

The incredible valley that is the Mat-Su valley today is flourishing with the towns of Wasilla and Palmer. It's one of our favorite places. Surrounded by some of the world's most beautiful mountains, the valley is fertile. With long days and plenty of sunlight in the summer months, the crops grow to enormous sizes. Just like the twenty-pound cabbage.

Even though FDR's project was real and we used the historical timeline of real events, our hero and heroine (and their families), Nasnana and Sadzi, our Pinkerton agent, the bank robbery in Chicago, the colonists' fear of the natives, and the criminal activity at the colony are all fictitious for the story.

But below are many of the real events and real people we used:

The hailstorm, July Fourth picnic and celebration, and the Matanuska River flooding (although we fictionalized and dramatized it for our story, it did flood, and it flooded the town of Matanuska) all happened. The actual telegram sent to Washington was taken from *Alaska Far Away*, seventy-five workers left in a single day, and many families left as well. The concert and performer in September were real, as well as David Williams's changing the positioning of the town, and all the generous Christmas presents for the families celebrating their first Christmas in the colony.

Dr. Earl Albrecht was indeed sent after the deaths of several children. But what is most fascinating is that this man did it all alone. Posted at the railway hospital in Anchorage, he came to the valley in July of 1935 and was the only doctor. An extraordinary man, he longed to be a missionary doctor to Bethel, Alaska, but was sent to Palmer instead in the midst of the Great Depression. Later in his career, he became Alaska's first full-time commissioner of health and also won the right for natives to be treated at Alaska hospitals. In addition, he's noted to have all but eradicated the plague of tuberculosis, which was widespread and extensive during that time among the native populations. During WWII, he ran the hospital at Fort Richardson with responsibility for more than 50,000 troops.

Our cast of characters included many other real people from this exciting time in our history:

The first baby born in the colony—Laura Norena Van Wormer

The Bouwens family and all their children (they were the largest family chosen)

Don Irwin—general manager of the ARRC
Eugene Carr—U.S. commissioner
Stewart Campbell—FERA administrator
Mrs. Lydia Fohn-Hansen—from the University of Alaska
David Williams—platted the town of Palmer
Reverend Bingle and the other two clergymen
Arville Schaleben—reporter for the *Milwaukee Journal*

As you can imagine, we had a lot of fun researching this story. If you'd like to see some of it for yourself, this Web site gives an aerial tour of the Valley in 1939: http://palmer historicalsociety.org/1939%20Aerial%20Photos.htm. Another favorite resource was the Alaska Digital Archives—below is a Web site with hundreds of pictures from the ARRC and the Matanuska Colonization: http://vilda.alaska.edu/cdm /compoundobject/collection/cdmg21/id/4336/show/3280.

The Palmer Historical Society was a huge help to us during the research of this book. http://palmerhistoricalsociety.org /colonyhouse.htm. The Colony House Museum is a charming place to visit, and if you are ever in Alaska, we highly recommend it!

The documentary entitled *Alaska Far Away* gives a detailed account of the Matanuska Colonization and also has interviews with a few of the original colonists and colony children.

Again, we'd like to thank you for joining us for *All Things Hidden.*

Enjoy the journey,
Tracie and Kimberley

Acknowledgments

Heartfelt thanks are due to many people, for each book takes a team to bring to this point.

First and foremost—to my Lord and Savior Jesus Christ. May you alone be glorified. This is for you.

Jeremy, Josh, and Kayla—my beloved family. I love you. Thank you for all the encouragement and support. I couldn't do this ministry without you.

Tracie Peterson—What a gift you are to me, precious friend! I'm so thankful to the Lord for crossing our paths all those years ago. How humbling to be asked to team with you and what an incredible, incredible honor. You have blessed me immeasurably.

Karen Ball—amazing editor, agent, and friend. You always challenge me and help me grow. So very thankful you are on this journey with me.

The absolutely incredible team at Bethany House—wow. Let me say that again backward—wow. Your love for the Lord, the written word, and your authors shines through. Thank you. Thank you. Thank you.

Dave Horton—it has been a privilege. Thank you.

Sharon Asmus—thank you so much for being such a wonderful editor to work with. What a joy!

Becca Whitham and Darcie Gudger—love you—thanks for reading in a crunch!

Arlene Benson Fox and Wayne Bouwens—real colony children—thank you for answering so many questions and sharing a bit of the actual account with us. It was so much fun to learn about you all.

Tracie Peterson is the author of more than ninety novels, both historical and contemporary. Her avid research resonates in her stories, as seen in her bestselling HEIRS OF MONTANA and STRIKING A MATCH series. Tracie and her family make their home in Montana.

Visit Tracie's Web site at www.traciepeterson.com.

Kimberley Woodhouse is a multi-published author of fiction and nonfiction. A popular speaker and teacher, she's shared her theme of "Joy Through Trials" with over 150,000 people at more than a thousand venues across the country. She lives, writes, and homeschools with her husband of twenty-plus years and their two awesome teens in Colorado Springs, Colorado.

Connect with Kim at www.kimberleywoodhouse.com.

If you enjoyed *All Things Hidden*, you may also like...

Three young women struggle to find love and a place to belong among the immigrant communities that first settled the harsh yet beautiful land of historic Minnesota.

LAND OF SHINING WATER by Tracie Peterson
The Icecutter's Daughter, The Quarryman's Bride, The Miner's Lady
traciepeterson.com

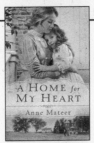

Sadie is torn when she is offered the position of matron at the orphanage where she works. She loves her job, but she also loves her beau, Blaine—and tradition dictates that she cannot have both. . . .

A Home for My Heart by Anne Mateer
annemateer.com

After three failed attempts, Everett Cline is not happy when another mail-order bride steps off the train—a woman he neither invited nor expected. But is she the wife he's been waiting for?

A Bride for Keeps by Melissa Jagears
melissajagears.com

More Romance From Bethany House

When Molly Zook's latest attempt to control her future backfires, will she finally learn to trust God with her life—and with her future groom?

Minding Molly by Leslie Gould
THE COURTSHIPS OF LANCASTER COUNTY #3
lesliegould.com

After a fire destroys her city, Mollie Knox struggles to rebuild her business while two men vie for her affections. Can Mollie rise from the ashes with both her company and her heart intact?

Into the Whirlwind by Elizabeth Camden
elizabethcamden.com

When Crockett Archer is forced off a train and delivered to an outlaw's daughter for her birthday, is it possible this stolen preacher ended up right where he belongs?

Stealing the Preacher by Karen Witemeyer
karenwitemeyer.com